I0690606

BIG GAME

First Edition

Published by The Nazca Plains Corporation
Las Vegas, Nevada
2009

ISBN: 978-1-935509-34-9

Published by

The Nazca Plains Corporation ®
4640 Paradise Rd, Suite 141
Las Vegas NV 89109-8000

PUBLISHER'S NOTE
Big Game is a work of fiction created wholly by *Lance Kyle*'s imagination. All characters are fictional and any resemblance to any persons living or deceased is purely by accident. No portion of this book reflects any real person or events.

Cover Male Photo, Antonio Balaguer Soler
Cover Background Photo, Sergey Khachatryan
Art Director, Blake Stephens

BIG GAME

First Edition

Lance Kyle

- CHAPTER 1 -

Simpson stepped onto the porch of his cabin into the cool of the dark, early African morning. He knew the weather would not stay that way. Soon the turning earth would bare itself to the sun and rising temperatures would make it advisable to seek the shade. Of course, he would not–he had more important things to do today. Mentally running through a checklist, patting himself down, he went over the necessary gear that he was to bring: a wide-brimmed hat for sun protection for his fair skin, sturdy three-quarter boots for snake protection, thick canvas shorts and shirt, water bottle, two-way radio. And his own conditioning: he had trained for months for this, running, lifting weights, not to mention target practice. He was ready.

As his eyes became adjusted to the dark–it must be, what, four in the morning?–he could make out the other buildings of the compound: the other cabins, only one or two of which were occupied at the moment–the main lodge–storage buildings–and the long, low, stone building with narrow windows with the sign out front that simply said "prey." Prey. So, where were they and where had they hidden themselves, out there in the dark? Five had been let loose, he was told. And he was to have only five rounds. He liked the challenge, though–it would make the gathering of a trophy even sweeter.

Breathing in the sweet, herbal, grass-scented air, Simpson gave thanks he had found this place. You could certainly never do such a thing in the States, or Europe, or... well, anywhere else. Africa, yes, if you paid enough and knew the right people and went deep enough into the bush. Which he had, all of that. Well, he was ready. Today, he understood he was to be the only hunter on the land. That was fine with him—more choice, less crowding.

DeGroot came walking up out of the dark, crunching on the gravel walks. "Did you eat, did you have coffee?" he asked, gruffly. Simpson nodded. He wasn't sure he liked DeGroot. Didn't matter. DeGroot had an experience, a product to sell that could be had no other place. Simpson wanted it and could afford it. End of story. The Afrikaner checked his watch. He nodded curtly at Simpson. "It is time. Here is your weapon." He thrust the high-tech looking gun at Simpson. Taking it, examining it, he found he was not unfamiliar with it, having used something very similar from the same manufacturer back in the States. He nodded his acknowledgement. "Five rounds," said DeGroot. "If you waste them, you are done for the day. They know that. You have until 1700 hours." Again, Simpson nodded, liking the camp owner even less. DeGroot added: "They were released half an hour ago. Remember, they might fight back. Good luck." Turning on his heel he walked away.

Simpson took a deep breath, cradling the weapon in his arm. Swinging it up to his shoulder, he found it equipped with a 6X scope and, sure enough, but five rounds. Well... again, he appreciated the challenge. Half an hour's head start... then it was time to head out. Already he could sense the curve of ultraviolet rays creeping over the horizon, the presence of the sun's power sneaking on ahead of it. A solitary bird cried out on the grasslands... or was it a bird? He would soon find out.

Shifting the weapon to carry it by its sling over his shoulder, Simpson walked over to the low stone building for "prey." He could hear faint sounds within, but they were not his quarry... not today at least. Looking at the dusty paths that led from the building were no help; they were well-trodden and confused with many prints. He pursued the path a little ways. It led directly to the perimeter of the reserve, marked here by a thick hedge of wait-a-bit bushes. Simpson knew that elsewhere there were high, barbed-wire fences keeping outsiders out—and the prey inside. Forget the honor system; barriers of steel or thorn made a real enclosure beyond which he could not go—nor could the prey.

2

Simpson edged along the perimeter for a while, scanning the interior of the reserve. He could make nothing out in the early dawn darkness. Taking a different tack, he followed a line of scrub bushes inland, dodging from clump to clump to avoid being seen. Thinking ahead, he filled his pockets with stones as he went along. Coming to a broad-trunked, spread-limbed tree, he scrambled up it and hid himself among the leaves in a spot where he could nevertheless make out the grassland around him. There he waited silently as the sun rose.

Before long the fiery sun rolled up over the horizon, bringing the African plains to life. He could make out mainly birds, but a few grazing animals went by in the distance: gazelles, springbok. There was only one kind of predator to worry about within the preserve. He pulled out binoculars and carefully scanned the horizon. Plains–a clump of trees–a flock of birds rising up from some bushes–more plains. Back to the bushes. Why did the birds fly? Simpson adjusted the focus. There beyond the green and brown was something else. It moved. He scanned around the area then back to the bushes. Still there. Taking his bearings and a landmark, he slipped down quietly from the tree and was on his way like a leopard on a scent.

From the tree to a ridge of rock that rose a bit above the plain. He peered over and scanned the bushes again. Unmistakable now, dark brown or black, a natural color but not of the earth or vegetation. He saw a line of vegetation behind which he could slink, over to his right. He slipped over to it, taking his weapon off his back and holding it to keep it from thrusting up into a line of sight. Closer he came, and closer, then found a taller patch of bush. He crouched down behind this cover, perspiring heavily from the effort as the sun began to assert its authority. Slowly, slowly rising up he took out the binoculars. His new angle made all the difference.

Crouched on his haunches and hands, looking in the direction of the tree where Simpson used to be, was a man no older than eighteen. His skin was a dark milk chocolate, his short cap of kinky curls jet black. He was thin but muscular, the rounded shoulder muscles narrowing down to skinny arms with high, thin, rounded biceps. His legs were wiry, muscular but thin. A simple brown loincloth covered his groin but did not conceal a firm, rounded, high bottom. The youth looked out of an almost Asian face, thin high cheekbones and almond eyes, in the direction of the tree. Simpson thought about it. He could be in range with another scramble, but was this the trophy he wanted? He was authorized to take just the one; maybe he should wait.

As he watched and deliberated, the lad shifted, rocking back and then scooting away, to his right, in an effort to outflank the imaginary enemy in the tree. Once he shifted, Simpson's heart stopped. The youth's movement uncovered a magnificent specimen: Heavily muscled, a shield-shaped chest above a thin, taut abdomen rippling with muscles. His skin was a beautiful coal black, shining with a light coating of oil and sweat. Perhaps twenty, this man crouched on his hands and knees, still looking at the tree, unaware of being observed from his flank. From this posture, the man's African bottom stuck out almost describing an angle, muscular and firm and out-thrusting. A white loincloth wrapped his private parts but seemed especially–full, somehow. The man's face was hourglass shaped beneath a mop of short, twisted tufts, a wide, deep brow, narrow, flat cheeks, and then a strong jaw and prominent, full lips with a wide, full nose. He stared intently through long, curling eyelashes in the direction of the tree.

Simpson's hasty judgment betrayed him. He should have stalked closer. Instead, confident that he could compensate for the range, he angled the cross-hairs of the scope up, braced against the stiff trunk of a bush, and fired. It was a mistake. A branch in front of the man was hit. Instantly, reflexively, the man jerked to his right and was off. Damn! Could he tell where the shot came from? Simpson's only hope was that the pair would think the shot came from the area of the tree. Or, he could hope that he ran into the three other prey. Where were they, he suddenly wondered, and looked around warily. They had no weapons, but there were stones, sticks... and five against one.

Watching over his own shoulder as well as ahead now, Simpson continued skirting low to the ground, carrying his weapon ahead of him and flat against the ground. Scrabbling along, he came to another clump of bush and reconnoitered. The two men he was stalking had moved off a couple of hundred yards and he could see them signaling furtively to someone even farther on. It appeared as if Simpson were following the trailing party of his prey. The younger, dark milk chocolate youth stretched his skinny body along the ground and slithered quickly across an expanse of high grasses while the magnificent coal black man kept watch, a stone in his hand.

It gave Simpson an inspiration. Reaching for a stone in his own pocket, he picked a time when both men were occupied in moving–and he hoped the other three were too far on to see him. Moving to a crouch for a better position, he wound up and threw the stone as far as he could in front of his prey but beyond them, in the direction toward which they were moving.

It worked. The thin youth froze, looking intently in that direction, making a motion with the palm of his hand to the closer prize whom Simpson had now decided was his main trophy. The man flattened his muscular body close to the ground and looked in the direction where the stone had landed, keeping stock still. From where he crouched, Simpson could see the high rounded hill of his white-garbed buttocks contrasting with the deep black of his skin. Slowly, carefully, Simpson used the moment of distraction to close in.

He slithered forward carefully, silently. Closer, closer. One hundred fifty yards, then one twenty-five. Two dark heads came up to look warily forward. Simpson paused, fetched out another stone, look beyond the men to where their companions must be—he still saw nothing—and flung the second stone as hard as he could in the same direction. Hearing a hit, the men hunkered down again, now indecisive as to what their next move should be. Slowly, carefully, inching along in the hot sun, heedless of flies and insects and the dust that occasionally blew across his face, Simpson got closer and closer. One hundred yards, then a little closer, and a little closer.

There was a sharp snap; he had crawled over a dry branch, breaking it. Simpson flattened himself completely, looking through a clump of grass. The two men were looking left and right warily, wondering if their enemy had flanked them, still unaware that he—Simpson—was coming up from behind. The white hunter dared not move. The men looked around—then the dark milk chocolate youth looked behind him and caught a glimpse of something unusual, a still but unfamiliar shape in the grass. Startled, he stifled a cry and gestured behind him. The larger, black man spun around on his haunches, fingertips on the grass, ready to spring away. Simpson reacted instintively, bringing the gun up, planting the cross-hairs on the man's dark chest right between two round, black nipples, and squeezed the trigger. A bloom of scarlet appeared on his chest, and there was a cry of dismay to the right.

Whipping out his radio, Simpson called in: "I have one down. Come collect him. I'll leave this on for you to triangulate on my coordinates." Then he sat up, resting in the tall grass as from one direction far away came the sound of the Land Rover and closer in the other direction was the sound of bare feet running away.

Later that evening, after dinner, cognac, cigars, and DeGroot's repeated congratulations, Simpson sat in the living room of his cabin clothed in a dressing gown before a small bundle of burning wood in the fireplace. Soft lamplight lit the cabin. There was a knock on his door. "Come in," he said, and DeGroot entered. He nodded at Simpson, his face carefully professional.

"Your trophy is being cleaned and prepared and will be sent right over," said the camp owner. "You did well for yourself, one of our best," he continued.

Simpson nodded, looking back at the fire and then at DeGroot. "Tell me," he asked, "what's in it for them? Why do they do this?"

DeGroot shrugged and looked into the fire. "Well, you know, life in the villages is very hard. If they escape five runnings they are paid handsomely, so handsomely that it seems like a princely sum when they return to their villages. Not all do return right away, some sign on for five more runnings. Nobody ever makes it to ten escapes," said DeGroot, smiling, shaking his head. "Although—although sometimes I wonder if some of them, a few, you know, actually don't try to escape. Life in the villages really can be very hard, you know, and maybe they see the consequences as preferable. At any rate," he said, shaking his head, "whether you choose to tip the, uh, staff for its services is up to you. They appreciate it. Frankly, they may expect it. A little goes a long way in the bush."

Simpson nodded. There was a knock on the door behind DeGroot, who turned. One of the camp staff stepped into the room, his head bowed and eyes carefully averted. Looking back into the darkness beyond the door he nodded—and into the soft light stepped the coal black man Simpson had tagged that day, the scarlet paint from the pellet now scrubbed off. In fact, his whole body was cleaned, glistening from a bath, tiny diamonds of water in his black tufts of hair—and he was entirely naked. He stood in the room, head bowed.

"Well, we'll leave you now," said DeGroot, and he and his employee left the room, carefully closing the door behind them.

Simpson sat, quietly appraising the naked black body before him. Slowly, the man raised his head and made eye contact with the white man in the chair. A smile, shy at first and then spreading wider, parted his full, moist lips. Slowly, the long, thick, purple black cock that hung halfway down to his knees began to rise, gradually arching straight out with a slight curve downward, over a dangling, full ballsack and beneath a small patch of dense, nappy pubic hair. The lamplight of the room played over the hills and valleys of his muscular body as he stood there, smiling, awaiting the consequences of having "lost." If this was in fact losing.

Simpson beckoned him forward. Coming to stand very close to the white man's chair, the black's penis was now rampant. Simpson bent over and took it into his mouth, sucking it, kneading the large dickhead with his lips. The man sighed, and whispered "Boss!" Simpson kept sucking as the man's hips began a slow rhythm back and forth, his wet, jet black tool riding in and out of the white man's pink lips. Simpson reached around and grabbed his muscular butt, pulling him forward closer still. Tentatively, and then more assertively when the gesture was not refused, the man put his strong black hands on Simpson's shoulders. Faster he rocked now, and then he dared to push the dressing gown off of Simpson's shoulders, which fell to the seat of the chair, revealing his white shoulders, chest, and belly. He slid his dark fingers over the unaccustomed white skin, wondering and exploring. With half-opened lips, through shuttered eyes the black man looked down at his dick going in and out of the pink lips until his semen rose within him. Crying out, he whispered fiercely "I come, Boss, I come," but still Simpson held on, and the black man bucked forward and spewed his semen into the white man's mouth, where it was swallowed greedily.

The black man was still shuddering, his penis still rampant, when Simpson rose and guided his trophy toward the bed. The white man pushed the black onto the bed on his hands and knees. Reaching for the tube of lubricant by the bedside, Simpson greased up his penis—but not the waiting, wrinkled black anus in front of him—and rammed his organ straight inside. The black man writhed and cried out, but did not move. Fully landed, Simpson began slamming back and forth quickly, conquering the man's butt as he had conquered his body, had earned the right to this privilege, earlier that day. His white thighs pressed against black thighs, ballsack swayed and slapped against ballsack, his red rampant cock sliding in and out of a hard, protuberant black butt. Simpson did not hold back this first time but came violently, roaring, pushing hard into the man and forcing him down, flat on the bed as his semen shot into the moist rectum. There the two lay as Simpson recovered breath.

Then the white man rose and extinguished the oil lamps, threw a few more logs on the fire, gathered up two snifters of cognac which he placed on a nearby table, and went back to the bed. He slipped under the covers beside his trophy, slid a palm over the broad muscular chest, tweaked a nipple, and then cupped the head of tufted hair in his hand. "What is your name?" he asked.

"Motumbo, Boss."

"Well, Motumbo, my name is Simpson. And this is just the beginning of a long weekend....."

- CHAPTER 2 -

"Mr. Simpson? Mr. Simpson?" It took a moment, but the forty year old man with the fair skin, salt and pepper hair, and blue eyes suddenly started and turned from the window-wall of his office to acknowledge his secretary, thirty yards away at the door.

"I have the Warner files, Mr. Simpson, let me just leave them here." The middle age woman, a picture of efficiency itself walked briskly to his desk, placed a foot thick pile of paper on a corner of the gleaming, polished mahogany, then withdrew. It took her a little while to traverse the distances on the thick carpet. Andrew Simpson sighed heavily, called back from the most pleasant daydream, a daydream in which a coal black man with a shield-shaped chest figured prominently. Simpson was moving now ever closer to a decision he knew he must make. He glanced quickly outside through the rain streaked expanse of glass at the grey Philadelphia morning sky. He looked at the departing form of his secretary, middle-aged and broad as a couch but deadly efficient. The thought flashed upon his mind that he had eschewed young, attractive help in favor of the older, the more mature, the more efficient—the less sexually complicated. How often had he fended off the ribbing of his colleagues with an appeal to that efficiency, to all the hours he billed for the firm? "Mrs. DeNiro," he said.

"Yes, sir?" she turned smartly and stopped.

"Thank you. Please ask Mr. Heliger to step in, if convenient."

"Yes sir," she replied, and then she was gone.

Simpson turned back to view the gathering autumn, the inevitable dusk, the reminder that each human must sooner or later go through fall and then winter. He wanted to turn back the calendar. He intended to do it soon, and perhaps today was the time. Ten minutes later there was a knock on his door, and Dandridge Heliger eased his grey eminence through the door and into the office. "Andy, wanted to see me?"

Andrew Simpson turned again and looked at him, pausing, considering. He gathered a breath and took the plunge.

"Dandy, thanks for coming. I... I am resigning my partnership. I can work out the details with Stone, he can do all the paperwork. Let's just say... let's say it's for my health." He looked again at the gathering grey.

Heliger stepped closer, but it took him a while given the vast ranges of Simpson's office. "Andy, can this be? Is it... is it serious? What... what can I do?" he rumbled in his patrician tones.

Simpson saw the opportunity to enact the perfect role for the circumstances. He sighed audibly, looked down, then up at the senior partner of the firm. "I have been advised to rest and to seek a better climate. I might get back into the game some day, and you know I'll miss... this..." he waved vaguely around him. "But it's something I have to do. I don't have a choice. Thanks for understanding." Heliger nodded, and the two shook hands.

It didn't happen right away. A week, a dozen meetings, and three trees worth of paperwork later, his condo on the market, his possession sold, his few relatives assured of his insanity, Andrew Simpson looked out of another window onto the hazy leaden Atlantic far, far below, as he winged his way toward Africa. Was he insane? He himself had to admit it: he was following the vision of his daydream, wrapped up in memories of the man he had met... the man he had won...in African months before. Was that man still there, did he even remember Simpson? Was this some adolescent crush? What were the odds that Motumbo had any recollection of Simpson? It was a crazy chance, and he knew it.

A whole day and two flights later he still was not at his final destination, but he was sound asleep at the airport hotel outside of Johannesburg, spending three days recovering. He never left the steel and glass confines of the modern hotel, far from the slums, far from the bush. He lived on room service, sleep, and fantasies. Finally, he bought–not rented–the Land Rover he had previously ordered and, loaded with the provisions he required, he set out in the direction of the future.

A four lane modern highway led to a two lane, which led to a dirt road which led to... the savannah. The crowded traffic gradually thinned, the last overloaded buses and crammed, rusty old sedans slowly thinning out. His speed slowed as the quality of the road deteriorated, swerving around potholes, taking narrow roads on curves where he prayed no other vehicle was oncoming. Simpson drove with the map and directions on the seat beside him and one eye on the GPS, consulting them every now and then, stopping from time to time to stretch his muscles, to eat the prepared food he had brought, to drink water and to look out across the rolling grasslands. Finally, as late afternoon shadows of the trees were lengthening, he turned down a dirt driveway marked by a small sign and, in a few minutes, pulled up to the compound he knew so well. The gates were shut. He blew the horn and after a few minutes a man he remembered came down the path from the cluster of buildings he could see on a hill. It was a man who had first brought to him, that night just a few months ago, his magnificent "prize:" Motumbo. He had never learned the name of the middle aged African who now approached, his wiry hair tinged with grey. But he recognized him and, after peering through the fence, the man nodded, grunted, and opened the gate to him. The African stepped up to his window.

"Welcome, Boss," he said, his face careful but inquisitive. "Boss De Groot, he gone. He leave you papers in the big house. Come in, Boss," he said. Simpson offered him his hand. The African looked at it in surprise, considered for a moment, and took it. He stepped back as Simpson pulled through the gate and stopped. As the African closed and locked the gate, Simpson stuck his head out. "Ride back up the hill?" he asked. Again a moment of appraisal, and the African nodded, then got into the car.

Simpson again extended his hand. "My name is Simpson. Andrew Simpson. And yours..." The African paused again for but a second, considering, wondering, and then said, "Thabo, Boss."

"We have met before, Thabo."

"Yes Boss," said Thabo, averting his gaze, looking straight ahead.

"Thabo...Thabo, I hope that you will continue working for me. But you don't need to call me 'Boss.' Simpson or, if you must, Mr. Simpson, or even Andrew will do. Thabo is your first name?" The African nodded, now looking with frank interest at the white man beside him.

"Well, I wish you would stay and work for me as you did for De Groot. But if it is 'Thabo' for me, it had better be 'Andrew' for you." Simpson broke into a broad grin. Thabo continued to stare at him as if a mythical beast had risen before him. Then he nodded and said, "Yes, Boss Andrew." Simpson chuckled; it could wait. The two drove the short distance to the buildings of the compound.

Stepping out of the car, Simpson looked around. "When did De Groot leave?" he asked.

"This morning, Boss Andrew," Thabo replied.

"Are there... Guests? Are we expecting any tomorrow or in the next week?"

Thabo hung his head slightly, shaking it. "We got one party, Boss Andrew. They to be here two more days. No other business. Boss De Groot...well, he not do so much with business, you know, Boss? Too much bottle in the last month," he said. Simpson nodded; he had received intimations of De Groot's impending collapse before. He didn't mind. He was not entirely sure he wanted to keep the business going as it had been. They drove a few more yards, and Simpson was compelled to ask the question he had been rehearsing for months.

"Thabo...do you remember Motumbo? He was... He and I... well..."

Thabo took mercy on him and nodded, looking away from Simpson. "Yes, Boss Andrew. Sometime he work, sometime not. Not a lot since you left. He in his village, Boss, not far." Simpson nodded, his heart beating more rapidly. They finally reached the buildings of the compound, pulling up to the largest dwelling, the caretaker's lodge. Now, it was his.

Turning to his luggage, and with Thabo's help, he unloaded the vehicle and moved his belongings into the caretaker's lodge. It looked as if De Groot had simply packed his own luggage and left. There were even cigarette butts in an ashtray. With Thabo's quiet assistance, Simpson had his belongings stowed away in good order before long. By then, night had truly fallen. The cries of the night birds and animals could be heard, some distant and some far off.

"You hungry, Boss Andrew? We got some springbok steaks" said Thabo. Simpson broke into a wide grin.

"That would be splendid, Thabo. And...our guests, have they eaten? Should I introduce myself?" he asked.

Thabo averted his gaze, his tone becoming carefully neutral. "They busy, Boss," he said. "They got a trophy this morning, been busy all day. I take food to their cabin later. And drink," he said, emphasizing the last word. Simpson thought for a moment, considering the meanings in what Thabo had left unsaid.

"Alright, Thabo, I will meet them tomorrow. I would love some dinner." Thabo brightened at this news and hurried off to prepare some food while Simpson continued to unpack. It was strange; it certainly looked as if De Groot had simply decamped with only his clothing, yet the space did not seem marked with another man's personality. It felt like home. With its wood construction, wild animal skins for throw rugs, rough-hewn furniture and massive stone fireplace, it seemed the perfect hunting lodge, yet it also seemed to Simpson as if he had lived here, not just since he began imagining it a few months ago, but forever.

Simpson had a small, bright fire going in the fireplace when Thabo returned with a covered tray. Thabo set in on the table and removed the cover, revealing a massive steak and vegetables. Simpson smiled broadly as he walked to the table, where Thabo was laying a single setting.

"It looks wonderful Thabo, thanks," he said. "Will you join me, have you eaten? It looks like enough for two."

Not for the first time, Thabo looked at Simpson in wonder. Then smiling shyly, he replied, "Thanks Boss Andrew, I ate. But....thanks. You eat, Boss."

"That's 'Andrew,' Thabo."

"You eat, Boss Andrew." Smiling again, thinking he might have to yield to the inevitable, Simpson sat. Surprised at his own hunger, he tore into the meal while Thabo watched with an air of satisfaction. After a few bites, he looked at Thabo. The African was not tall, of tough, wiry build, flecks of grey in his close cap of kinky hair. His broad, fudge colored face broke into a smile.

"Thabo, who is still working here, since De Groot left? Who is on staff?"

"Yes, Boss Andrew, we got me, the cook, two cleaning women they come in from the village once a day, Zama the night guard—he walkin' round outside with the shotgun at night—and three, uh... three of the prey, Boss." At this last mention Thabo's gaze shifted away from Simpson's. In embarrassment? In deference? Simpson wondered what Thabo thought of the business De Groot ran...the business Simpson himself had bought. "Oh, and the doctor from the government post down to the village, he come over whenever we got new clients or...prey, Boss Andrew. He test 'em, make sure everybody healthy." Simpson nodded again. It was a wise arrangement. He decided he might press the issue of "prey" a bit.

"And the prey...the young men..." Thabo's eyes caught Simpson's more directly for a moment, then flickered away again. "Three of them. Is one with the clients?" Thabo nodded and murmured yes under his breath. Simpson continued: "What kind of people are these clients?"

Thabo looked hard at his employer, appraising, assessing. "They not so good men, Boss Andrew," he said. "Russians. They drink a lot. We's had some good clients from Russia but...not these ones."

"When do they go?"

"Day after tomorrow they last day, Boss Andrew." Simpson nodded, but determined to keep his eye on them. And he had some hard thinking to do about whether to continue "the business." Pushing back from the table, he thanked Thabo, who smiled in satisfaction and collected the dinner things. As Thabo moved toward the door, Simpson walked up behind him.

"Thabo, please introduce me to Zama," Simpson asked. Thabo nodded. On the way to the kitchen, he whistled loudly. A tall, rail thin man in his forties seemed to materialize from the darkness, his own dark color congealing from out of the shadows. Over his shoulder he carried a semi-automatic shotgun. Thabo introduced Zama and his new employer. Zama was a man of few words, carrying himself with an air of formal elegance and restraint, but Simpson reflected that he would not want to be on the wrong side of the gun. With a slight bow, Zama blended again with the night shadows.

Simpson told Thabo he wanted simply to walk around the compound. It was not large, and the outer fence was clearly visible, piled mud and earth in some places, high chain link with razor wire in other places. Thabo nodded and suggested, needlessly, that Simpson not go beyond the fence.

"Should we tell Zama I am out and about?" asked Simpson.

Thabo grinned broadly. "He know where you are, Boss Andrew. All the time. You can't see him, he can see you." Simpson nodded, both reassured and disconcerted at the knowledge of Zama's armed omniscience. He and Thabo bade each other good evening, and then Simpson began to walk slowly around the compound. It was just as he had remembered. From the building marked "Prey" came a soft light and the soft sounds of men's voices in quiet discussion…. these men would be "released" tomorrow, running from the predatory Russians…or enticing them? Simpson had never been sure during his visit, and De Groot seemed to imply some ambivalence on that score.

Simpson walked from building to building, then down the path that led to the more remote clients' cabins. He thought he recognized the one he had occupied, then a couple that stood empty. Then, at the end of the path, was the cabin occupied by his sole "guests," a soft light showing at the windows. The sound of men's voices could be heard as he came nearer, stepping softly, voices not in conversation. There was a cry of pain, not agony but discomfort. A harsh chuckle, then another in a different voice. Instructions growled. Something said urgently in a voice with unmistakable African tones. Then the sound of a slap on flesh, and a gasp. Teetering between concern and diffidence, between knowledge that the Russians had paid for their pleasure and a concern for the nameless African who was yielding it, Simpson paused. Then, in spite of himself, he stepped silently down the packed earth path toward the cabin. Nobody had bothered to curtain the windows. Simpson peered around the corner of a window and looked inside.

In a softly lit room stood a large, fleshy white man, nearly bald, with a jowly face covered with moles and warts. His rolls of flesh were partially covered by the black man he held in front of him, holding the African by his upper arms, the man's back to the white man's front, pulling the dark body into his fleshy torso. The African looked very young, eighteen barely. His skin was a medium brown that seemed darker in the light, highlights of dark honey here and there. The young man was slim but with a taut, muscular body, well defined chest and abdomen. His lips were two full rolls of flesh beneath a rounded, flared nose. A cap of tight peppercorn hair covered his head atop a slender neck. The youth's penis was dark and long, half-erect now beneath another small patch of peppercorn curls, beginning to arc out at an angle in front of his body above a heavy ballsack that hugged tightly to his body. The youth's hairless skin glowed in the soft light.

Another naked white man, at least a decade younger than the big man who held the African pinioned, strutted up and down in front of their black "captive." This man had a full shock of blonde-white hair, and a well developed, muscled body. He was talking incessantly, softly, and evidently in Russian. The youth could not have understood him, but the dark eyes of the captive African followed the younger man, maybe in fear, maybe in anticipation, it was hard to tell. Twice the younger Russian stopped to run his hand over the black youth's hairless chest and torso, each time pausing to pinch and twist the youth's purple dark, cone-shaped nipples, the young African wincing each time. And once...the Russian slapped the youth's face with an open hand. Simpson started, and some impulse in him wanted to burst into the cabin, but he held himself back. The two white men had paid for this, and the African had known what he was getting into...and would be paid himself for his troubles. Still, Simpson had a bad taste in his mouth about it.

A few more minutes of this passed. The younger white man's penis was now fully erect and purple, sticking out at attention. A thin thread of precum swung from the tip as he walked. To tell the truth, the African's penis was fully erect as well, arcing a little upward despite its length and weight. The heavy white man remained where he was, but continued to pull the African in toward him, grinding his groin into the black man's firm, protruding buttocks as he held the youth by the arms. In spite of himself, in spite of his disapproval, Simpson's own cock had begun to swell.

The white men exchanged some words, and suddenly the large white man pushed the African forward onto his hands and knees on a nearby bed. The heavy white man's penis could now be seen, also erect, beneath heavy folds of abdominal flesh. Reaching quickly for a tube of lubricant, the large white man greased his shaft liberally. Then stepping back up to the African who was on knees and elbows on the bed, the heavy white man put his erect tool to the prominent bottom of the black youth and push, hard. The African cried out, raising his head up and grimacing. The heavy white man pushed forward on the man's thin but muscular shoulders, pushing his head back down, and continued to push his groin into the firm black butt before him. The African groaned and squirmed but did not resist. There was a pause, and then the white man began pushing in and out, back and forth, his heavy flesh making a slapping sound as it connected with the chocolate flesh kneeling before him.

Now the other white man jumped onto the bed in one quick motion and positioned himself at the African's head. He reached down and lifted the black man's chin, aligning the thick, rolled lips with the leaking head of his rampant cock. The African was gasping in pain from the assault on his rectum, but he understood what was required of him. Opening his mouth, he took the younger white man's cock into his mouth. The black youth was now being fucked fore and aft by the white men, his own cock turgid and full, swinging almost down to the bed beneath his groin, his own midnight ballsack slapping against the testicles of the heavy white man who was pistoning in and out of him from behind.

Again, the heavy white man pushed the black man on his back, and then began slapping the rounded buttocks between which his rampant red cock was sliding in and out. Each thrust brought another slap, each slap harder than the last. The white man whose dick was being sucked held the African now by both ears, tweaking and twisting them, now by the head, digging his fingers into the tight, crisp hair, now slapping the black man's thin, muscular shoulders. The bed creaked with the increasing rhythms of the two whites. The African who was captive between them moaned and squealed softly, but was powerless to escape being fucked from both ends.

With a mighty push and a shudder, the heavy white man came, pushing forward, nearly toppling the black youth as well as the younger white man at the other end. His breathe seethed and he slapped the black youth's butt twice, quite hard, then shuddered, then stood still, breathing heavily, his eyes closed. It took the younger white man a few minutes and then he also came, bucking his hips as his cock poured semen into the black youth's mouth, a gurgling sound of frantic swallowing coming from the captive's throat. The younger white man held that position, shuddering, and then pulled out, a trail of white semen coming from the black youth's thick lips as the red penis pulled away. The younger white man collapsed down onto his back and panted heavily, catching his breath. With an audible plop, the heavy set white man pulled his own wilting dick out from between the firm, rounded black bottom. With one push of his arm he swept the black youth off of the bed, then staggered forward to collapse next to his younger compatriot. Both white men lay side by side, panting, each one now reaching out to softly stroke the body of his companion, the younger man running his fingers over the mounds and lobes of the heavy man's flesh. The African picked himself up off the floor and walked stiffly to a chair in the corner of the room. There he sat, his own penis still erect and unrelieved, awaiting further instructions.

Simpson could take no more. He knew the Russians had paid for this, but he had a bad feeling about their treatment of the African, who sat gingerly on the chair, eyes closed. Simpson pulled away from the window and walked back up the path as quietly as he could. He was glad the two were leaving soon.

In the caretaker's lodge, in what was now his own bed, Simpson quickly fell asleep. But his dreams were all of a very dark, beautiful man with a shield-shaped chest, and when he awoke he found, to his wonder, that even at his age he had had a wet dream in the night.

Simpson rose and showered, dressing quickly. When he emerged, he saw that Thabo, alerted by the light in the lodge, had laid out breakfast. The black man was just preparing to depart.

"Good morning, Thabo," said Simpson.

"Morning, Boss Andrew."

"The Russians...are they hunting again this morning? Should I greet them, speak to them?"

Thabo's face was carefully composed. "They not go out today, Boss Andrew, they say they keep Little Mandla another day. Sometimes they clients, they do that, pays twice, if the one they catches agrees."

"Little Mandla...that was the name of the one they were with?"

"Yes, Boss Andrew, they say he OK with that."

"Did you hear that from Little Mandla himself?"

"No...no Boss, I didn't no hear, but Little Mandla, he take care of hisself." Thabo's face was still cautiously neutral.

Simpson considered, but decided that if Thabo was alright with the arrangement, he would be too...for now. Sitting down to his breakfast, Simpson gathered up his courage to say what he had planned to say.

"Thabo...I want to go visit Motumbo. Can you tell me how to find him? Is it easy enough?"

Thabo looked appraisingly at the white man, interest and comprehension growing. "Sure, Boss Andrew, not hard to get to his village. If he there. I think he is. You drive out?" Simpson nodded. "I fix food and water for you...and a gun, you need a gun out there," he said. Simpson nodded again and thanked Thabo, who likewise nodded, then left. Simpson quickly ate his breakfast. Finding a hat and a jacket to ward off the sun, Simpson walked out into the morning that was already warm and sunny. He was pleased to see that Thabo was just gassing up his vehicle, and that a basket of water and provisions had been stored in the back. Walking to the vehicle and peering in, Simpson recognized a Winchester in .458, well oiled, nestling in the gun rack behind the driver's seat.

Thabo gave directions, which did indeed seem clear. The two men rode down to the gate, shaking hands again as Thabo stepped out to open the gate and let Simpson through, then close it behind him. The men waved to one another as Simpson drove off, slowly for the sake of the terrain, quickly for the sake of his impatience, in the direction of Motumbo's village.

A Boner Book

- CHAPTER 3 -

Simpson's Land Rover bounced and jostled its way down the dirt path from the camp to a marginally better road, and turned right at the intersection. He drove with Thabo's directions and a map in the seat beside him, alternately scanning the landscape and consulting his guides. Twice he swerved out of the way to miss oncoming buses, each one loaded to the gunwales with people and possessions, crates and luggage and adventurous riders even strapped aboard on top. Once again he turned, off of the branch road and onto another "road," an impacted dirt path, really, that would take him to Motumbo's village. He was surprised to see that it was not as far as he had feared. Two hours of careful driving brought him at last to the village.

If he had imagined grass huts or mud shelters, he was mistaken. Western culture had infected Africa, along with the strange economic patterns it had introduced that turned so many once self-sufficient societies into famine-prone market economies linked to far-off stores in Europe and the States. The village was a collection of structures made of wood framing, some with grey wooden sides, some with rusted, half-painted tin or aluminum sheets for walls, corrugated iron or peeling plywood for roofs. A few houses seemed more prosperous: square, cinder-block structures with small patches of garden surrounding them, occasional stray electrical lines running here and there to a lucky few, the scent of coal fires for cooking breakfasts still lingering in the air. Some vehicles were parked next to these structures, most of them pickups, none of them new. Even at this hour, the local shebeen was open to sell beer and packaged snacks, and seemed to be the busiest location there. One or two ramshackle huts advertised themselves as cafes, and smoke curled from stovepipes sticking out of their side walls. An open air stand sold fruit under an awning. The sound of metal striking metal came from a nearby all-purpose mechanic and repair shop. Stray chickens and small children dressed only in shorts scattered here and there. Women drew water from a central pump, and men in old but clean clothing sat here and there in the shade. A few curious people stared in his direction. De Groot had been correct, months ago: life in the villages seemed to be hard, and other than the shebeen, cafes, and mechanic, there seemed to be no organized businesses or places of employment. Simpson pulled the Land Rover over and took in the scene. He could well imagine the young men of this village, and dozens like it, coming to De Groot...and now himself...for employment.

So he was here. And somewhere nearby might be Motumbo. And Simpson's heart was suddenly, unaccountably, beating hard, hard to match the hardness of his constricted breathing. Simpson, who had stalked Manhattan courtrooms like a lion, seeking whom he may destroy, was sitting alone in his vehicle at the edge of a dusty African village like a boy on his first date, afraid to go ring the doorbell. Andrew Simpson had planned his exit from his firm, he had planned the liquidation of his assets, he had planned the purchase of De Groot's operation and had made the move. But his fantasies about this moment had remained that, just fantasies. Now in the moment, he realized he had no clear plan of what to do. Perhaps he had envisioned Motumbo laid out naked and beckoning on a halfshell, ready to be scooped up and taken off. Struck with his own foolishness and utterly at a loss as to what to do, Simpson sat in the gathering heat and breathed deeply, trying to regain composure and to make a plan.

As he sat composing himself and thinking, hope appeared in the form of two teenage boys, seeming to be about sixteen each, wearing clean but torn shorts and t-shirts. Padding up quietly in the dust, in their bare feet, the two materialized right by Simpson's car door, broad grins splitting their handsome dark faces with white. They had come to inspect the spectacle that had appeared near their homes. Simpson nodded at them and smiled, and then realized that he had no idea whether the people here spoke English. He had none at all of their own language, whatever it may be. Motumbo spoke some

English, enough to get by…. to get by in De Groot's context… but that might be a more specialized use than these boys were accustomed to!

"Good morning," Simpson essayed. The boys giggled and looked at each other. With a start, Simpson realized they were twins.

"Good morning" they each replied, very carefully, even with exaggeration… Were they mocking him or trying to get it right?

"Do you speak English?" he asked.

One of them, with a beautiful deep dark complexion, button nose, and sparkling eyes, took half a step forward. "Yes, I learn English in school!" he said, his thin chest thrust out proudly, each word carefully molded and carefully laid in the space between them. His companion, not so brave, continued to grin and nodded vigorously.

"I am Andrew Simpson," extending a hand.

Delighted with their success so far, the boy scrunched up his cute features in thought and then replied, carefully, extending his own hand. "I am Thatho Ndebele. May I present to you my brother, Mthobisi Ndebele." Each word was labored over and proudly uttered, as he gestured grandly at his shyer brother who giggled again but stepped up to have his hand shaken.

Simpson smiled broadly. "Where do you go to school?" he asked, pushing his linguistic luck. The two boys stared intently at him, quickly huddled, a mixture of English and non-English words were whispered back and forth, and then Thatho grinned again, stood stock upright once more, and replied, each word its own event:

"We go to Mission School. Nearly graduated. Mission School, three miles there!" and he pointed to the east.

Simpson nodded. He stepped out of the car and summoned his courage for his next question.

"Do you know a man named Motumbo? He is tall, like this," raising a flattened palm to a little over his own height. "Motumbo," he repeated. "I… I do not know his family name," said Simpson, feeling a little crestfallen and a little stupid at the admission. He might at least have asked Thabo before he left. "He is, maybe, twenty years old." The boys gaped at him, struggling to absorb this enormous amount of information in a strange language. "Motumbo," Simpson repeated, helplessly, wordlessly and hopelessly indicating the man's height again.

The boys scrunched up their eyes and turned to each other, whispering again in consternation. Suddenly, the shyer one's face was alight with revelation and he whispered even more urgently to his brother. There was more discussion and nodding, and then Thatho turned triumphantly to Simpson.

"We know Motumbo. Motumbo Sisele. He is our—" another pause and whispered consultation—"he is our cousin."

Simpson nodded, smiling. "Will you tell me where his house is? Where does he live?"

More whispers, then enlightenment. "Yes, we can take you. You will come?" Thatho turned as if to lead the way up the dusty street. Simpson quickly gestured toward the Land Rover.

"Would you like to ride?" he asked.

The boys reacted as if they had been invited to board the space shuttle. Grinning hugely, they gingerly entered the vehicle on the passenger side, sliding on the front seat with Mthobisi on the outside, Thatho in the middle, both sitting as erect as kings, looking left and right in hopes that their friends might see them. Simpson admired their youthful beauty and enjoyed their physical proximity, but that was not what he was here for. "That way," said Thatho, pointing down the road. As the Land Rover rolled slowly away, Simpson was aware of what a spectacle they made, and what fame the boys were gaining by being conveyed in this enchanted chariot.

The distance was not far at all, but the house stood on the other side of the little community, on the edge of the little village as it melted away into bush country. It was one of the better ones, cinder block, with a new, corrugated metal roof, surrounded by a chain link fence, a tidy garden, and wonder of wonders! its own water pump in the yard. Simpson thanked the boys gravely, and they all shook hands once more around. Fishing into his pocket, he found some money to give them—it was clear from their reactions that it was a princely tip—and the boys leaped from the car. But they did not go far. Huddling at the corner of a nearby building, they hung around to see what new drama would unfold.

Simpson wondered the same thing himself. He stepped from the Land Rover, breathing hard and slow to calm his racing heart, and stood in front of the fence gate, staring at the door. Summoning his courage, he opened the gate and shut it behind him, then took the few steps to the front door, hesitated, and knocked. He could hear a soft voice—or perhaps two—inside, the scraping of a chair on the floor, footsteps. The door opened.

Inside stood an attractive young woman of about twenty, her hair an inch-long cap of wiry black hair, tobacco colored skin that was smooth and flawless, a heart shaped face with bee-stung lips, a cute, broad, rounded nose, and a figure so attractive it almost tempted Simpson. His heart sank. He had imagined having to get reacquainted with Motumbo, he had imagined having to woo him to return to the camp, but for some reason it never entered his mind that he would have female competition. All confidence drained right out of him. Nevertheless, to avoid looking the complete fool, he found voice.

"Good morning. My name is Andrew Simpson. Is Motumbo here?"

The woman looked puzzled and curious, staring intently with her bright/dark eyes under long, curling lashes at this white stranger. Perhaps she doesn't speak English, Simpson thought. "Motumbo?" he repeated. The woman started at the familiar name and grinned, shook her head yes, said a few words in a language Simpson couldn't place, and darted back into the house, leaving the door opened but a crack. There were voices within. A moment passed, the door opened again, and there he stood.

Simpson's breath was momentarily taken away; Motumbo was as handsome as he had remembered. He still kept his hair in a short mop of twisted tufts above an hourglass-shaped face with a strong jaw, full, luscious lips and a broad nose, dark eyes shining brightly under long lashes. Motumbo had on a loose-fitting shirt and khakis that did not disguise his powerful physique, a shield-shaped chest tapering down to what Simpson knew to be rippling abs, and a tight compact pelvis with, Simpson also knew from experience, a high, rounded, firm African butt behind. The African stood tall and regally in his own doorway as if it were the entrance to a palace. Simpson was for a moment at a loss for words.

In that moment Motumbo looked blankly at him, and then a flash of recognition spread over his handsome features, followed by a look of curiosity and appraisal. Simpson recovered voice, and they spoke together, over one another: "Boss!/Motumbo, I don't know if you remember..." Both stopped, then laughed softly. Simpson continued.

"Motumbo, I don't know if you remember me. We, uh, met...we met at De Groot's a few months ago. You were, uh....you were working there and...uh..." How to describe what had passed between them? "We spent the weekend together" he concluded, lamely.

Motumbo nodded, smiling but with an air of reserve. "Yes, Boss, I remember. I go to...I work at De Groot's maybe five, six time...not so many!" Was it an explanation, a self-justification, an apology? "Your name, Boss....Sampson?"

"No, it's Simpson. Andrew Simpson. Please call me Andrew, not Boss," he said, extending his hand. Motumbo nodded and extended his own, enfolding Simpson's hand in warm strength. Then he released it.

"Why you back, Boss? Uh, Andrew... Why you back? You are De Groot's again?"

"I, um, I bought the place from De Groot. He is gone now. Can we," said Simpson looking left and right, "can we talk privately? Can we walk down the road?" he asked, nodding in the direction of the dirt road that led away from the house in the direction of the bush. Motumbo also looked left and right, shrugged, said something in a soft voice to the woman inside the house, and stepped down off his porch, closing the door behind him. They walked a few steps in silence as Simpson gathered his thoughts; out of the corner of his eye, he thought he could see a flicker, the boys shifting position around the corner of the nearest building so as to continue spying on him.

Motumbo broke the silence. "You want me come work for you...Andrew? At De Groot's?"

Simpson evaded the question momentarily. "Do many men from around here work at De Groot's?"

"Oh, some, Andrew. De Groot, he ask we who work for him, find him others. They have to be," and here he smiled and ducked his head, "they have to be good to look at, you know?" Simpson nodded. "So, Boss...so, Andrew. You come here to ask me to work? I don't know, you see I got—"

Simpson interrupted him, quickly placing his hand on the thick arm of the man beside him, then withdrawing it. "Motumbo, I... if you want to work, alright, but....Motumbo, that's not why I came." Motumbo looked at him with interest; they were away from any houses now, and perhaps the increased privacy unlocked something in Simpson. It came gushing out: "Motumbo, since I was here, I could think of nothing but you. I know, you were working when we...when we were together last time. I know you have....worked for other men at De Groot's. I know you have other things, other people in your life," and now a sense of futility and despair began to wash over Simpson. What was he doing here? He pushed on: "I didn't know if you would even remember me. But you, I, you were the only thing I could think of for months. In my thoughts, my dreams. Motumbo....I know this must be embarrassing for you, but I came back because I want you. Well, I want to be near you, I mean... if you need to work for me, alright, but..." His language was beginning to fail him. He stopped, half-turned and looked at the tall, nearly coal black African almost in despair. "I came back because I want you," he half-whispered, hopelessly.

There was a silence. Not smiling, Motumbo regarded the white man deeply. Simpson held his gaze for but a moment, then dropped his head. Not unkindly, Motumbo spoke:

"Boss...Andrew....This my life here. I got house, a woman, do a little work." Simpson nodded agreement, hopelessly. "What you think, you come back and I give up all and come with you?" It was as much an honest query as an accusation. Simpson hung his head and shrugged; it was exactly what he had fantasized, and the absurdity of his situation was growing stronger every moment. Motumbo continued, a little bit of steel in his voice now: "Boss, you not own me."

Simpson shook his head violently. "No, Motumbo, I don't and I don't want to. That's exactly what I don't want to do. I just...I just want to be with you. Maybe not all the time, I don't know. If you want work, you can...it doesn't have to be with...with other men. Your woman...." he shrugged again, hopelessly. "I just wanted to see you and to invite you to be at De Groot's. I think I assumed a lot, and I am sorry for that. But I...I couldn't stop thinking of you." His heart was twisting slowly inside of him.

Motumbo stared at him for a moment. Then he turned and walked back to his house, Simpson a step behind him. They walked in silence until they reached the gate in the fence, and then Motumbo turned to Simpson. "Boss... Andrew...I think about it, alright? I think, really, I will." Simpson looked at him directly, trying to interpret his emotions; the African's eyes were not unkind, but they betrayed no thoughts. Simpson nodded, they shook hands again—Simpson holding on as long as he could before Motumbo broke off—and then Simpson turned and slowly walked back to the Land Rover. When he got into the cab he could see Motumbo standing on his front steps now, hands on his hips, watching Simpson. He turned the key in the ignition and was about to put the car into gear when once again, the twin boys popped up almost as if by magic by his side of the vehicle.

"Boss," said Thatho, "You are at De Groot's now? You De Groot now?" Simpson smiled gently and nodded. That was the whole trouble, wasn't it? He was De Groot now, and he didn't want to be, not with Motumbo anyway. How do you change the direction of a boulder once it has begun rolling downhill? Thatho continued: "You want to hire us, Boss? We are strong!" He puffed his skinny chest out, as did his brother.

Simpson couldn't help but smile, even in his grim mood. "I'm afraid you have to be eighteen. Maybe some day. Thanks, boys, for the help," he said, and put the car in gear. The boys pressed forward eagerly and said, "No, eighteen just last week!" Skeptical, Simpson nodded absently and looked back. Motumbo was no longer on the step, but he thought he saw a shadow at the window as he turned around and headed back down the street.

In a shady grove of trees a few miles back toward the main trunk road, Simpson pulled over to drink some water and pick at the food that Thabo had prepared. He had no appetite. Not for the first time, the ridiculous nature of his situation had dawned on him. What was he doing here, he wondered, also not for the first time. Protected from the rising sun by the shade, he sat in the vehicle lost in thought until sleep came upon him, and he dozed.

The sun was settling in the west when Simpson awoke with a start. Time to move on before four or two-legged predators gathered. He retraced his path and eventually pulled up in front of his own gates just as the sun had dropped below the horizon. Thabo walked quickly down to let him in.

"How was your day, Boss Andrew?" Thabo asked, his face and voice carefully composed, as they drove up toward camp from the gate.

Simpson sighed. "Alright, I suppose. Thanks for the directions. I found Motumbo."

There was a moment of silence, and Thabo looked sideways at Simpson a few times. Thabo said softly, "Motumbo a good man." Simpson nodded, and all of a sudden felt close to tears. "Yes, he is," he replied.

Once inside his own lodge, Simpson washed the dust of the day off; by then Thabo had delivered his dinner. A sense of sadness and longing had come over him. But going over the conversation from earlier in the day, he realized that Motumbo had not absolutely rejected him. He just wanted to think, wasn't that what he had said? Hope, perhaps foolish hope, began to regroup within him. He sat thinking over the remains of his dinner, then decided he would take a stroll around the premises in the cool evening air.

Once again, the only lighted guest cabin was the Russians', and Simpson once more approached it stepping gingerly. He was going to give himself the guilty pleasure of spying on them once more. Sidling along the side of the building, he came again to the open, lighted window, and peeked inside. What he saw froze his blood.

Little Mandla sat naked in a chair, his arms tied behind to the back of the chair, and a cloth gag in his mouth. The young African's legs were likewise tied to the legs of the chair. And from both of his nipples a line of blood ran down his abdomen. Fear could clearly be seen in his eyes, and he was squirming against his bonds.

Both Russians were naked, fully erect. The older, fatter one carried a bottle of vodka in one hand, nearly empty now. He prowled the outer perimeter of the room, constantly slurring some words. And in his other hand he carried a knife. The younger Russian also held a knife, and was speaking to Little Mandla in what were clearly taunting tones. His penis was fully erect, a furious purple rising from beneath a dirty blonde bush of pubic hair. And then the taunts stopped and he stepped up close, held the tip of the knife to one of Little Mandla's nipples, and pressed. There was a squeal from the bound and gagged African, a violent struggle against his bonds, and a fresh line of blood began running down from his chest. The fatter Russian was now masturbating as he took in this spectacle.

Simpson was already pulling the hunting knife that he had, fortunately, not removed from his belt after the day's journey. He rounded the corner of the building and opened the unlocked door, throwing it back with a crash. The room smelled of alcohol, semen, and fear.

"What the hell is this?" he roared. Both Russians jumped back. Little Mandla closed his eyes, whether in pain or relief Simpson did not know. Simpson strode up to the bound African in two steps and began cutting at the ropes with his knife. In a flash, he was aware of movement from two directions, and looking up he saw both Russians coming toward him with their own knives extended. Simpson took a step back, certain his end had come, utterly unused to knife fighting and trying to formulate a plan.

There was a loud metallic click from just behind him and he swiveled quickly to see what new threat it meant. It was Zama, the click having come from the safety on his semi-automatic shotgun being thumbed off. The tall African meaningfully pointed the weapon first at one Russian and then at the other, as Simpson ducked down into a crouch to be out of the line of fire. Drunk as they were, neither of the clients wanted to go to a gun fight with a knife. They dropped their weapons and put their hands up, looking both sheepish and wary. From outside came the sound of quickly approaching footsteps.

Simpson rose and darted forward to Little Mandla again, cutting loose the bonds and pulling off the cloth gag. Little Mandla started up, speaking rapidly in a language not English, clutching at Simpson and then swinging around behind him, putting the white man between himself and his captors. By then Thabo had burst through the door, his hand on the grip of a 1911-style pistol in a holster on his belt. He whistled softly at the scene, then cried "Aaiiieee!" at seeing Little Mandla's wounds. He quickly took the youth by the arm and led him away, backing out of the cabin.

"Thabo, please see to Little Mandla's injuries," Simpson called after him, urgently. Then turning to the Russians, he said in a clear, cold voice. "You will leave tomorrow at dawn. Until then, do not leave the cabin." Turning to Zama, who still held his weapon on the two, Simpson said, "Zama, if you see these two outside tonight, shoot them." Zama grinned wolfishly and nodded, then disappeared out the door and into the night as quickly as he had come. Simpson looked at the two Russians and then loudly, ostentatiously spat on the floor between them, turned on his heel and left, slamming the door shut behind him.

Ahead of him, Thabo was leading Little Mandla toward the main offices. Zama had completely disappeared into the night, but Simpson had no doubt of his vigilant presence. His thoughts churning, Simpson stomped, head bowed, toward his own cabin. Once inside he poured a stiff drink of whisky and threw himself onto a couch to sit, pondering.

He sat there a long time. Was what the Russians had done so much different from his own past actions at De Groot's? How thin a line was that, to "tag and bag" someone and then think you had actually come to own a wild animal of the African plains? An animal on which you could work your will in any way. Simpson slugged back another swallow of his Scotch as doubts about his own behavior vied with a return of longing for Motumbo in his head.

Perhaps an hour passed in this way, and there was a soft knock at the door. His hand on his belted knife, just in case, Simpson opened the door a crack. It was Little Mandla. "Ah!" Simpson cried and swung the door wide. The young African was alone, now wearing shorts but no shirt, scabs from the few nasty punctures forming in his nipples under a light coating of antiseptic gel. Simpson grabbed him by the hands and pulled him inside.

"Little Mandla! Were you hurt anywhere else? I am...I am so sorry," he said. "Oh! Do you speak English?"

Little Mandla smiled and nodded. "Little bit, Boss. I not hurt anywhere else, Boss, these," and he nodded at his chest, "these be OK soon." Still holding hands, Simpson nodded at the youth and then sighed deeply in relief. Little Mandla smiled hugely and then looked quite serious.

"Boss...Boss, you save my life." And then his face clouded over and he burst into a great sob. It was the tension of the close escape breaking into relief. Tears streamed down his handsome chocolate face as his shoulders heaved silently. Although about eighteen, he was basically still a boy inside. Simpson pulled him closer but slid to the side, one arm around his smooth brown shoulders and the other around his thin, meaty tube of an abdomen, to hold him gently without touching the wounds on his nipples. Little Mandla laid his head of tight peppercorn curls against Simpson as he continued to fight down his sobs, shuddering, while Simpson murmured soft, meaningless words to him.

Finally the storm passed, but they held that position. Simpson turned his face slightly to nuzzle his lips and nose into the youth's tight, crisp hair, which exuded a slight coconut aroma. Little Mandla's breathing slowed, he shuddered and sniffed, raising his hand to wipe his nose. Then he stirred and held his head up, looking directly into Simpson's eyes.

"Are you alright?" the white man asked.

Looking steadily at Simpson, Little Mandla nodded silently, sniffling. They held each other's gaze a moment more, and then Little Mandla turned into Simpson, reaching his hands up behind the white man's neck, and pulled his head slightly down. Little Mandla pressed his lips, two full rolls of brown and maroon softness, to Simpson's. His fingers clasped behind the white man's neck, fingers entwined in his silky hair. Hesitantly, then with growing feeling, Simpson's hands caressed the youth's smooth, rounded, muscular shoulders as their tongues met between lips, tongues sliding over teeth, Simpson sucking the black youth's full lips into his own mouth and feeling his own caressed in return.

Little Mandla unfastened the button on his own shorts and pulled them to the floor in one move, then eagerly unbuttoned Simpson's shirt, and then his trousers, as all the while they explored each other's lips, tongues, mouths. In a second they both stood naked. Days of pent-up lust rose in Simpson, and he felt his penis rising quickly, then stop as it met a barricade. It was Little Mandla's own long, rampant cock. Purple black and purple pink, their erect rods batted each other as the two men, now breathing heavily and softly moaning, continued to kiss. Then Little Mandla unclasped his hands from the white man's neck and brought them down to seize both their rods together, black and white tools held tightly in his double-fisted grasp, rising straight up between them.

Little Mandla took the lead, which Simpson was willing to grant him, not wanting to initiate anything that would further harm him. And it seemed as if relief and gratitude had given the African youth a powerful passion as well. The boy led Simpson quickly to the nearby bedroom, gently pushing him down onto the bed. The youth quickly swung over him, tail to toe, and held his purple black, iron-hard, leaking cock over the white man's mouth even as he seized Simpson's reddish penis in his own mouth. Looking up, Simpson took as much of the African youth's penis into his mouth as he could, as he enjoyed the view of the boy's tight, firm bottom, clean starfish of a rectum, and heavy, nearly black, rough-textured ballsack which was now drawing up tight against the African's body.

Together, the white man and black youth set up a rocking movement, riding the waves of lust, desire, and relief. Hands grasped thighs, Little Mandla slid his underneath Simpson's butt and dug into the hip muscles, while Simpson clutched the firm, tight bottom of the African hard and sucked furiously even as he pumped his own penis up and down, in and out of the full lips and warm mouth of the black youth who hovered above him. Both took care not to harm Little Mandla's injured nipples in the course of their passion. Pumping and writhing, each one moaning and unable to speak for having a mouth full of his friend's swollen dick, the two rode the rhythm of their passion. Sweat broke out in the warm African air, coating their bodies. Little Mandla broke first, his moans becoming squeals as he shuddered and bucked, pushing his long, heavy penis down into the white man's mouth, Simpson swallowing furiously and trying not to choke. And then it was his turn, the tingling electricity gathering in his thighs and loins and then shooting up to fill the sucking mouth of the African. The white man dug his fingers even more tightly into the high, firm bottom muscles of the youth, while Little Mandla's grip on the white man's bottom tightened. Each one seething, pushing, moaning, they held that position until first Little Mandla and then Simpson collapsed, spent. The African youth rolled off, panting heavily, to lie on his back on the bed, while Simpson likewise struggled to catch his breath as he gently stroked the chocolate, muscular leg beside him.

After a few minutes, Little Mandla rose and, in the outer room, extinguished the lamps. Then he returned to lie by Simpson on the white sheets in the pale moonlight that streamed in from the window. The African youth snuggled up close to Simpson, laying his crisp-haired head on Simpson's shoulder, Simpson laying his arm around the youth's back and hugging him closely. Little Mandla winced once or twice as he found a comfortable way to lie without hurting his nipples and then, his arm across Simpson's abdomen, he feel fast asleep. Simpson's head swirled a few minutes more, full of thoughts and images of Motumbo, of the two boy brothers from the village, of the crisis with the Russians and then of this moment of unlooked-for grace and bliss with Little Mandla. And then, giving it over to what was to be, he drifted off to sleep, his breathing matching the cadence of the boy in his arms.

- CHAPTER 4 -

Simpson awoke in the cold predawn, aware of a duty he needed to perform. For a moment, he nuzzled the face of the sleeping chocolate colored eighteen year old next to him, gently kissing Little Mandla's full, ripe lips. The boy startled awake and half sat up, but Simpson pulled him back down and whispered, "Sleep. Stay here and rest. I will be back." Moaning with contentment and smiling, Little Mandla settled back into the bed as Simpson kissed him once more and then slid out into the chilly morning.

He dressed quickly and stepped outside in time to see Thabo pulling a pickup truck up in front of the Russians' cabin. Simpson pulled his Land Rover up behind it, taking care to lock the doors as he stepped out. Zama loitered nearby, shotgun at the ready. Simpson jogged over quickly; this was his job to do. He huddled with Thabo and Zama, the former armed again with his pistol, then went to work. The sun was just cracking the eastern sky as he pounded on the door to the cabin. There was silence, so he pounded again. The sound of a chair being knocked over, what might have been a bottle dropping to the floor and rolling, a few footsteps...and the door opened.

The older, fatter Russian swayed in the opening. He was fully dressed but not entirely stable on his feet. His face was puffier than it had been the night before, and a wave of alcohol-soaked air floated out of the cabin from behind him. He stood silently glowering at Simpson.

"Right then, cheerio, pip pip, up and at 'em!" Simpson cried in his best false-English accent. The irony was completely lost. The big Russian staggered out of the cabin, followed closely by his younger companion, who looked to be in no better shape than he was. They were careful to ignore Simpson as they walked past him, but seemed to make a point of brushing Thabo back. The younger one, in the rear, jerked his thumb back over his shoulder toward the cabin and said "bags" to Thabo. Then the two walked to Simpson's Land Rover, tried the locked doors, and then leaned back against the vehicle. The big man pulled out a cigarette with shaky fingers and began smoking it.

Thabo turned to walk into the cabin, and Simpson went with him. The place was wildly disordered, although the damage did not seem to be permanent. Thabo and Simpson each collected the men's bags and emerged from the cabin. They walked to the pickup truck and slung them in the back. That brought some life from the Russians, who pushed away from the Land Rover and swarmed toward the pickup, loudly protesting. Simpson wheeled around and put his face in the face of the younger Russian...he could not have stomached it for the fatter one...jerked his thumb over his shoulder in the direction of the pickup truck and shouted "In!"

Both Russians stood stock still, murderous looks gathering on their faces. Once again, the steely click of Zama's safety being thumbed off got their attention. Staring at them with an impassive face, Zama swung the barrel from them to the pickup truck. Furious, the men leapt into the back of the truck. Then the older, fatter one spoke, an angry grumble:

"You vill be sorry. Ve sue you. Ve send men vith gun."

Simpson roared with laughter. "Sue us? We already have your credit card debited. It will be debited again for the damage to the cabin and for Little Mandla's medical expenses. Men with guns?" He threw his head back and howled. "There is no Russian mafia here and we both know it. As for these threats, two can play at that game. The minute I return from dropping you off I will post information about your visit here all over the web. How does gay sex with black men play in Moscow, boys? Now sit down and shut up!" The Russians, already pale from drink and dissolution, turned sheet white and collapsed as much as sat in the bed of the pickup among their luggage. Thabo got into the cab to drive, with Zama sitting beside him, shotgun in arms.

Simpson pulled his .458 from out of the Land Rover, ostentatiously worked the bolt, stuffed a round into the chamber and put it in full view, on the dash of the vehicle. Both cars pulled out of the compound, the truck in the lead.

It was barely light by the time they reached the main road, still two-lane, to Johannesburg. There they stopped. As per their plan, Thabo, Zama, and Simpson got out and motioned the Russians to exit, pulling the luggage out from around them. This brought loud protests from the departing clients, who had been assuming they would receive a ride all the way to the Joburg airport. They were not answered. The group had not long to wait. From out of the dim light lumbered a bus, which Thabo flagged down. The vehicle was crammed full of people and belongings, even the roof being covered. Onto that roof Thabo and Simpson threw the luggage, while Zama glared at the Russians, shotgun at the ready. Simpson gave the driver some money and instructions. The clearer the realization as to what was happening became, the louder became the Russians' protests. But to no avail...at last, Simpson and Thabo pointed meaningfully toward the crowded interior. Howling with indignation, the two Russians crawled aboard and crammed themselves in among the African people, the latter now fully enjoying the joke, laughing, and taunting the new arrivals. Off the bus went, trailing fumes and smoke, leaving Simpson, Thabo, and Zama to collapse in howls of laughter and congratulatory handshakes all around.

Upon their return to the compound, Simpson asked Thabo to charge the Russians' credit card an exorbitant amount for every conceivable charge they could imagine. Cleanup to the cabin was already underway from help hired to come in for the purpose. Simpson made a mental note to do something nasty in cyberspace to the two offenders, and then with a sense of a job well done, entered his own cabin again.

There he found Little Mandla, dressed again only in shorts, by the table, a breakfast already prepared. Simpson thanked him profusely, and insisted that he sit down to share the meal with him. He relayed the story of the Russians' departure, with suitable embellishments, and by the end of the breakfast Little Mandla was laughing as hard as Simpson. The two settled into a companionable chuckling. Little Mandla smiled at Simpson and ducked his head.

"Thanks, Boss...Andrew," he said softly, his eyes averted, "You are a good man." Simpson reached over to cover the youth's hand in his, squeezing it softly. After a moment, Little Mandla rose to remove the breakfast things, Simpson rising also to help. As the youth turned, Simpson caught his breath. He had not noticed his back before, but beneath the beautiful chocolate skin were darker discolorations here and there: bruises, and recently made.

"Little Mandla!" Simpson cried. "Did those men do this to you?" He brushed his fingertips as lightly as he dared over the puffy, damaged skin. Little Mandla held still and nodded his head, whispering "Yes."

"I did not notice last night," said Simpson. "I am sorry…I am so ANGRY!" he cried. "Does this often happen to the men? We must stop this and close the camp immediately, this is terrible!"

Unexpectedly, Little Mandla wheeled around with a look almost of fright on his face. "Oh, Andrew! No, please not to close camp. This not happen often, really. You close camp…how we work?"

"But Little Mandla, it's wrong. You could have been killed. Nobody should make a living being beaten. Really, we must!"

"No, Andrew, please! Me, the other men, what we do then?" Little Mandla's expression of concern matched Simpson's look of horror. The two stood for a moment staring at each other. Then anguish over the immediate situation of Little Mandla's injuries overcame Simpson, and he reached out to pull gently on the youth's arm.

"We will discuss this later. But come, I have something for those bruises." Simpson took Little Mandla back into the bedroom, and slipping into the attached bathroom he found some arnica gel that he had brought in anticipation of cuts and bruises in the African bush. Gently, oh so softly, he applied the cooling, slippery ointment to the bruised areas of Little Mandla's back. Around and around his palm slid on the slick surface of the discolored skin. The youth whispered "thanks, thanks" in a soft rhythm as Simpson did his work.

Seeing that some of the bruises ran down below the waistband of Little Mandla's shorts, Simpson reached around from behind and unbuttoned the garment, which fell to the floor. Applying the gel to these lower bruises, Simpson was relieved to see that they went no further than the upper hips. He sank to his knees as he worked, facing the high, firm buttocks which showed a darker, deep chocolate color. Simpson took the opportunity to surreptitiously inspect the youth's anus, which did not seem damaged from the Russians' attentions, for which he was thankful.

"Alright, turn around please," Simpson said softly, gently guiding the youth by the hips. Little Mandla turned slowly, revealing a full erection. Simpson stopped, awed by the simple perfection of the organ, like some beautiful flower, the head a bud ready to open, a lighter pinkish brown peeking out of the receding foreskin, swaying on a long, veined shaft. Little Mandla's heavy, very dark ballsack was drawn up tight against his body, and a small patch of dense peppercorn curls clustered around the top of his magnificent organ. Little Mandla put his hands over his rigid cock and murmured, "Sorry, Boss, it have mind of it own."

Simpson let his gaze travel up the eighteen year old's smooth, muscular tube of a body, just the hint of abdominal muscular development giving way to two thin slabs of chest muscle with purple black nipples now standing in little cones dotted with scabs from the night before. He was relieved to see no bruises on the youth's front side, evidently the Russians had done their work only on his back. Simpson's eyes rose until he caught and held the boy's gaze, looking down at him with gratitude...and maybe love?...from beneath long, curling lashes. Simpson smiled, and laying the tube of ointment aside he gently removed the strong brown hands from covering the organ. It sprang up again. Simpson grasped it by the shaft, sliding his hand up and down it several times, which made Little Mandla moan and mutter "O! Boss! Andrew! You no have to..."

By way of reply, Simpson took the head, now fully emerged and glowing from a coating of precum, into his mouth, flicking it with his tongue, his lips going back and forth over the sensitive flared top of the cockhead. Then he moved his hands from the shaft to grasp the African youth by the back of his legs, being careful to go no higher so as to avoid further damage to his bruised skin. Pushing his head forward, Simpson took as much of the rampant penis into his mouth as he could, causing Little Mandla to throw his head back and moan in sheer pleasure. The youth's hands moved to Simpson's shoulders, then to entwine themselves in his silky hair, to caress the white man's head which was giving him so much pleasure. Sucking strongly, Simpson bobbed his head up and down, trying to take more of the shaft and swollen dickhead into his mouth with each cycle. Up and down he went, scooting closer to the boy's trembling brown thighs, up and down as Little Mandla lolled his head from side to side, moaning softly.

Simpson felt a quivering in the youth's strong leg muscles, heard a quickening and then a catch in the African's breathing, and then Little Mandla tensed and pushed forward. Two, then three, then four shots of semen spurted from his throbbing shaft into Simpson's mouth, where they were swallowed greedily. Little Mandla was lost in ecstasy, quietly intoning a rapid chant in his own language, his fingers holding Simpson's head like a vise, quivering and pushing, and then it was over. The youth slumped, gasping for breath. Simpson slowly moved his head back and forth, swallowing, draining the penis of its white liquor, as Little Mandla gasped out his thanks between ragged breaths.

Finished, Simpson released the turgid penis with a plop, looked up and smiled at the boy.

"Andrew! I do that for you now, yes?" said Little Mandla, a huge smiled playing on his face.

"No," said Simpson, "you need to rest now. I...I just wanted to do that for you. I like you, Little Mandla...a lot," he said. "But you rest." Rising, Simpson took the youth gently by the arm to the nearby bed and eased him down between the sheets. Settling on his side to spare both his back and nipples, Little Mandla nodded and murmured thanks again, then soon was asleep.

The youth would stay that way for most of the day, sleeping off the physical and emotional trauma of the night's assaults. In the meantime, Simpson stalked off in the direction of the main offices, and to the computer. Going to every chat room and usenet group he could think of, posting pictures and commentaries to every service he could find, he did what he could to ruin the macho reputations of the Russians, and he did it with a vengeance. When he was finished, thinking he had done what he could, he paused for a moment to imagine with relish the long bus trip the two culprits were probably just now finishing, crammed in tightly among Africans. He shared lunch with Thabo and some of the cleaning help, talking about general subjects, and then stretched out for a nap on a couch in the office, wanting not to disturb Little Mandla back in his own cabin.

Awaking refreshed from his nap, Simpson found Thabo arranging some stores in the back of the main offices. "Thabo, could we please talk? About the future of this place?" The African nodded and followed Simpson back to the couch, where they sat.

"Thabo, I don't know if you saw, but Little Mandla is bruised all over his back. Those men must have beat him as well as cut him. We can't have that, Thabo. I...I am thinking of not having any more clients here." Simpson immediately saw a look of growing alarm in Thabo's face, and rushed to quiet it on the basis of his own interpretations. "Don't worry, Thabo, you will always have a job here. Zama, also. Maybe we could...maybe we could host photo safaris, or a bed and breakfast, or..." He knew the minute he said it that his last suggestion was as lame as it could be, but Thabo was looking increasingly worried.

"Boss Andrew, no! what all the men do? Men come here from villages, earn good money, get tips from clients, no close, Boss Andrew!" Simpson stared at him.

"But Thabo...look, Thabo, I will be the first to admit that the idea of hunting down real men and then possessing them, sexually, even for a night or two, was powerfully attractive to me. It is why I came here. But I don't think it was a worthy motive. I think it can bring out the worst in people, Thabo. See what the Russians did? And isn't it demeaning for the men?"

"But Boss Andrew, most men, black and white, know it a game, they come to play, you know? Then they have fun with men they catch, with being catch. Please, Boss..." Simpson looked at him in consternation. First he exploited these Africans himself for his own pleasure, now he was in a position of telling an African what was in his best interest. It was intolerable.

"Thabo...there are 'prey' still here, right? I have not see them, but they are still here?"

"Yes, Boss Andrew, I was gonna ask, what we do with them, but two still here: Strello and Mandla...Big Mandla."

"Can we go talk to them, ask their advice?" Simpson asked. Thabo nodded and rose, leading the way into the afternoon heat toward the lodge with the word "Prey" on the outside. Simpson did not know what horror he would find within: men chained to walls, dirty mattresses on floors, whips. Thabo knocked, then pushed open the door...to Simpson's surprise it was not locked from either the inside or outside...and led the way in.

The lodge was not palatial, but was at least the quality of a good American motel, with room service. It was air conditioned. The outside door opened onto a large, comfortable room with two exercise bikes and a treadmill in one corner, two television sets, several couches and tables, two large refrigerators, a computer, stereo, and a pool table. At the far end of the room were two doors. One was half ajar, revealing a clean, comfortable bedroom (if a bit messy, with an unmade bed and clothing on the floor) beyond. On one side of the lodge was a door leading to a kitchen and laundry area, on another a door leading to two bathrooms. Two men lounged on one of the sofas wearing shorts and t-shirts, watching television. They jumped to their feet as Thabo and Simpson approached.

Thabo rattled off an explanation in an African language, taking enough time to have explained the whole issue, Simpson was sure. Then he turned to introduce Simpson to his two employees. "Boss Andrew, this Mandla," he said, indicating a massively muscled, dark brown man. Big Mandla, in his early twenties, stood a little over six feet. Great lobes of muscle bulged from under his t-shirt, and a gap between shirt and shorts revealed mounds of developed abs. An oval head sat atop a thick neck, with head trimmed very close, almost shaved, small ears like seashells, thick lips and broad nose. He extended a big paw at the end of a heavily muscled arm and enfolded Simpson's hand in a surprisingly gentle shake. A smile creased his dark face, bringing a flash of masculine beauty and friendliness to this mountain of muscled steel. "And this Strello," said Thabo.

Strello looked to be about eighteen. His skin was a rich, oiled tobacco brown, a deep color with honey highlights, simply a beautiful and smooth complexion all over. Strello stood about five feet, ten inches. He wore a beater t-shirt that revealed a well developed, stocky but entirely muscled body; if anyone deserved the expression "built like a fireplug," Strello was it. A one inch cap of kinky hair covered his head and surrounded a handsome, boyish face, pug-nosed with thick, flat lips that seemed to press outward as if to be kissed. His handshake was firm, and he held Simpson's hand perhaps a beat longer than necessary, looking into the white man's eyes, seeming to appraise and examine him.

The introductions over, Simpson determined that Mandla and Strello could speak some English, then invited everyone to sit around a table. Thabo opened one of the refrigerators and brought out beers for everyone. Simpson broached his idea of closing the camp, explained the dangers and his view of the indignities it offered, told of Little Mandla's injuries. As with Thabo, both men looked increasingly concerned as he went on.

42

"Boss Andrew, I never hurt here. I go out, oh, mebbe ten times...caught three times!"said Mandla; and here he blushed a dark maroon beneath his chocolate skin. "But it good, Boss Andrew...the white men, they pay well. Nobody hurt me."

Simpson regarded his massive frame and thought that likely nobody would try to harm Mandla. He turned to Strello. "And you, Strello?"

The youth noded his head emphatically. "Nobody hurt me, Boss, I caught five times. Really, it not so bad. It a little fun," he said, and actually giggled.

"But listen," Simpson pressed on, "do you want to make money like this? People are using you."

Mandla looked perplexed. "But Boss Andrew, I see on television, people in your country...you from States? Yeah, people in States 'used' also. People in factories, they hurt, killed sometime. Everybody use somebody, Boss. This fun! Besides," he added, more seriously, "De Groot's best place to earn good money around here. People in villages, they wait for money from here, Boss Andrew! We even make a little just waiting here," Mandla explained, a point which Thabo agreed to by nodding.

The conversation continued in that vein through their beers and another round. It was clear that it was not as cut and dried as Simpson had thought. But he could not escape his misgivings about a business based on hunting down Africans, even with paintballs. As he talked less and listened more, he also began to think about alternatives. As the men began on their third round of beer, he leaned forward.

"Alright, listen. I have some ideas. So far De Groot's...and you know, I think we will just keep that name...De Groot's has been based on men coming here... white men...and hunting Africans, correct?"

"Boss Andrew, some Japanese come sometimes," said Thabo. Simpson nodded.

"Alright, well...must it always be that way? There must be men in the world who would want to come here and BE hunted." The men looked thoughtful. "What if men from other countries wanted to come here and have African men hunt them down and 'possess' them for a weekend? I think there may be a market for that," and thinking back to his experiences of some clubs and bars in the greater Philadelphia area, he could not help but grinning at the thought of several chocolate queens he knew or knew of who would pay lavishly for such an experience.

"Or how about men coming here to organize into teams for paintball combat," he continued, "with the winning team 'possessing' the losers for a few days?" Mandla, Strello, and Thabo were now clearly thinking hard about the possibilities. "We could hire men from the villages, and pay them well, to referee such combats. In addition to doing what you have been doing before, of course, sometimes, with men hunting...with men hunting you," he nodded at Mandla and Strello. "We could advertise all sorts of interesting and creative ways to use the land here for these purposes," he said. The Africans immediately broke out into an animated discussion in their own language, and Simpson could tell from the nonverbals that the talk was enthusiastic.

"Boss Andrew, these some good idea," said Thabo, turning to him to speak for the group. "Maybe even get more customers, hire more men from village, you know?" Simpson nodded enthusiastically. "You and me, we work on it Boss, advertise right away!" said Thabo. "Can we get business soon, Boss Andrew?"

Simpson thought about it. "It might take a couple of months. Most men cannot just drop plans and come, although perhaps a few will. But Mandla and Strello, and you, Thabo, and Little Mandla and everyone here can stay on until then...we can fix the place up, get it ready, you know? Prepare the land for team combat. Add sleeping quarters."

The three Africans huddled again, speaking quickly and enthusiastically. Thabo announced a general agreement, and there was congratulations and toasting all around. Simpson rose from the table, followed by Thabo.

"Well, we begin work tomorrow. I will prepare some ideas tonight. Can we get some more workers from the villages to come help with preparations?" Thabo nodded, and Mandla and Strello rattled off several names of men they knew with needed skills. With a plan agreed upon, Simpson and Thabo turned to go. Mandla shook Simpson's hand quickly, but again Strello's grasp lingered on, and, squeezing Simpson's hand, he actually winked at him and said "later tomorrow, Boss Andrew" in a whisper. Simpson felt a stir in his groin, but was not entirely sure he had read Strello's meaning correctly, so he simply nodded.

The sun was setting as Thabo and Simpson walked back toward the main offices. Simpson collected some cold food as dinner for himself and Little Mandla. Thabo agreed that Simpson's lodge was a good place for Little Mandla to rest overnight, then the youth could return to the "prey" lodge with the other men. Simpson carried the meal back to his cabin and entered.

Little Mandla was sitting on a couch, leaning forward a bit so as to keep his bruised back free from contact with the leather, watching television. He leaped to his feet, a huge smile splitting his handsome, chocolate face.

"Andrew! I sleep most of day, Andrew. I think I better….these," he said, looking down at his nipples, "not hurt much now. Back a little better."

"That's great, Little Mandla! You need all the rest you can get. Please stay here tonight again, then you can return to your own room tomorrow." The youth grinned and nodded agreement. "Eat!" said Simpson, gesturing at the food he was laying out on the table. Both men helped themselves and sat companionably on the couch to watch the show, a syndicated rerun of an American crime drama. What must people in other countries think of the States from watching such crap, Simpson thought. Putting the food away, they continued watching similar shows throughout the evening. During breaks, Simpson explained the new plan for De Groot's to Little Mandla, who seemed delighted with some of the schemes and puzzled with some others, but was generally accepting. The youth seemed relieved to find that his employment would remain secure.

Even though he had rested all day, Little Mandla was still tired from his ordeal, so Simpson suggested that they retire early. Simpson took a quick shower, followed by Little Mandla. Simpson remained naked, and as the youth emerged from the shower the white man helped to sponge his body dry gently, then applied two small dollops of antiseptic to cover each nipple and again rubbed some arnica gel onto the lad's bruises, which were turning some interesting colors. As Simpson ministered to the lad, both men developed half erections, a fact each acknowledged silently with looks, nods, and chuckles. Finishing his task, Simpson stepped to the bed and slid between the sheets. Although his erection was tenting up the covers, he would not force himself on the African youth during his recovery.

But Little Mandla had different ideas. The boy walked to Simpson's side of the bed and bent over, kissing Simpson on the lips. "Thanks, Andrew, Boss, for everything," he whispered, nuzzling Simpson's face with his full, ripe maroon brown lips. Half kneeling on the bed, Little Mandla ran his fingers through the white man's silky hair, then down his neck to caress his shoulders. Passion rose strongly within Simpson, but he was hesitant to touch the youth in return, for fear of further damaging his injuries...but his fingers slid lightly over the youth's unharmed thighs and arms.

Both men were panting from their prolonged kissing, from explorations of tongues and lips, when Little Mandla reached to the bedside table and produced some lubricant which he had evidently found or placed there earlier. He whisked back the sheets and Simpson's reddish, iron stiff penis sprang up. Little Mandla greased the rigid organ well with the lubricant, then bent slightly and oiled his own rectum. Little Mandla then sprang upon the bed and positioned himself above Simpson's organ, facing the white man, and placed the swollen red cockhead against his own anus. Wincing a little, Little Mandla lowered himself...the cockhead pushed against his starfish and then pushed through. Little Mandla gasped, waited, and then lowered himself some more, slowly, until Simpson was fully inserted and Little Mandla squatted above him. Simpson could see the scabs on the boy's nipples but not the bruises on his back, and in this position neither set of injuries would be exacerbated.

Smiling down at the white man beneath him, his back erect and shoulders held back, Little Mandla's face took on a dreamy look as he began to move up and down on Simpson. The white man was meanwhile in ecstasy, his rigid rod fully engorged in the warm bottom of the African youth, the firm, tight butt of the boy bouncing up and down on his thighs. Simpson clutched the youth's firm thigh with one hand and with another clasped the purple black, rigid penis that was slapping his abdomen and chest, leaking precum down onto his skin. Simpson began pumping the youth's organ in time to Little Mandla's rhythm of rising and falling. Both men were breathing heavily, gasping, muttering in their own languages, their eyes drinking heavily of each other's delicious bodies with the different and delightful skin tones and hair patterns. Simpson began pushing his pelvis up and down to match Little Mandla's rhythms, and kept pace with pumping the rampant purple black rod in his hand.

Little Mandla came first, crying out, pushing forward even as he tried to keep up a rhythm of bobbing up and down on Simpson's cock, spraying the white man's chest with drops and globs of thick, white sperm. Simpson himself was so close that the break in Little Mandla's rhythm did not delay him much. He now pushed his pelvis up strongly and roared with sexual delight as, deep inside the black youth's gut, his rampant penis pumped dollops of semen.

Simpson's hand gripped the chocolate thigh tightly, while his other hand slowed, milking the last of the African's semen from the thick tube. Then both men slowed and stopped, quivering, the final waves of ecstasy washing over them. And then Little Mandla slowly leaned forward, Simpson's rod still inside of him, and laid his forehead on Simpson's shoulder, now running his fingers through the white man's silky hair. For a few moments more both men held that position as Simpson's rigid cock slowly retreated back down the shaft of Little Mandla's anus, and then plopped out. Little Mandla giggled, leaned forward some more to kiss Simpson once again, and then flopped down beside him on his side, pulling the sheets up over them. Once again with arms around each other, the two men drifted off to sleep: Little Mandla quickly, Simpson but a few minutes behind him, caressing the kinky head that lay on his chest...but thinking thoughts of Motumbo until sleep overtook him.

A Boner Book

- CHAPTER 5 -

Simpson awoke with the dawn light, still entwined with Little Mandla who continued to sleep soundly. The pleasure of their physical closeness warred with his sense of purpose, but duty won out. That, and a sense that Little Mandla needed to rest more than he needed another passionate coupling such as they experienced the night before! Simpson slipped out of bed as quietly as he good, leaving the youth still asleep. He washed and dressed quickly and quietly shut the door behind him as he left his lodge to step out into the African dawn.

Going to the main offices, he found Thabo preparing breakfast. One or two of the cleaning staff came and went, exchanging greetings with Simpson. The two sat down together, and over game steaks and eggs, and steaming coffee, Simpson began to lay his plans. Armed with paper and pencil, Simpson sketched out rough drawings, jotted down some specifications, and questioned Thabo about materials and resources. As the scope of Simpson's plans were explained, and the boldness of some of his concepts made clear, Thabo alternated between head-scratching wonder, laughter, and polite skepticism. Still, an agreement was made to press ahead with a scheme to transform De Groot's into a kind of sexual entertainment paradise unknown before. It was agreed that Simpson would handle marketing and booking while Thabo would oversee the physical changes and staffing additions that would be required.

As they parted to go their separate ways, Simpson paused and turned to Thabo. "Will...will you be calling for construction help from all the villages around here?" he asked. "For staff to be trained for the new games?" Thabo nodded, looking intently at Simpson; he seemed to know where this was headed.

"From Motumbo's village?" asked Simpson casually, looking away, seemingly occupied with a spot on a nearby window. Thabo grunted agreement. Simpson nodded. The two waited a moment. "Perhaps Motumbo will want to come back to train, or to bring some recruits with him," said Simpson, as nonchalantly as he could.

Thabo continued to look knowingly at him, then nodded and added in a kind, soft voice, "Perhaps, Boss Andrew. I ask 'specially for him when I call."

Simpson simply nodded, but could hardly contain the big sigh he breathed within himself. "Call?" he asked Thabo. "Are there phones?"

"Cell phones, Boss Andrew, lots people in Africa got cell phones. No land lines, but lotsa towers, cell phones!" And at that, Thabo slipped away to go about his business. Now Simpson really did sigh out loud, and headed for the computers.

Using his own skills, and calling on some friends connected with some agencies back in Manhattan, Simpson soon put together an impressive marketing campaign online. He was targeting a very special demographic that was nevertheless globally distributed, and he took great care in presenting an appealing and professional image for De Groot's. It took all morning. Simpson could hear Thabo come and go, the sounds of the voices of the staff, even what he thought were Big Mandla's and Strello's voices. The whole camp was buzzing with activity, even with as small as staff as it had; and the staff was soon to grow larger.

Simpson and Thabo ate lunch. They each discussed their progress, and then Simpson announced his intention to return to his own lodge for a nap before returning to work. He helped Thabo to clean up the lunch things, added one or two more touches to a web site he was developing, and then walked down the dusty path toward his own lodge.

Shutting the door behind him, he peeked into the bedroom to see a patch of dark brown skin beneath the sheets. Little Mandla must have needed more recovery time than anyone thought if he were still sleeping. Quietly, Simpson slipped into the room and closed the door. Removing his clothing, he pulled back the sheets and pulled back the bed sheets. The man turned over; it was Strello.

Simpson gasped in surprise; Strello pulled a face, then burst into a chuckle. His boyish face, broad pug nose, and deep tobacco brown skin was as beautiful as Simpson remembered it.

"Little Mandla, he need sleep Boss Andrew! I send back to lodge, take place for him!" said Strello. The eighteen year old whipped the sheets completely off, exposing his naked body. Not overly tall, he was extremely muscular, dense lobes and ridges of hard flesh flowing like lava across his frame. Wide, flat, maroon brown nipples clung to the lower edges of his rounded lobes of chest muscle. A narrow valley descended through small hills of abdominal muscles to a slightly outie navel, then followed a thin line of short body hair to a patch of dense, kinky black hair around a very thick, heavy penis that was half erect and visibly moving toward full rigidity. Simpson looked in awe at the splendid sight and simply slid down onto the bed beside the boy. Strello lost no time. Leaning over, he put his wide, flared and moist lips over Simpson's, sucking the white man's mouth passionately, pushing his tongue down and playing across his teeth, sucking Simpson's tongue back into his own mouth. Strello's now iron hard cock slapped against Simpson's thigh, as the white man's own dick grew hard and red.

Strello played the aggressor, rolling over to lie on top of Simpson, their hard red and purple black cocks aligned straight up between their torsos, each leaking precum mixed together to make their skins slick as they slid around, squirming. Strello tweaked Simpson's ears and ran his dark brown fingers through his silky hair, while Simpson grabbed tufts of the black youth's dense, inch-thick cap of hair and pulled his head down. Simpson, usually the more active one, was simply overwhelmed by Strello's insistent conquest of his body, and he made the split second decision to let happen what may.

The black eighteen year old broke off their long kiss with a pop, a string of mixed saliva trailing from his mouth to Simpson's, as he pushed himself off the white man with one shove of his muscular arms and rocked back on his haunches. He spread Simpson's thighs and then pushed them back up against the white man's chest. Simpson felt a moment of fear...it was all happening so quickly, and Strello's swollen dick, which he was now greasing with lubricant, really looked too big for the thing that was about to happen. But Strello was not to be denied. One hand on the white man's thigh, the other on his own massive, thick dick, Strello pushed Simpson back again and placed his swollen, flared cockhead at the entrance to Simpson's rectum. There was an initial push, then another, and the black boy's cockhead entered.

Simpson writhed and cried out, pushing the palms of his hands against Strello's hard, rounded chest. The African youth paused, looking intently into the face of the white man he had impaled beneath him. Simpson breathed steadily and, when the pain passed, nodded to the black boy above him. Strello quickly and deliberately pushed in another two or three inches, then halted again as Simpson cried out and pushed against his chest. Another wait, another push, and Strello was completely inside Simpson.

The white man had been entered before, but never by anything so large. Strello positioned himself above, his tan palms spread out on the bed on either side of Simpson, resting on the white man's thighs which were pushed straight up and back, his knees nearly to his chin. Then slowly, slowly, moving a bit at a time, Strello began sliding back and forth. Then faster, until a steady rhythm was achieved between the two of them, Simpson arching his pelvis up as much as he could to meet the thrusts of the mighty black rod that was sliding in and out of his ass. Simpson's pink palms pressed against the rounded, hard chest of the African who rode above him. Their eyes locked into each other, looking deep into one another, sharing this moment of the greatest intimacy possible, merging into one another. The black boy's bubble butt rounded and then clenched rhythmically with every piston cycle of his dick, a large dimple forming in the sides of each hip as he pushed his shaft down into the white man.

Simpson came first, the stimulation on his prostate combined with the friction of Strello's lower abdomen against his rod proving too much for him. The white man's red dick was arching up along Strello's abdomen, and when Simpson cried out and moaned, tearing at the kinky hair he had clutched in his fingers, his penis shot out a spray of white cum that dotted the tanned white and tobacco brown chests of both men. Stimulated by the tightening inside Simpson, now Strello cried out and bucked forward, holding still for a second as he pushed deep inside the white man with all his strength, then quickly fanned his hips and pushed again, then again, as a second and third wave of white spunk flowed down into the man beneath him. Through it all, they never broke their locked gaze, seeing deep into the other man, so different and yet so much the same, two strangers come from thousands of miles apart to fuck themselves into one being.

Then Strello collapsed, his still hard rod sliding out of Simpson, and rolled over onto his back. Simpson flopped over and put his arm around the heaving brown chest of the boy and held him tight. Semen was all over their torsos now, running down in rivulets, running from out of Simpson's winking asshole onto the sheets as well. Heaving and gasping, but now slower, the two caught their breath and, as peace descended on them, slipped off into sleep.

Simpson woke with a start an hour later, which brought Strello to consciousness as well. They looked at each other, a little in surprise, then both laughed. They kissed, but Simpson broke it off. There would be plenty of time for this and all good things later, but there was work to be done now. He sprang from the bed and showered. Strello pushed himself into the narrow stall just as Simpson was stepping out, the two sliding against each other on the water from Simpson's body, chuckling. As each one finished dressing they left the lodge to continue their work, exchanging one more quick kiss before opening the door.

Simpson worked on a marketing and advertising plan the rest of the day, interrupted by the placing of orders for supplies at Thabo's requests. As evening approached, Simpson suggested to Thabo that all the staff on the premises be invited to dinner. Thabo agreed, and one by one everyone but the redoubtable Zama, faithfully prowling the perimeter like stalking Death, came into the main lodge for a meal. Simpson was introduced to all the remaining staff, every one of whom had been busy all day with the new plans. Questions about the future were asked and answered, suggestions offered and considered. Strello sat a few chairs away from Simpson, but the two exchanged grins from time to time. Big Mandla and Little Mandla sat on either side of Simpson, the iron hard, massive thigh of the big man pleasantly rubbing up against his own from time to time, while Little Mandla punctuated a laugh or a story with a gentle hand laid on Simpson's arm or shoulder. After an hour or so, Simpson realized with a start that he felt as if he belonged here. De Groot's was coming to seem like home, and these men like family.

There was more work in the evening hours as every man there had caught a sense of excitement. Returning tired but satisfied to his lodge, Simpson found Strello undressing. The black youth gave him a questioning glance.

"OK, Boss Andrew?"

"OK, Strello, but maybe we can just hold each other. I am very tired." Strello nodded a happy agreement, even though his dick was half erect. The two slid into bed and held each other loosely, companionably, gently exploring each other's facial features and hair with soft fingers, enjoying the moment of freedom and license. Some gentle kisses then, and, arms around each other, they fell asleep.

Strello stayed in Simpson's lodge for another two days, the men alternating between passionate and then gentle sex, sometimes Simpson taking the passive position and sometimes being on top, pounding the black boy's high bubble butt for all he was worth. By mutual agreement and with no rancor, they agreed after two days that Strello would return to the "Prey" lodge, with many a promise to continue enjoying their pleasures in the future. After all, neither man wished an exclusive or permanent relationship with the other… and often, as Simpson ploughed in and out between the firm, rounded buttocks of the black boy beneath him, or lay impaled by a thick, purple black cock, he imagined Motumbo in place of Strello.

On the second day, to Simpson's surprise, first inquiries and then reservations, with deposits, began arriving by email. The first arrivals were six weeks out, which was just time enough to complete the changes planned for the physical space. Teams of experienced "prey" could also be recruited for training in the new "games" to be offered.

On the third day, a convoy of trucks from Johannesburg pulled into the compound and offloaded supplies for the planned constructions and renovations. As if by magic, within an hour of their departure came workers, some on foot from nearby villages and some in rattletrap pickups and flatbed trucks from more distant settlements. In all, about twenty men would eventually arrive, making a sizable, willing, and effective workforce. Empty guest cabins were converted into dormitory space for the men. Half a dozen women also arrived to cook and clean and…to tell the truth…provide sexual alternatives and outlets for the men who were so inclined.

Thabo, a good general for the purpose, began organizing parties for the new construction, and soon the sounds of sawing, drilling, and the whines of power equipment, could be heard all over the camp. Meanwhile, in between managing the business side of the operation, Simpson felt ready to move toward training those who would be involved in the new entertainments at De Groot's. These were not necessarily the same men as those skilled in construction. After some consultation with both of the Mandlas, Strello, and Thabo, it was agreed that it was time for Thabo to put out a cell phone summons to some select invitees. One of the new buildings was already finished, and others were in the process of preparation, so a new phase of training was called for. The experience "prey" would of course assist, lending their expertise.

A group of three men arrived first, each one young and handsome. It was clear why they had been chosen in the past to serve as "prey." Simpson explained the new plans, and they were delighted, pleased with the prospect of new income, pleased with the variety of new roles they were to play, pleased with the power they would soon sometimes experience after their recent careers as "prey"...although they all quite agreed that they were willing to run in the bush again if the money was right!

The group of sexual staffers, as they were now being called, had grown to five. The doctor from the nearby clinic came and tested every conceivable candidate for sexual contacts for disease. The sexual staffers and Simpson were returning one evening from a day of training and practice on the land, hot and thirsty but excited at the new prospects. Simpson noticed an unfamiliar pickup truck that had just pulled up, a thin curtain of dust still hanging in the air in its path. Coming closer he saw two men step out of it. One of them was Motumbo.

Unable to believe his eyes, his heart pounding, Simpson walked quietly up to the truck. Motumbo was pulling a bag out of the back...actually pulling luggage out! Simpson stopped a few feet away and Motumbo, not yet noticing him, continued speaking in a low voice to the other man. Then they shook hands and the other man got back into the truck and began pulling away. Motumbo waved him off, then turned around...and saw Simpson. The two froze for a moment, regarding each other.

"Evening, Boss."

"Andrew."

"Evening, Andrew. Thabo call, say there is work. For the games, for the 'hunt,' you know." Simpson nodded, then extended his hand. Motumbo took it, carefully watching the white man all the while, looking deeply into his eyes, trying to read his face.

"So, I here, Boss...uh, I here, Andrew."

"Just to work?" The big man shrugged, and a slight smile crept onto his face.

"Who knows, Andrew?" There was another pause...the two kept their handshake grip...and then Simpson spoke.

"I am glad you are here, Motumbo. I have missed you. I think about you all... well, it is as I told you before." The tall man nodded, cocked his head slightly to one side, still inspecting Simpson. Then he released the handshake and picked up his bag. For effect, he looked around him, as if he had never been there, and asked nonchalantly, "Where I stay?"

Simpson looked down and said, his voice throaty with tension, "You could stay with me, if you want to." Motumbo looked piercingly at him. He set the bag back down.

"You pay me, Andrew? Boss? This for pay?" Simpson's head jerked up and he looked directly at Motumbo, a wave of passion and impatience washing over him.

"No, Motumbo, it is not for pay. Not this part. If you want work with the hunts, the games we will put on, yes, I will hire you. I will not pay you for sleeping with me. I want you, Motumbo, as a person, not just your body. But I want your body also."

Motumbo's eyes widened a bit and the smile slowly, slowly floated back onto his features. "OK, Andrew," he said. "OK...maybe we try it, yes? My friend," and he jerked his thumb in the direction of the departing truck, "he go to Joburg, back in a week to pick me up, so we see then, OK?"

Simpson nodded. He felt as if he had passed an important test. Then before Motumbo could react, he stepped forward and picked up the luggage. Looking into the startled face of the African, Simpson said, "I would be honored if you would follow me to my lodge, Motumbo...to our lodge." Astonishment warred with pleasure on Motumbo's face, but he nodded and followed a step behind Simpson, who carried the bag to the waiting lodge.

The two entered the cabin, the door closing behind them. Simpson set the bag down and then simply stood there, looking hard at Motumbo. The longing in his eyes was as plain as if he had spoken it aloud. Motumbo paused a moment, looking searchingly at the white man, who still made no move. Then Motumbo took one step nearer and reached out his arm, to lay one strong, large hand on Simpson's shoulder, which he squeezed. With a shudder, Simpson moved into the African's strong body, laying his head against the strong shoulders, encircling the chest with his arms and hugging tightly. Motumbo pulled Simpson into him, nuzzling his silky hair with his face, returning the embrace. For a long moment they stood like that while two thin tracks of tears ran down Simpson's face.

Motumbo reached down to tilt Simpson's face up a little to his own, and seeing tears grunted softly, then wiped them away with his thumb. Then bending his beautiful, strong face down, Motumbo kissed Simpson's mouth. For a long time they stood there, embracing each other, dancing with their heads and their mouths, lips and tongues exploring lips and tongues, their breathing becoming heavier, their organs straining within their pants. Then Simpson unclasped his arms from around the strong upper torso of Motumbo and began unbuttoning his shirt, which was soon open and fell away. Motumbo in answer tugged up Simpson's shirt from out of his pants and, breaking their embrace, over his head. The two returned to another embrace, tighter now as naked skin met naked sin, Simpson's body of average musculature meeting the hard, meaty contours of Motumbo's shield-shaped chest, feeling the hard hills of muscles down his back on either side of the valley of his spine.

Falling to his knees, Simpson quickly unclasped the trousers of the man before him, pulling them and his undergarment down to fall around the African's shoes. The heavy, massive, purple black organ sprang out to meet him, bigger than Strello's, a noble organ of midnight strength and power. Raising it up with one hand, Simpson took first one and then another of the massive testicles beneath into his mouth, gently sucking at the rough but hairless ballsack, running one hand up and down the thick shaft of the heavy organ. Motumbo grasped Simpson's shoulders and moaned with delight. Then Simpson took the heavy organ into his mouth, gnawing the large, flared dickhead with his soft lips. Now Motumbo threw his head back and cried out softly in ecstasy. For a few moments Simpson slid his head up and down on the massive shaft as Motumbo pushed forward, muttering to himself in an unknown language.

Then rising, Simpson quickly slid his own pants off, kicking them and his shoes away as Motumbo did the same. Reaching out to grasp a dark brown hand, Simpson led Motumbo to the bedroom, impatiently throwing back the covers and flinging himself onto the bed. So often in charge of every aspect of his life, Simpson now led but he led in giving himself to this African of whom he had dreamed so many nights. Seizing the tube of lubricant nearby, Simpson impatiently dabbed some onto and into his own anus while with his other hand he patted the bed between his legs, signaling where Motumbo should position himself. Grasping the rampant, thick purple black rod, Simpson slicked it liberally, mixing lubricant with the copious flow of precum now running from the piss slit. Then throwing himself back onto the bed, Simpson drew his legs up and gestured to Motumbo to come forward.

With great gentleness in one of such muscular strength, Motumbo placed his cockhead against Simpson's anus and pushed softly. The next few minutes were a great struggle, and had Simpson not been with Strello now and again over the last week or so, he could not have received something so large. With many starts and stops, each man impatient but each communicating physically with the other, Motumbo was finally landed deep inside Simpson, who lay gasping flat against the bed, sweating. Then the white man opened his eyes, which had been closed, and nodded and smiled at Motumbo who sat quite still, on his haunches, his massive shaft impaled inside Simpson.

Slowly, then more quickly, Motumbo began sliding in and out, in and out. Moving from off of his haunches, he stretched out over Simpson, pushing his own legs back straight. Simpson's legs locked by the ankles around the broad brown back and pulled the pumping buttocks in closer, while he wrapped his tanned white arms around the strong brown shoulders and held on as if he were drowning. Faster now, Motumbo pumped in and out, in and out, then bent his head forward to kiss the white man beneath him passionately. Then Motumbo lowered himself entirely onto Simpson, pressing his face into the white man's hair, gently biting his lips, kissing his face, grasping him by the shoulders. Both men were pulling each other closely together, locked in a tight embrace, brown skin sliding on white skin on a sheet of sweat and Simpson's precum, holding tight as Motumbo's orgasm came upon him suddenly. Clutching Simpson fiercely, Motumbo's whole body clenched, his pelvis tilting to push his penis its whole length into Simpson, the white man pulling the African's heaving, bucking body desperately down into him.

To Simpson it felt like receiving a gift or a sacrament; this strong African had given him the gift of his seed, deposited deep inside of him. The white man felt on the verge of tears, a moment he had thought about for so long having come true. But then Motumbo, his breath still ragged, pulled out with a plop and slid down the length of the white man's slickened torso, stopping to take his rock hard red cock into his mouth. Stimulated from his massive fucking, it did not take Simpson long. Placing his legs under the arms and then over the back of the black man who had swallowed his penis whole, Simpson thrashed on the bed, bucking his hips up and down, holding the nappy-haired head above his groin tightly in his hands, and when he came it was with a mighty eruption, shooting months worth of pent-up desire into the African's mouth, shouting and groaning uncontrollably.

Motumbo milked every drop from the rigid red shaft as Simpson trembled and gasped, and as he slid up to lie alongside Simpson, saw that the white man was sobbing soundlessly, tears of relief and fulfillment again running down his cheeks. Now chuckling outright, crooning a soothing sound, Motumbo again wiped the tears away with his fingers, kissing the white man softly. The peace that comes from release slowly settled on the room, and the two figures on the bed drifted away into sleep.

- CHAPTER 6 -

Opening his eyes in the early dawn light, Motumbo tensed. Everything was strange, the room unfamiliar. Looking around he saw the rustic furniture, heavily made from unfinished, varnished raw wood, the horns and heads of hunting trophies on the walls, the polished wood floors with animal skins for rugs. Then he noticed the white man next to him. For a moment his thoughts went back to the times he had been the trophy for white men who came to De Groot's, going back a year or so now. Was this one... and then he remembered. This was Andrew, the strange white man who came back, who came back looking especially for him. What did it mean, who was this man, and what did he want?

Motumbo turned on his side toward the sleeping white man to look at him more closely. He had been little chance to do this sort of thing in the past. Most of the men who "won" him had seemed to prefer that he keep his eyes averted, that he act passively. It was not especially his nature, but it did not last long and the money was good, it was more than good. But this Andrew, he seemed different. Motumbo listened to the white man's soft breathing and gazed at his body intently, trying to unravel the mystery who was sleeping beside him. A mixture of off-white, light tan, and light rose colors played on his skin. The man's body was muscular but not as heavily developed as his own.

A mop of light, soft hair spread out on the pillow from his head. Motumbo reached out tentatively to touch it again, as he had the night before. Gently, he entwined his fingers in it, marveling at the strange texture. He leaned into it and smelled it, pressing his lips to the cornsilk texture. And then Andrew awoke with a start, and turned toward the African whose fingers were still in his hair. He smiled, and Motumbo smiled in return.

"Motumbo," he said, and turned toward the African. Lying on their sides facing each other, the men lightly embraced, their morning semi-erections lying against each other's abdomens, now slowly growing harder. Each man traced the features of the other with his fingers, exploring the differences in facial features and hair, but recognizing the underlying similarities and the bond between them. Slowly, Andrew moved forward to kiss Motumbo. Lips caressed lips, tongues met and slid around and then past each other, ran along teeth in the other's mouth. Lips so full and lips more thin sucked and slid on each other.

Hands grasped both penises together and slowly pumped, while other hands reached around to caress muscular bottoms. The two slid even tighter together, sharing the faster tempo of their breath, feeling each other's chests rise and fall now. Eyes looked deeply into eyes.

Turning half away, Motumbo found the lubricant and began smearing it on Simpson's rigid red cock, while the white man closed his eyes and moaned. The African reached behind himself and lubricated his own asshole and then, nodding at Simpson, rolled over onto his belly, cocking his hips up, laying his cheek on the sheets. He was offering himself up in the way Simpson had done the night before. The white man had taken him like this on their first night, months ago, but now the black was giving himself as a gift, not as a prize that had been won.

Softly whispering the black man's name, Simpson slid up and over the African's strong thigh and positioned himself behind his upturned bottom. One palm supported his body on the sheets while his other hand guided his cock to the wrinkled dark purple brown asshole. Simpson pushed the flared cockhead and then pushed again. It popped inside. Slowly, as Motumbo quietly gasped and moaned, Simpson pushed himself all the way inside, then craned his torso up and over Motumbo's body, supported by both hands on either side of the waiting black man beneath him. His rigid red cock was now firmly buried in between the hard bubbles of Motumbo's butt. It was a wonderful sight.

Simpson began to rock, moving in and out, the slick, glistening purple red dick sliding in and out of the African's anus. Motumbo moaned softly in time to the rhythm of the thrusts.

As he pushed in all the way, Simpson's muscular lower belly and upper thighs slapped against the meaty cushion of the rounded African butt, pushed hard against the man's sensuous flesh. As he pushed in, Motumbo cocked his pelvis back and up, rolling the meaty hams up to meet his white lover's thrusts. Faster and harder Simpson pumped, now slamming forward to push as hard as he could, pulling out almost all the way and slamming forward again. Like a train chugging at top speed toward a cliff the white man pistoned in and out, in and out, and then with a wild howl pushed forward and held it, grinding his groin into the African butt as he spurted his cum deep into the black man's gut. Gasping and cursing quietly, Simpson held his position, grinding into the ass, and then slumped in utter exhaustion, breathing heavily, lying on the muscular African's back, his face on the fleshy shoulders. Catching his breath, Simpson kissed and licked the deep, dark skin, tasting it, tonguing it.

Recovered, Simpson leaped off and grabbed the lubrication, smearing it on his own anus. Turning Motumbo over onto his back with the other hand, Simpson greased up the enormous purple black pole that now sprang up into the air. Simpson moved quickly over the African's lower abdomen and grasped the huge, rigid black cock, positioning it against his own bottom, and then sat back quickly. The pain was intense as his rectum took the whole organ in at once. Simpson, completely impaled, sat quietly for a moment, looking down at the magnificent shield shaped chest and hills of abdominal muscles below him, his softening cock dribbling the last of his semen onto the African's muscular belly. Motumbo crooned soothing words and ran his dark hands over the white man's thighs and chest. Then Simpson nodded, and first slowly, then quickly, began riding the African cock inside of him, rising and falling, rising and falling.

Motumbo's powerful hips and thighs pushed up to meet Simpson's downward motions. His knees on either side of the black man, Simpson bounced up and down for a while, then leaned forward to kiss the full maroon brown lips. But half of Motumbo's organ was still inside of him, and the black man was now freed to thrust upward with even more vigor. Simpson now held quite still, kissing and sucking Motumbo's lips, while the big African did all the work, thrusting up and down, up and down, until he also cried out, muffled by the white man's mouth that was over his, and pushed up, holding it, while a fountain of cum sprayed up inside of Simpson. The African pulled back and then thrust again, and then again, spurting again, and then collapsed back flat on his back. Simpson put his head to the side of the African's, cheeks pressed tightly together. The magnificent black cocks remained in his ass a few minutes longer, then with a plop fell out as it deflated from iron rigidity to mere meaty weight. Simpson pushed his legs back, entwining them with Motumbo's, and stretched out on top of the African. Moments passed in silence, and then Simpson half rose to look at Motumbo's face. Both men smiled, then chuckled, then laughed softly...but neither one could have said what they were laughing at. No words were spoken, but in time, with one accord, they rose and showered together, tidied the room and dressed. Then, making small talk about the weather and the plans for the new De Groot's, they went out into the morning light and toward the main offices.

There they found Thabo and some of the staff nearly done with breakfast. Some good natured ribbing about the lateness of their arrival, some pointed comments about what could have delayed them...Motumbo and Simpson took it in good humor, and exchanged many quick, meaningful looks between themselves.

There was more discussion about the new plans, Motumbo being made fully aware of the new activities and facilities that were planned. It was clear he was impressed, and also clear that he was aroused by the escapades promised in the new plans. And so began a week of steady activity and preparation. Each night, and during the day when they could, Motumbo and Andrew Simpson returned to their lodge and threw themselves into the bed, powered by a strong passion. Each new coupling offered a chance to experiment, to explore each other's bodies. When not riding the tidal wave of their sexual passions, they spoke of small matters, each resolutely staying within the moment: how the training and renovations were coming, which of the staff were working out and which were not, what changes needed to be made.

Little Mandla, up and about and healing, and Strello, both kept a managed distance from Simpson during this time. Oh, they risked occasional winks, or arranged to be standing in narrow hallways that Simpson would need to pass through, and neither could keep from the occasional suggestive joke, but neither one was possessive. Both knew they would get another chance at sharing Andrew's bed, and in the meantime there was no lack of other outlets in the busy camp.

All the while, business began pouring in by way of the Internet. Requests for reservations even sooner than the projected starting date were pressed upon Simpson, and mindful of the need to generate a cash flow, as well as proud of the progress that had been made, he began accepting some reservations that would be very soon. The activities desired for these early bookings then received top priority in the training and construction that was going on. The week marched forward as the time of the first bookings became sooner and sooner, and before long the end of Motumbo's promised seven days were approaching, the day his friend would stop on the way from Johannesburg to take him back, if that was what he wanted.

It was on the evening before the day of Motumbo's friend's return that, sitting at a late private dinner in their own lodge, each spent from a hard day of work and the athletic lovemaking they had just shared, Simpson took the plunge and raised the question that had been hovering over them all week.

"So…Motumbo. Your friend, he comes back tomorrow?"

"Yes, Andrew." Motumbo cocked his head and looked carefully at Simpson, his eyes half hooded by his long lashes.

Simpson nodded. He waited. He tried a different tack.

"Motumbo, does your wife…your woman, does she know what you do here?"

Motumbo nodded. "Yes, Andrew, she know. Is OK, long's I come back, you know? She like the money."

"But she wants you to come back."

"Yes, Andrew. From time to time. That my home." And here he looked aside. Simpson glanced sharply at him and sucked in his breath. Another moment passed.

"Are you going back tomorrow then, with your friend?"

"Maybe. Maybe yes. Yes, I think so, Andrew." Motumbo was looking at the floor now. Another moment passed, and Andrew pushed his chair back suddenly and rose to his feet.

"Motumbo...you already know this. I don't know how else to say it. I need you. This last week has been...it has been what I dreamed of back..." And he gestured vaguely in the direction of what might be Philadelphia. "Motumbo," he continued with rising energy, "if you need to go back to see your wife, alright, I understand. Maybe I need a break sometimes too, OK?" Motumbo looked up quickly and flashed a smile, while a wintry grin crept across Simpson's otherwise pained features. "But Motumbo...I need you. Come back." He sat down heavily, took a deep breath, and said it: "I love you."

Motumbo stared hard at the white man, and then put his thick, large brown hand over Simpson's. The "L" word hung all by itself in the space between them as Simpson's heart thudded out a passing moment. "I like you also, Andrew." Well, there it was. The lesser "L" word. Simpson sighed softly. Motumbo continued: "I must go tomorrow. But I be back, yes, I promise. You know...I can't stay here always." Simpson gulped and nodded, turning his head and wiping his cheek on his shirt. Composing himself, he turned back to Motumbo, whose face showed a mixture of pain, resolution, compassion... and maybe the "like" he had just expressed? Could it become more, over time?

"I know, Motumbo," Simpson said. "Go, but come back. Or," and he sat up straight in his chair, "or can you bring your wife here? We can find a space for the two of you."

Motumbo gave a not very encouraging shrug. "I dunno, Andrew. That her home. Her own house, y'know? I ask, but I not think so. Andrew," he said, squeezing the hand again, "I be back soon, OK? Lotsa money to be made, guests come soon. And I got a idea I tell you about when I come back."

Simpson turned his hand over to entwine his fingers in Motumbo's. Looking down at the interlocked fingers, light and dark, he thought he had never seen such a beautiful sight. He nodded and smiled, and whispered "OK." They sat there in silence a few minutes more and then made for the bedroom where, long after their passion was spent, as the oil lamp burned the last of its fuel and guttered into a thin curl of white smoke, Simpson lay awake, caressing the crispy haired head of the sleeping man next to him as it lay on his chest, an occasional tear making its track down his cheek.

Simpson put on a brave face the next morning when, an hour before noon, Motumbo's friend pulled up in the compound. Simpson and Motumbo exchanged a brief embrace in the lodge, then Simpson waited and waved in the door of the dwelling while Motumbo entered the truck, which rumbled off into the distance leaving a cloud of dust in its wake. Simpson stared after it, sighed, and headed for the main lodge. The first reservations for guests were now a week away, and planning was proceeding apace to be ready for the unexpectedly early new business.

All that week Simpson threw himself into his work. Strello and Big Mandla were the team that would "entertain" the first guests, and Andrew avoided the temptation to have sex with either of them by keeping them and himself in a constant state of exhaustion from work. The night before the first guests were to arrive, everyone flopped into their own beds early and slept long into the next morning, while Thabo went alone to pick up the guests from the nearest town of any size, where their bus would deliver them. By the time Thabo pulled back into the compound in the afternoon, everyone was up and waiting.

Two slim, blonde and fair-skinned twenty-something men stepped out of the car. Simpson consulted his notes again: James and John Leggett, 24, twins, Brits from London. Further down was the notation that they were advertising creatives. Simpson set the notes aside and strode forward to play the good host. Introductions were made all around, Simpson making sure that key members of the staff were also introduced. Then he asked Thabo to take the men to their lodge to settle in. He knew that a nurse would be waiting there to draw blood for the mandatory STD test that everyone at De Groot's, staff and guest alike, took on a regular basis.

Later that evening, Simpson greeted the Leggetts at a dinner of wild game in the main lodge. The twins' manner was a trifle twee for his tastes, a little too willowy and languid, a bit too much of the Aubrey Beardsley thing, but then they weren't there for him and they were paying good money. Simpson went over the terms of tomorrow's games, and both men seemed to understand the rules completely. At the end of the dinner, Simpson bade his guests a good evening and counseled a good night's rest, to which they agreed. He himself, after scouting the territory, slipped unobtrusively down to his own lodge and turned out the light quickly. Still saddened over Motumbo's departure, he was not in the mood tonight for a frolic with Little Mandla or with Strello. Plus, Strello at least needed to save his strength. Simpson quickly slipped into a dreamless sleep.

Before dawn the next morning, Simpson was up early, first to knock softly at the door of the "Prey" lodge, where he spoke softly with Big Mandla and Strello to make sure they were ready. Then turning onto the path to the Leggett's cabin, he saw they already had a light on. They opened the door to his gentle knock, and stepping in he saw that they had just finished their light breakfast. They were clothed and equipped as well, and had been just about to emerge. All three men stepped into the early morning coolness, where Simpson turned again to assess the twins' state of readiness.

Each was clothed in light tan, or "flesh" colored skin tight breathable spandex, with sturdy sneakers on their feet. Each had a light cotton hood to cover their heads. Each had a small rucksack with some food and a bottle of water. They were the first to take advantage of the new program of attractions at De Groot's. They were going to be prey. The Leggetts represented the flip side of Simpson's own adventure some months ago, with the exception that their clothing would protect their fair skin from the African sun, a necessity for them if not for the rich, dark skins of the Africans Simpson had pursued before. Simpson led them to a small gate at the perimeter of the compound and, offering some last words of advice, ushered them through it into the wild lands beyond. They were off and running.

Simpson waited half an hour and then, as expected, saw Strello and Mandla walking down the path, clothed in sturdy shorts and shirts with snakeproof boots and broad-brimmed hats...and armed, each one, with a serious-looking paintball gun. The three men laughed and joked, each one exhilarated in his own way at the new game. Simpson made sure their radios were working, then led each one to the fence and out into the wild.

The Leggetts did not last until noon. Unaccustomed to the rugged landscape, scratched (but in minor ways) by thorns and brambles, first one and then the other took his paintball, splat! in the middle of his chest. Tired and hot, and anticipating the consequences of their capture, neither seemed to mind. Thabo and Simpson drove out to pick up the Leggetts, who were made to sit in the back of the truck while Strello and Mandla, grinning from ear to ear and swinging their paintball guns like trophies, sat in the four passenger cab with Thabo and Simpson. Back they went to the compound, where the twins and the two Africans, temporarily going their separate ways, washed up, drank water, and ate lunch. Then Strello and Mandla took up residence in a new lodge especially built for the purpose, and waited.

In the early afternoon, Thabo knocked on the door of the hut where Strello and Big Mandla were waiting. Strello opened it. Both he and Mandla were clothed in simple athletic shorts and T-shirts. Thabo led into the house the two blonde twins, James and John Leggett. Each was naked, freshly scrubbed, with their hands loosely bound behind with a soft cord. Their bodies were slim and willowy, no fat but only a boyish wash of thin muscle over their long frames. Straight blonde hair hung over their ears. The twenty-four year olds' complexion was cream and light rose. Beneath a patch of dirty blonde pubic hair, each had a half erection that swayed and bounced as they stepped into the lodge, eyes cast down. Thabo, barely able to suppress a smile at the reversal of the usual turn of events, announced to Strello and Mandla that their two trophies from the morning's hunt were here, and were theirs to do with as they pleased. Then he withdrew.

Strello and Mandla exchanged a quick glance of victory and anticipation, then slowly walked around the captive white men, whose erections were slowly growing. Walking behind them, Mandla swatted first the one and then the other, hard, on their rosy round bottoms, leaving a red mark where his hand struck. The twins each gasped, but kept their heads downcast and did not object. Strello, also standing behind the twins, slipped off the cords that bound their hands. Returning to stand in front of them, Mandla prodded James in the chest and said, "Remove my clothing." James sank to his knees in front of the large African and slipped off his sandals. Then he rose and tugged up and off the huge black man's T-shirt, to the best of his ability. Mandla's massive frame was more apparent with his shirt off, the great lobes of his chest and dense abdominal padding making him a formidable sight. Thick shoulder and neck muscles rose to the close-cropped head of hair. The big man, standing over six feet tall, regarded from beneath hooded eyes and curled lashes the naked white man, several inches shorter than he. "This, too," he said, snapping at his athletic shorts. James sank again to his knees, his now rigid red cock bouncing, and tugged down the shorts, which fell to the floor. A massive, thick, purple black penis popped out, curving out from beneath a dense patch of kinky pubic hair, above a heavy scrotum containing two nuts the size of golf balls. Mandla reached down and grasped his organ, then taking a step forward began to gently slap James's face with it. As the huge cock stiffened it also began to leak precum, and Mandla painted the white man's face with it, leaving a pattern of glistening clear liquid on and around his button nose and rosebud lips, streaking the blonde hair hanging down over his forehead.

In the meantime Strello, still standing behind the naked John Leggett, had stripped off his own T-shirt and thrown it aside. He stepped up close behind John and pulled the blonde man back into him, clasping him in front, running his dark brown hands over the thin cream and rose chest and belly, burying his face in the silky blonde hair. "Pull my shorts off" he growled into the ear of the white man, who stood about his own height. Reaching back, John tugged down the athletic shorts, which fell to the ground. Strello kicked them and his sandals away. His thick, heavy cock, black as midnight and smooth as satin, was fully erect and pushed downward between the two men. Strello ground the thick, meaty shaft in between John's rounded, rose and cream colored buttocks while at the same time he ran his hands down the slim abdomen of the white man to pause at the bush of silky pubic hair, then to grasp the long, slim, iron hard rod that now stuck straight out from John's body.

For his part, Mandla now sank his fingers into the thick blonde hair of the white man who was kneeling in front of him and moved James's rosebud lips to his thick, flared cockhead that was dribbling precum. James opened his mouth and Mandla pushed forward, gagging the white man, but still the African shoved his enormous dick into the waiting mouth. "Take it!" Mandla commanded fiercely. James squirmed, his palms pressing against the muscular tree trunks of Mandla's thighs, as he gagged and swallowed in an attempt to accommodate the thick sausage that now slid against the back of his throat.

Strello pushed and ground his swollen dick into the ass crack of the squirming white in front of him, smearing John's reddish asshole with the precum that oozed out of his black cock. With one hand Strello pawed the white man's thin chest and belly, pulling John's body back into his own, while with the other he pumped the rigid red cock, spraying drops of precum from the end of it. John's breathing became harder and harder, his legs began trembling, his hips bucking in the rhythm of the black hand that slid up and down his pole, and then with a shout he spouted out a long rope of cum, then another, that dotted and splattered the floor in front of him. No sooner had the last drop landed than Strello roughly pushed the white man to the ground in front of him. John fell onto his hands and knees, his still erect rod slapping the wood floor, and Strello dropped immediately behind him. He placed his thick black cock at the entrance to John's rectum, already slick with precum, and with no other lubricant gave a push. John cried out and lowered his head, sinking down onto his elbows, but Strello had his hips and upper thighs in his strong hands and would not let the white ass escape. Strello pushed his thick dick all the way forward in one mighty lunge as John cried out, writhing in pain.

Fully landed, Strello waited, balanced on his knees, pulling the round pink butt toward him by the hips.

"Why this happ'nin' to you, eh? Why?" Strello roared at John. The white man sobbed and gasped, and choked out, "Because you won me, sir."

"What I do to you now, eh white boy?" Strello shouted, jerking the pelvis toward him even tighter.

"You...you will fuck me, sir."

"Call me master, boy."

"Yes, master. You will fuck me, sir" gasped John. And at that Strello immediately lunged forward into a frantic pumping, fucking the pink, rounded ass in front of him while John gasped and slobbered, covering the floor in front of him with his tears, saliva, and leaking precum. Harder and faster, pumping like a piston, Strello ploughed the white man's butt.

All the while, Mandla had begun moving his swollen dick in and out of James's mouth as the white man continued to kneel in front of him. James gagged and struggled for breath as the huge rod slid in and out, in and out, never fully landed because its size was simply overwhelming. Mandla's eyes shifted back and forth between the sight of Strello power fucking the white man on the floor and the blonde head into which his own black dick was sliding. And then the tingling began in his thighs and belly, the gathering of the storm, and Mandla cried out, pushing forward and into James's mouth farther than ever before as the white man squirmed and pushed in desperation against the black man's massive thighs and belly. Mandla's head rolled back and his eyes rolled up in his head as he shot great gouts of semen directly down the throat of the struggling white man in front of him. The minute his ecstasy had passed he pulled his great organ out in one movement, leaving James gasping, semen dribbling from a corner of his mouth.

Mandla, still panting, reached down and pulled James to his feet, then with his great strength lifted the white man up into the air by his hips. The rigid red cock came up to Mandla's thick, maroon brown lips and the black man lunged at it with his mouth, taking the whole long, slim length of the white man's penis into his mouth with ease. James supported himself with his palms flat on Mandla's thick shoulders and held on for dear life as Mandla's head pistoned back and forth in a blur, sucking the white man's cock.

On the floor, Strello's hips were fanning back and forth, his hands still pulling John's round bottom to him, until a very sudden and violent orgasm slammed through Strello unexpectedly. He roared and pushed, lifting John's knees off the ground as he pulled the white ass back toward him to receive the heavy offering of white spunk. John cried out again, still unused to the very size of the black tool that now pumped semen into him. James, lifted up to Mandla's mouth, now threw his own head back and howled as he shot his load into the African's mouth, quivering and shaking as the black man drained every drop. Animal howls filled the lodge for a minute's time.

Strello pulled out of John, leaving a thin trail of semen running from the end of his dick to the white man's gaping asshole, and stood up as John collapsed to the floor, moaning, his tortured anus gaping wide. Mandla gave James one last suck and then dropped the white man on top of his brother on the floor. The two blonde twins curled into each other's arms, whimpering. The two Africans broke into laughter, exclaiming loudly in their native tongue and shaking each other's hands. Then the victors in the day's hunt went to a nearby table, their dicks still swollen and leaking fluid, to celebrate with the bottle of whisky that had been left there. On the floor the twins caught their breaths and huddled together...but as the physical pain subsided, slowly and then more broadly a pair of satisfied grins spread across their faces. James looked at John and winked. John nodded back. They had lost, but they had won; the consequence had been what they had hoped for even if it was what they had feared, and it surely topped anything the club and bathhouses of London had ever offered. At the table, Strello and Mandla planned the next bout...it was going to be a long night. A blessedly long one.

- CHAPTER 7 -

Simpson and Thabo couldn't help but laugh, just between themselves. For the rest of that day and into the evening, and then beginning bright and early the next morning, the sound of bedsprings squeaking, howls and roars of ecstasy or anguish, and guttural sounds of animal rutting came from the new lodge in which Strello and Big Mandla had their way with the blonde British twins, James and John Leggett. It just never let up. Although it would not have been Andrew Simpson's style, he quite understood the attraction the experience held for the willowy young white men, for he had met plenty of white men who wanted nothing more than to be dominated by a muscular black man. Strello, built like a brick outhouse, and the massive Mandla, certainly fit that description of muscular. Having "won" the two Brits by hunting them down with paintball, they now ploughed their sore pink asses without mercy, and filled their mouths with their massive dicks on an hourly basis. Only food passed in, and scraps passed out, of the lodge.

The second evening things were a little quieter, although the sound of an occasional grunting, or a yelp of pain every now and then, could still be heard. And the next morning, which was to be the last day of the twins' stay at De Groot's, dawned with even more peace and quiet, with only an occasional thump to be heard.

That afternoon, Thabo and Simpson were sitting in the main lodge discussing plans when Little Mandla entered, grinning ear to ear, a handful of folded slips of paper in his hand. He sorted through the wad and pulled out two, then presented them to Thabo and Simpson, saying "It gonna be a party!"

Thabo and Simpson looked at each other and shrugged, then at the paper. In block pencil printing was an "announcement" from Big Mandla and Strello inviting them to a "party" at their lodge in the evening. The two men looked at Little Mandla and then the three broke out chuckling.

"Are you going also, Little Mandla?" asked Simpson. The youth nodded happily. "Well, what's it about?" Little Mandla winked broadly, put his finger to his lips and winked again, then continued on his appointed rounds to hand out invitations. Thabo and Simpson shrugged at one another once again, but agreed to go see what the party could be, and what connection it might have to the blonde British twins.

After a light dinner, Simpson walked down to the guest lodge at the appointed hour. He met up with Little Mandla and Thabo on the way, along with a couple of the staff, Gift and Justice, to whom Simpson nodded cordially. The compound was not quite as populated now as it had been earlier during construction; now all was in readiness, and the number of men around was lower.

At the lodge, Thabo, a little in front, knocked. The door opened, flooding a soft light into the night. Big Mandla filled the doorway, completely naked, his dark skin shining in the artificial light. With a great ceremonial wave, he motioned for his guests to enter. Inside the lodge was a sight to behold.

The door to the guest lodge opened into a great room, and just beyond that was a single bedroom, with the door opened wide. Stepping to that inner door, the guests caught their breaths: the two twins were on their bellies, naked, with pillows stuffed under their pelvises so as to present their round, pink bottoms to the world. The two blonde men were spread-eagled, hands tied to the headboard and feet tied to the footboard lightly with soft cords. They could probably have escaped…if they had wanted to. In the center of each round, upturned bottom was a glistening gob of lubricant over their exposed anuses, which were winking slightly open; it was clear that the activities of the previous two days had stretched them significantly.

"Come, you get drink!" said Big Mandla, motioning to a table back in the great room, where an equally naked Strello was pouring out whisky over ice cubes in glasses. Each guest helped himself, his imagination racing to comprehend what was in store for the evening. Toasts to De Groot's, to Simpson, to every person there were offered up, and the party gradually became looser and merrier. Big Mandla topped up all drinks and then said, "Come!" He led the way into the bedroom. Apparently these five guests were all that were coming, and they crowded in a companionable way around the bed.

"Strip!" said Strello, and he and Big Mandla walked from guest to guest, encouraging them to discard their clothing, tugging at a shirt or belt where necessary. Had Simpson been sober he might have objected; only Strello and Little Mandla in this group had seen him naked, and Gift and Justice were practically strangers. They were both in their mid twenties. But with a little encouragement from their hosts, the guests gradually shed one and then another piece of clothing, joking and laughing with one another, until soon everyone in the place stood naked.

Simpson had nothing to be ashamed of in the physical endowment department, but he had to be impressed by the muscular beauty of the naked Africans who surrounded him, most of them sporting half erections in the sexually charged atmosphere. Gift and Justice were of average musculature and height, each with a long, weighty penis, Gift's curving to the left markedly as his erection grew. Little Mandla he had seen (and more than seen) of course, and exchanged knowing smiles with the youth, whose shaft was now rising straight out in front of him. Simpson also looked with interest at Thabo, still trim and taut in middle age, his pubic bush salt and pepper like the crisp hair upon his head. And Thabo was also half erect. Simpson had wondered more than once about the older man's sexual proclivities. How many times had Thabo led a naked man to a lodge to be enjoyed by other naked men, and yet what were Thabo's own fantasies? Did he enjoy the "Prey" crew, and they him, when guests were not around? Thabo's growing erection seemed an indication of some strong interest, at least, in men.

Strello and Big Mandla proposed one more toast, which everyone threw back in short order, and then with a nod at each other and no further ado, they led the way back into the bedroom, where each of the two hosts scrambled up onto the bed between the outspread legs of the two blonde twins. Squatting on their haunches, they lubricated their own fully rigid, midnight black shafts and pressed them to the well oiled anuses of their white conquests. Two days of being ravaged by the Africans had prepared the white men for this. Strello and Mandla slid quickly in, and while the white men cried out, and John exclaimed "Master!" they seemed not to experience the agony that might be expected from being impaled by such huge organs. As Strello and Big Mandla pushed all the way in and then began slowly pumping, the rest of the men gathered round. Some of them rubbed the legs, arms, or hair of the blondes on the bed even as they were being fucked; Simpson reflected that it was possible that Thabo, Gift, and Justice at least had not seen a naked white man before. Strello squatted on his haunches still, his long shaft clearly visible as it slid in and out of the red asshole in front of him, and the men looked closely to savor the sight, some bending over to eye the sliding shaft closely. Big Mandla stretched himself out fully on top of the blonde he was fucking, covering his pale body entirely with his weight, the Brit crying out "Master!" but not otherwise protesting. Mandla's strong legs entwined with the slim legs of the white man as his butt pistoned up and down, up and down, and he slipped his arms underneath the blonde beneath him to hug him tightly, nearly squeezing the breath out of his conquest. Strello shifted to extend his legs straight back, but held himself up off of the blonde man beneath him so he could still look down and see his thick black shaft moving rhythmically in and out, in and out. Strello came first: quivering, then picking up speed tremendously, then crying out and pushing forward, grinding his pelvis into the pink upturned bottom below him as he shot his cum into the blonde's asshole. He held that position, shuddering, and then pulled out, his dick still erect and dribbling cum.

Gift was standing right beside Strello as he slid from the bed, and Strello slapped him on his naked butt and grinning, motioned him to take his place. Needing no further encouragement, Gift took Strello's place and, without any more lubrication, slid his own heavy penis completely inside the waiting white man's anus. A look of wonder spread over Gift's features as he flew into a very rapid rhythm of fucking, his dark chocolate bubble butt rolling upward as he pushed in, rolling downward as he pulled back, a sheen of sweat and oil spreading across his beautiful fudge dark skin. Holding himself on one hand, Gift entwined his fingers in the blonde's silky hair, then ran his hand across the man's heaving pink and cream back, as he fucked even faster.

Big Mandla at that pointed roared and, still hugging the blonde man tight, pulled even tighter, a squeal coming from his sexual victim as Big Mandla tensed and shot his semen down into his "property" for that week. He lay there quivering for a moment, then quickly rolled off the bed to sit on the floor, his still-erect penis bobbing about and leaking semen. On the floor, he slapped the thigh of the man standing closest to him: Little Mandla, and jerked with his thumb toward the bed.

Little Mandla took Big Mandla's place as Gift, too excited to hold it for long, came with a roar. Little Mandla's slim, boyish butt now fanned back and forth in a furious rhythm, a dimple in the side of each rounded buttock appearing and disappearing as his bottom clenched and unclenched with the rhythmic pumping. Gift was barely recovered before Justice, seething with impatience, nearly pulled his friend off the bed and jumped into place himself. Justice remained on his haunches, his long, thick midnight black dick sliding in and out of the gaping pink bottom in front of him. There was no longer any question of lubrication, each white man's rectum was fully lubricated by now with semen. Justice's hands slid up and down the flanks of the white man he fucked, then they slapped the rounded pink buttocks, at first tentatively, and then in time to the rhythmic pumping of his shaft. Smack! Smack! Smack! The pink flesh became redder and redder the longer he fucked.

Those who had not yet had their turn were nearly beside themselves with expectation. Those who had already cum sat on the floor, recovering breath and joking, or they continued standing by the side of the bed, penises slowly deflating, offering advice to their friends and taunting the white men. The sound of the outside door closing distracted a couple of them. They realized that Strello had opened the door and had now admitted Zama. The tall guard laid his shotgun on the table, abandoning his post for a moment, and quickly stripped off. His tall, lean frame sported a hard ebony rod that was extremely long but not so thick. As Zama entered the room, Little Mandla cried out frantically and, bucking two and then three times, slammed forward into the white butt beneath him. Zama was instantly aroused, and did not even wait for Little Mandla to recover. The youth was still quivering, lying atop the blonde, when Zama pulled him off, cum still flowing, and set Little Mandla on his feet by the side of the bed where the African youth slumped to the floor, chest still heaving from his labors. Zama plunged into the butt beneath him and began fucking him in a curious circular motion, his high, rounded bottom cycling like a wheel, his gyrations enabled by the great length of his penis: he could stay landed inside the white butt no matter how he moved!

Zama and Justice labored mightily side by side, Justice showing more staying power than his friend Gift, and the two came at the same time after about ten minutes of serious fucking, each one pitching and bucking forward, grinding their groins down into the white asses. Each lay there another few minutes panting and heaving. But mindful of others' needs, each also pulled out before their erections had subsided, and slumped to the floor to add the dribbles from their own penises to the streaks and puddles of slime that had collected everywhere. And that left Simpson and Thabo.

The two men looked at each other, nodded, and climbed onto the bed. Two red anuses positively yawned open before them, rivulets of white cum running out of each one and onto the bed. Simpson and Thabo, acting in tandem, positioned themselves and, placing one reddish pink and one purple black rod at each anus, pushed in. Of course, they slid all the way in with no more than a grunt or a sigh from the well-fucked white men beneath them. Each now rode inside his respective white rectum on a thick coating of African cum.

How many hours had Simpson and Thabo spent together working on the business of De Groot's? Those hours of physical proximity and mental connection; it may have prepared them for what was happening now. For Simpson and Thabo, inches apart, shoulders and knees rubbing from time to time as they pumped in and out of the upturned assholes, looked not at the blondes beneath them but at each other. Their eyes met the other one's, or ran up and down the body next close at hand, Simpson admiring the muscular tautness of the middle aged man, Thabo enjoying the differences presented by the white man fucking another white man next to him. Their hips fell into the same rhythm, in and out, in and out, as both men held themselves up off of the blondes with their hands on the bed. Both men smiled at each other as their rhythms increased, and both saw the secret unfolding in the other one's eyes, saw the coming crisis, saw the moment in which the eyes lose focus, and then refocused hard again into each other as the explosion occurred, both at the same time. Roaring at one another with heads turned in each other's direction, Thabo and Simpson poured their cum down into the blondes beneath them, but in the spirit they were fucking each other.

No one else needed a turn...indeed, Zama had already dressed again and returned to his duties...so Simpson and Thabo were allowed to recover while resting on top of the blondes, still looking at each other. Thabo tentatively brought a hand up and touched Simpson's cornsilk hair, and when that was not refused, he entwined his brown fingers in it. Simpson reached over to run his hand over his friend and colleague's close-cropped hair, so crisp and delightful it was like biting into an apple, and the two men chuckled together at the moment of discovery. Then, as the moment passed, they also rose up and got off the bed. There was a round of applause all around as they, and then the other men, stood up and bowed. Comments and critiques of each man's performance were offered in fun, and friendly insults traded back and forth. The men took turns showering in the nearby bathroom, then gathered around the table for another drink. At some point, Strello untied the blondes who limped into the bathroom, a positive river of semen running down the backs of their legs, but with smiles on their weary faces. Cleaned, the blondes were likewise invited to the table to drink, and their own good health was proposed and their special kind of stamina celebrated. It was the most unusual party Simpson had ever attended, and the most enjoyable. It was late into the night before all the men staggered back to their lodges, including the blonde Brits, who were "released" by the grateful (and almost affectionate) Strello and Big Mandla to rest and prepare for their journey home the next day.

Midway through the next morning the British twins, positively glowing from their time at De Groot's and seemingly none the worse for wear, were loaded into the truck for Thabo to return them to their bus stop. Simpson and Thabo greeted each other cordially as they met at the truck, but it was a greeting with an extra layer of shared experience and, perhaps, a little sexual tension. Simpson loaded the twins down with brochures to distribute back in the UK, while they each expressed their thanks effusively and promised to send more business to De Groot's than they could handle. Simpson waved after the departing truck until the cloud of dust hid it, then walked up to the main lodge.

He met Strello and Big Mandla on the way, vacating the guest lodge on the way back to the "Prey" house. In the distance, Simpson could see a cleaning crew heading for the guest lodge; it would need sandblasting after last night! The three men stopped to laugh and recount the exploits of the previous night. With "professional" interest, Simpson also discussed the whole process of the hunt and the days that had followed, to make sure that it was an experience that might appeal to others…and to determine the kind of appeal it would be. Their discussion took some time, and it was approaching lunch when Simpson finally made it to the main lodge.

Simpson, Thabo, and Guest were sharing a bite to eat when the official De Groot telephone…a cell phone, of course…rang. Thabo answered, spoke a few words, and handed it with a smile to Simpson.

"Hello?"

"Hello, Boss Andrew, it Motumbo here."

Simpson caught his breath and a smile involuntarily broke out. Seeing it, Thabo smiled and nodded gently.

"Motumbo...good to hear your voice. So...what's happening?"

"Andrew, you know the 'Ball Room' fun we plan? When it happen first?"

Simpson rose to consult a calendar on a nearby desk. "In a week, actually." He summoned his courage. "Want to come back for it? I had thought Little Mandla would take that one, but..."

Motumbo broke in. "I come back, sure, but I got different idea for 'Ball Room,' you gonna like, Andrew. See you in day or two. Bye." And he rang off.

Simpson took the phone from his ear and stared at it. The news that Motumbo was returning was good, but the new idea he had promised was mystifying. The "Ball Room" was one of the new attractions that had been planned, requiring its own new, small building. Simpson resolved to be open to whatever was presented. Thabo looked at him quizzically. As nonchalantly as he could, Simpson shrugged and said, "Motumbo is coming back, in a day or two. He has some new ideas." Thabo nodded, smiling, as the silence between them lengthened, and then burst out into a cackle, rose, patted Simpson hard on the shoulder, and went about his business, still chuckling to himself.

Motumbo did not come that day, nor the next. Simpson found good reasons to work by himself and to turn in early and alone, despite clear signs from the other men who had been at the party that a threshold had been crossed and a new openness reached in terms of sexual possibilities. But Simpson wanted to save himself for Motumbo, at least this once.

It was in the early afternoon of the next day that Motumbo pulled up in a pickup truck, driving himself this time, and rumbled to a halt at the end of a trail of dust in the compound. Emerging, he smiled broadly at Simpson and enfolded him in a bear hug. Was this still "like" or had it become something else? Had Motumbo missed him? Simpson simply could not tell. But as they talked for a moment exchanging pleasantries and news, Simpson kept an arm halfway around the big African's waist, and Motumbo did not object. Eventually, Simpson asked about the news.

"So, Motumbo, your new idea for the Ball Room...?" Motumbo nodded and grinned, then whistled loudly. Simpson had paid no further attention to the truck after Motumbo had emerged from it, but now he turned around and beheld, exiting from the passenger door, the two twin brothers, Thatho and Mthobisi, who had first guided him to Motumbo's house in their home village. The boys presented themselves grinning ear to ear, standing erect with chests thrust out, and with great ceremony shook Simpson's hand. He was glad to see the boys, but...and then it dawned on him. He wheeled back around to Motumbo.

"Motumbo, you don't mean them, do you? They are just boys, they are kids, they are underage."

Motumbo threw back his head and laughed. "Andrew, they jes look young for their age. They got papers, from government, eh? Both eighteen, just. And Andrew, they know what up...they...they done it, eh? OK?" Motumbo grabbed his crotch lightly, by way of clarification. Simpson made as if to protest again, and Motumbo continued. "They not been here, not De Groot's, but Andrew, everybody, they do it by they age, OK? And," and here he played his trump card, "they need the money, they family need the money, real bad, OK?"

Simpson turned again to look helplessly at the boys who continued standing there, smiling. So young, and they looked so small, in comparison with American boys! "Show me your papers," he said. Proudly they offered up quite official looking documents, stamped and embossed. Sure enough, eighteen. Simpson thought for a moment. If they were in fact eighteen but look no more than sixteen, the possibilities were intriguing.

Motumbo touched Simpson on the arm.

"Come, I sleep in your lodge?" His dark face split into a huge grin. As he suspected, that distracted Simpson sufficiently. Simpson nodded vigorously and turning, led the way to his own lodge, Motumbo close by him, both of them chattering all the way about the first new adventure a few days before, Motumbo laughing out loud at Simpson's description of the sexual exploits involved. Simpson opened the door to his lodge and led the way in. He turned after a couple of steps and there stood the two boys inside the doorway... evidently they have followed the two men from the truck. Each had a small sack of possessions. Simpson's jaw dropped in surprise.

"Motumbo, really, do they know what they are doing?"

"Andrew, they perfect for Ball Room...so small, so light, so slippery!" Gracefully, Motumbo took a step toward the door and swung it shut. Simpson looked with consternation at Motumbo and the twin black boys. Then matters took a truly unexpected turn. Motumbo muttered a word in their language to the boys, who instantly began removing their own clothing, despite Simpson's strangled yelp of "Wait!" In a flash, the boys stood completely naked, grinning from ear to ear, before the two men. Motumbo himself had a knowing grin, and was eyeing Simpson closely to see what he would do.

Simpson had never especially had a thing for adolescent boys, although he could not deny the appeal of a few he had seen. But then, he had never really been in a situation like this: two slim young teen twins, barely eighteen and slight as boys, with the lightest padding of muscle on them, chocolate brown skin of flawless complexion and no body hair except for a little patch of pubic hair above their penises. And what penises, for their ages! Not as big as the adult Africans, nevertheless they gave promise of the magnificent organs they would become. Both curved out and downward and would have seemed average on many an adult white male of Simpson's acquaintance. On the boys' thin frames, they seemed oversized, as if the long, meaty organs had rushed into adulthood ahead of the boys. Simpson's gaze wandered from these magnificent organs, curving out and a little down as they now rose into erection, and lingered over the rest of the boys' bodies. Standing erect with shoulders back, their bodies described the perfect S curve of so many Africans who stand proudly tall, shoulders back and chest thrust forward, belly curving gently in front, then rounded, high-rolled buttocks in back that were so prominent it seemed as if they were being pushed backward, offered up for fucking. The twins were simply physical perfection, beautiful faces with full, bee-stung lips and button noses, long curling lashes, and that deep chocolate color you could sink into with your eyes. Simpson was smitten and he knew it; the bulge in the front of his trousers was evident to everyone.

It was surely evident to Thatho, who stepped forward and in a flash unbuttoned Simpson's trousers, then before those had reached the floor, tugged his underwear down to follow. Smiling hugely, Thatho looked intently at Simpson's organ which was rapidly growing larger, more erect, and redder. The boy ran his fingers through his patch of dirty blonde pubic hair, and it occurred to Simpson that neither boy might have seen a naked white man before, much less touched one in this way. Mthobisi stepped forward and gently cupped Simpson's ballsack, hefting it, as his brother wrapped a slim brown hand around the reddening shaft and slowly, deliberately pumped it. Simpson had no breath to object, he was totally caught up in the moment.

Mthobisi, with a glance back at Simpson that might have been one of yearning, stepped over to Motumbo and quickly unfastened his pants and underwear as well, soon exposing the African man's own stiffening purple black rod. Motumbo whipped off his own shirt and tugged at Simpson's sleeve to indicate that he should do the same. Simpson complied, and both men stood naked with the naked brown twins in front of them. Each boy was now sliding one and sometimes two slim brown hands up and down the midnight black and the purple red penises, both men now grasped the boys' thin, naked shoulders to steady themselves as their breathing increased and they began moving their hips back and forth.

But more was to come. First Thatho, and then his brother following his lead, leaned over and took each man's penis into his mouth. At first, they closed their full, maroon brown lips over the flared heads, greedily sucking off the gathering precum. Then they slid as much of each penis as they could into their mouths. Neither boy took either organ whole, but they took enough to give the men the most intense pleasure. Without applying their teeth, each boy now sucked the penis of the man in front of him, while he bobbed his head up and down. Each boy grasped a man by the waist, now by the hips, as each man kneaded a thin brown shoulder, cupped a slightly curving bicep, or clasped a crisp-haired head in his hands. Faster and harder the boys sucked, Simpson and Motumbo's hips were now swinging back and forth, and then at the same time each man came, crying out, pushing forward, while each boy sucked and swallowed noisily and pulled their heads back some to avoid being gagged. One spasm and then another wracked each man as he shot his semen into the warm, waiting mouths of the brown boy in front of him. When each one was finished, the boy carefully sucked each dick dry, then stepped back, licking their lips and smiling hugely again.

Simpson, amazed, was still breathing heavily, his penis still turgid even as his erection flagged. He look at the boys, then at Motumbo, who was looking at Simpson closely despite his own ragged breath.

"I'll be damned," said the white man. "I think they really would be good in the Ball Room." To which statement Motumbo nodded and grinned in agreement, and the boys whooped with glee.

- CHAPTER 8 -

Andrew Simpson woke up with an incredibly heavy feeling, and an urgency to use the toilet. But it took only a moment for the disorientation to pass. The heaviness was the fact that Motumbo was still on top of him, having fallen asleep after his orgasm the night before. And the urgency to use the toilet probably came from the fact that the African's massive rod was still inside Simpson's rectum, so long and heavy that even in its flaccid state it remained where Motumbo had left it after his last quivering spasm the night before.

Simpson pushed up and over, and Motumbo turned onto his back, his penis plopping out of the white man. But the African did not awake. Quietly, Simpson slipped from the bed and padded across the floor out into the great room on his way to the bathroom. On the way he passed the sofa on which Thatho and Mthobisi slept, having been put up there for the night in the absence of any better lodging until further plans could be made. Having relieved himself, Simpson walked softly back toward the bedroom, stopping to look at the eighteen year old boys on the sofa. Their boyish good looks really were attractive, but he still had some lingering doubts as to whether they should be employed at De Groot's.

Simpson slipped back into bed and into the semi-conscious embrace of Motumbo. For another hour or two he dozed, coming more fully into consciousness as the first light of dawn crept into the lodge. Sensing Motumbo's gradual awakening as well, Simpson nuzzled the big man on the face and neck. A soft chuckle announced Motumbo's awareness of his attentions, and powerful black arms around him pulled him in a little tighter.

"I'm glad you're here," whispered Simpson. Motumbo grunted and nodded, then hugged a little tighter. A moment passed. "But Motumbo," Simpson continued, "Thatho and Mthobisi...alright, they are sexually experienced. But really, they are very young, only just eighteen. Blow jobs, sucking us, yes they do that well. But if they are the Ball Room team, they will need to do more than that, you know." Motumbo nodded and grunted noncommittally. "Have they," Simpson continued, "have they, you know, taken it in the butt? Can they do that?"

Motumbo chuckled and reached around to squeeze Simpson's hard buttock. "That way, Andrew?" he asked, and laughed out loud. Simpson snuggled in even closer, giving Motumbo's slowly swelling cock an encouraging squeeze.

"Yes, that way, Motumbo. You know, it would come to that. Maybe they have fucked each other, but a fully grown man?" Motumbo grunted again. He paused a moment, then pushed himself up on one elbow, turning his head toward the door. Simpson listened as well. There was the sound of stirring from the great room. Motumbo cleared his throat and called out the boys' names loudly. There was more sound from the great room, a couple of low voices, then the sound of padding feet. The boys appeared naked in the doorway, rubbing sleep from their eyes.

They were a beautiful sight, and once again, Simpson felt himself aroused by their youthful appearance. Even just awaking, the boys held their muscular curved tubes of their bodies erect, shoulders back, slim, upturned buttocks protruding behind. Their morning erections made their nearly man sized penises seem even larger and more outsized than Simpson had remembered from the night before, now curving out and a little down from underneath sparse little patches of pubic hair. Their skins were a rich, deep, flawless chocolate, a color infused with life as is so often the case with the young, a fudge color you could eat over ice cream. Motumbo spoke to them in their language. They both laughed and answered, punctuated by light jabs at one another, some animated gestures, and at one point Mthobisi squatted down and then stood up again quickly, which brought a hoot of laughter from Thatho. Motumbo turned to Andrew.

"Andrew, they say they do it with other boys they age, not men. But they say, no big deal. I don't know, Boss...what you think? Shall we test?" Motumbo broke into a huge grin. Simpson, still reticent but now tempted nearly beyond endurance, didn't know what to say besides smile back in wonderment. Motumbo answered for him. He whipped back the sheets from the bed, leaving the two men naked on the mattress, their morning erections, now growing, being fully apparent. Motumbo spoke to them again in their language and the eighteen year old twins, giggling with laughter, bounded over to the bed, piling into it between the two men in a squirming mass.

For several moments the men, turning inward, cuddled with the boys, tickling them, squeezing them, enfolding them in light bear hugs, kissing and nuzzling their necks and ears while the boys in their turn mock-struggled with Motumbo and took this chance to explore Simpson's physical differences, his unaccustomed cornsilk hair and light complexion. The boys placed their fingers on his thinner lips, and remarked on the scattering of body hair that was new to them. Soon, playfulness led to foreplay. The boys began to tease and then to squeeze the men's penises, which brought them to full, iron erection. The men, tickling the boys, tickled down to their hairless ballsacks, and then grasped their mannish dicks, now also growing fully erect.

Motumbo reached first for the lubricant, for after all this escapade was also a working session to find out whether the boys could handle the consequences of some of the games at De Groot's. Motumbo flopped onto his back and began greasing his midnight black, meaty pole that stuck straight up, slathering lubricant on it from its wide base to the flared cockhead now poking out of his foreskin. Then he reached over and grabbed Mthobisi, who had sucked his rod the previous day, and hauled the boy over to squat above his organ, knees on the bed on either side of Motumbo's hips. Mthobisi took his position with a grin, but cast a wistful look at Simpson and the white man's towering organ. Seeing what was planned, Simpson oiled up his own rigid red shaft, but he did not have to encourage Thatho, who was in place before the white man could direct him to do so.

Now began the time of trial. Wincing and gasping, both boys squatted above the men's pelvises and tried impaling themselves on the man-sized organs. Each man was helpful but insistent; a customer, after all, would be less gentle than this, and the boys needed to show that they could handle it. Not surprisingly, Thatho achieved a breakthrough first: with a yelp, the head of Simpson's organ slipped inside, and the boy slowly lowered himself all the way down, finally settling his firm, rounded buttocks on Simpson's pelvis. Slowly, tentatively, still wincing but breathing hard with growing lust, Thatho began pushing up and sliding down, up and down, on Simpson's dick.

No such luck with Mthobisi. A little more shy than his brother, tears started from his eyes as he tried to accommodate Motumbo's huge organ, but it wasn't any good. No matter how hard he pushed, no matter how many comforting words to relax were spoken by Motumbo, the African man's huge dick was just too large. Seeing the difficulty, even as Thatho was beginning to pick up his rhythm, Simpson realized that his relatively smaller penis might work where Motumbo's did not. He quickly suggested that the twins switch. Thatho objected, and had to be half-pulled off of Simpson by Motumbo, but eventually he settled over the African man's penis. Mthobisi, wiping a tear but with a smile of glee, shifted over and positioned himself over Simpson.

Now the drama was repeated, as Thatho struggled to accept the larger African meat. Mthobisi struggled and strained to take Simpson. Once again, the white man proved capable of penetrating the African boy above him first. With a cry, Mthobisi pushed his rectum down over Simpson's cockhead, and then with another cry he slid all the way down in one motion, landing now on Simpson's pelvis, shuddering and breathing hard but fully encasing the white man's dick in his bottom now. Not far behind, and opened up by Simpson's dick before, soon Thatho yelped as Motumbo's fat cockhead popped inside his anus, then moaned as he settled on the African's pelvis, squirming at the huge sausage stuffed inside his gut.

There was a moment of waiting, of tentative movement, of each man insistently but gently pushing up with his pelvis, and then the boys began to swing into a rhythm, up and down, up and down, then faster, now landing down with force so as to receive the grown dick as far up as it would go, now rising up until the man's cockhead was only just inside the anus, then back down again. In the meantime, each boy's own nearly man-sized cock was fully erect, and spraying precum as they bounced up and down. Simpson and Motumbo each grasped the dick of the boy they were fucking and began pumping it in time to the boy's rhythm. Each boy was now stimulated more than they had ever been, their bottoms stuffed full of oversized man-dick and their own penises being rapidly pumped. Each man used his second hand to fondle a hard, rounded buttock, to tweak a nipple, or to support a boy with palm splayed flat on a chest. Mthobisi could not take his eyes off the brand new sight of Simpson's pale fist wrapped around his own purple black cock, and Thatho kept looking over at the spectacle from time to time also.

Being more forward, Thatho came first, crying out and spraying cum all over Motumbo, the white splats decorating the man's dark fudge skin on his belly, chest, and face. Thatho's rhythm faltered as he came, shuddering and quivering, and he almost pulled off of Motumbo entirely, but he recovered quickly and returned to his rhythm, even faster now as his hips pistoned up and down even as his quivering dick leaked semen as it slapped Motumbo's belly. It took Mthobisi another moment but then he, also, growled in a deep voice belying his age and tensed. As luck would have it, he shot a rope of cum directly into Simpson's face, and Simpson, seeing it coming, opened his mouth in anticipation, being rewarded by a shot, and then another one, of eighteen year old African cum in his mouth. It was enough to put Simpson himself over the edge, and roaring, pushing up and gripping the boy's thigh with all his might, Simpson ejaculated up into the African boy, filling his rectum with thick semen even as the boy was still trembling and quivering from his own ecstasy. Finally, Motumbo came, bucking upwards and pulling Thatho down onto his pelvis as he filled the boy with spunk, bucking again and then again. At the end, the boys fell forward onto the cum-spotted chests of the two men, laying their small heaving chests against the heaving bellies and lower chests of the men, as all four fought their way back to normal breathing. Each man gently embraced and stroked the boy above him, feeling his beating heart through the thin wall of muscle.

Eventually, the two men and two boys got up and showered, squeezing as many into the shower stall as they could, the boys laughing and hooting, everyone's penises fully recovered and semi-erect as they slapped against the other slippery bodies beneath the warm falling water. But there was work to do, and they contented themselves with looking and the occasional squeeze. Drying and dressing, the four made their way to the main lodge, where the boys were introduced to Thabo and the rest of the crew that was around. Simpson explained the plan to use the boys in the Ball Room to Thabo, who also expressed concern for their youthful appearance, but when informed as to the demonstrations of their "qualifications" the day before and that morning, and when he inspected the documentation of their real ages, he shrugged and, chuckling throatily, agreed that they would add a special allure to the Ball Room. The question had to be decided soon, though, the next guest was but five days away and the boys had to be trained.

By luck, Little Mandla came into the main lodge about that time. He had been the previous choice for the Ball Room, being smallest on the staff. Simpson introduced the twin boys to him and suggested the change in plans. Little Mandla did not mind at all, as he would have plenty of opportunity for other service. Although eighteen himself, he seemed a little older. At Simpson's request, he agreed to take the twin boys to the Ball Room structure and begin training them. As they were leaving, Motumbo whispered in Simpson's ear, Simpson nodded, and made one more request. He asked the boys to stay with Little Mandla in the "Prey" lodge. Part of their training would be daily butt-fucking by Little Mandla, whose ample but not grotesquely large penis would keep the boys loosened up but not sore for the guest who would arrive a few days hence. After that, the guests would keep the boys loose and limber. Everyone agreed to the plan with glee, and off went the boys under the care of Little Mandla.

Thabo took himself off to attend to a project, leaving Simpson and Motumbo alone in the offices. The two men eyed each other quietly. They had not really talked since Motumbo's arrival yesterday about the question that had been hanging over them for weeks now, Motumbo's status at De Groot's. Simpson slipped his hand along the table at which they both sat and covered Motumbo's hand, squeezing it.

"How is your wife, Motumbo?" he asked.

The African grinned broadly. "She OK, Andrew. She say some day she want to have a baby, she tell me!"

Simpson's heart skipped a beat; he didn't know what this would mean. "Oh! Well, that's wonderful. If she gets pregnant, would it be your first child?"

Motumbo grinned again and shook his head. "Nah, Andrew, I think I got maybe two more, but them by other women. I don't see them much no more. If she get baby, our first together, though." He seemed filled with anticipation, and Simpson could well imagine that he was capable of attracting and then impregnating every young woman for miles around. But the question remained unanswered, and Simpson had to summon up his courage and pursue it.

"So, Motumbo...does that mean you will have to be with her more than at De Groot's? I...I just need to know for staffing...Oh, hell, Motumbo, I need to know for myself. I'm happy for you, it's wonderful to start a family, but..." He trailed off. Motumbo nodded, looking at him thoughtfully, then slipped his hand out from under Simpson's to lay it over the white man's hand, reversing their positions, squeezing Simpson's hand now in his turn.

"Andrew, having baby, that women's work. She maybe be a mother, she come, stay in house, there be women things all over house. Maybe better I stay here more often, not all time, but more, y'know? If you can hire me."

"Just for hire, Motumbo?"

There was a long pause. Motumbo's face turned a little serious and a little gentle at the same time. When he spoke, it was in a voice almost as soft as a whisper. "No, Andrew, not only for hire. For you and me, y'know? Not all time, I gotta go back sometimes, but, for me and you. How you say it?"

"I say it, 'I love you,'" said Simpson.

Motumbo nodded, smiling. "That!" was all he said. Dammit, thought Simpson to himself, can he not come out and say it? Was this against some African rule of macho manhood to say he loves me? Well, be content with this small step forward for yourself, he thought, and turning his hand upside down underneath Motumbo's, the two locked fingers, squeezing gently.

In the early afternoon, shortly after lunch, Simpson, Motumbo, and Thabo walked over to the Ball Room to inspect the facility and to see how the training of the boys was going. Simpson mentally patted himself on the back as they approached the Ball Room: it was an inspiration, if he did say so himself. The building was a single, large room, about the size of any of the lodges' great rooms. The main entrance (other than a couple of fire escapes) was from a porch and door built halfway up the side of the structure. The three men walked up the stairs to the porch, and there they found Little Mandla with an actual bucket of lubricant, greasing both naked boys who stood giggling, penises half-erect, as they turned, bent over, lifted arms, and generally helped in making themselves slick from head to toe. Little Mandla seemed to be enjoying the process as well; the front of his trousers was tenting out in his excitement. In a moment the boys were thoroughly greased. Little Mandla opened the door to the Ball Room and ushered them in.

The Ball Room was a single huge box filled with perfectly transparent, extremely lightweight plastic balls, each about the size of a basketball, each rigid but full of holes and hollow. The interior walls contained lights at intervals, and a strong air conditioning system pulled comfortable air through the structure. The idea was that a person could wriggle into the mass of balls and be suspended in space, completely surrounded by balls. Because they were so lightweight, and because of the combination of lighting and air flow, one would never feel claustrophobic or suffocated even though you were always completely surrounded by the balls. The visual effect was arresting, also. The balls acted as hundreds of prisms defracting the soft light. If someone else were in the Ball Room with you, it was possible to see them as a distorted, indistinct mass, and the farther away they were from you the more indistinct they became although one could always make out something even at opposite corners inside the structure.

Little Mandla, clothed, and the boys entered a tiny space just inside the outer door to the Ball Room. The outer door was secured, then an inner door opened, which filled that entry space immediately with the balls. They were now inside the playing field. The men still outside on the porch could look through a series of glass observation ports and see what was going on inside. Little Mandla repeated instructions to the teen boys again. They had been told in principle what would happen, but in practice they were hesitant to push into the room. Still, with encouragement from Little Mandla, first Thatho and then Mthobisi pushed, swam, or flew off into the mass of balls. Thoroughly greased, they soon discovered how easy it was to move through the mass of lightweight balls, how much like having wings, how much like being a fish in the sea. Before long the sound of whoops, laughter, and shouts could be heard as the boys went diving, climbing, slithering all around the mass of spheres. Their dark brown shapes could be made out, but indistinctly, as they moved now here and now there. Little Mandla called out encouragement and advice to them. In this and later training sessions, the boys would become accustomed to easy movement in the space. And when a guest arrived...ah! that was the fun part. A guest would be allowed to enter the Ball Room a minute after the boys were released, thoroughly lubricated and naked himself, and would swim or fly after them in pursuit. Catching a boy meant you could enjoy him then and there, buoyed weightlessly in the atmosphere of balls. It was an attraction that was drawing lots of registrations already online.

The next few days were, Simpson realized, the only calm period that De Groot's would see for weeks if not months. Online marketing had done its magic, and multiple parties were making reservations for the different attractions offered by the resort. A full calendar loomed, promising hard work but also riches and fun for all concerned. The staff was hard at work finishing construction and training for the array of entertainment that was offered.

And each night, Simpson and Motumbo returned alone to their lodge. Simpson used all his arts and cunning to woo the big African further: candlelit dinners, soft music, the best South African wines and brandies, and of course sex that was as full of torrid passion as it was of love and tenderness. Every morning they awoke in each other's arms, beginning the day with a slow, loving waltz of love.

The evening came when Thabo drove up into the compound with the first of a long line of guests, Felipe Almodovar, a Spaniard. About thirty, of olive complexion, loose black curls of hair and blue eyes, Simpson could see that he likely charmed everyone he met instantly. Simpson came out to greet the guest, returning his firm handshake and frank smile, then introduced him to Motumbo and other members of the staff who had come out to see the newcomer. Felipe had a good command of English, although it was moderately accented. Thabo escorted him to his own lodge where he would unpack and be tested for STD's, as standard procedure. A couple of hours later, Almodovar, Simpson, Thabo, and Motumbo sat around a festive dinner table in the main lodge, the guest getting to know them and they their guest. The games would start the next day.

It was at a reasonable hour of the morning that Simpson went to fetch Almodovar from his lodge, where he had enjoyed a good breakfast. The two walked up the path to the Ball Room and climbed the stairs to the entryway porch, where Thatho and Mthobisi were already waiting with Little Mandla. The boys were introduced to Almodovar and they shook hands with him as if at the start of a business negotiation, politely formal with one who was about to do his best to catch and fuck them. Simpson could tell by the sparkle in Felipe's eyes that the boys had been the right choice for him. Simpson asked the boys to strip, and then made the same request of Felipe. The Spaniard could not take his eyes off the slim, brown bodies of the boys that emerged from their clothing, nor could they conceal their curiosity when Felipe's muscular, olive-toned body stood naked before them.

The boys' two nearly man-sized penises were already bobbing, semi-erect, as Little Mandla helped them to slather lubricant all over themselves. Felipe gazed at them like a wolf, never taking his eyes off of their slim, muscular, brown teen bodies. Little Mandla opened the entry door, ushered them inside, pulled the lever that opened the interior to them, then pulled another lever that cleared out the entry space for Felipe. Then Little Mandla turned to Felipe and began lathering him with lubricant, a process both he and Felipe enjoyed if their erections were any indication, a wet spot showing on Little Mandla's trousers. He opened the outer door, explaining the rules once again to Felipe. Before he closed the door, he bent down and strapped a tube of lubricant to the Spaniard's ankle. Then, daring to slap Felipe's butt lightly, Little Mandla closed the outer door, opened the inner door, and then went to an observation port to watch the fun with Simpson.

Felipe's eyes adjusted quickly to the soft lighting as the inner door opened and he entered the space full of balls. In the middle distance, some thirty feet away and fifteen feet apart, could be seen two twisting, wallowing brown shapes as the boys, giggling and whispering to each other, made their way into the ocean of balls. Felipe pushed into the mass. It took him a moment to become accustomed to how it felt, to develop a technique for movement, but before long he was swimming or flying in pursuit of his quarry. He decided to pursue one brown shape, not knowing which one it was, but not really caring. The boy could see him coming as well, and dodged here and there, once just barely escaping Felipe's grasp. His brother taunted the Spaniard, once sneaking up behind him and pulling on his foot, but Felipe knew he would deal with that one in good time. Closer and closer he came, edging his target boy into a corner, until with one final lunge he grasped an ankle with one hand, the calf with another, and hauled the giggling boy in.

It was Mthobisi. Caught, he gave up willingly, joining Felipe in laughing at the fun. Floating weightlessly in the sea of balls, Felipe pulled the boy to him, kissing his full, bee-stung lips, tasting the rounded soft flesh of each lip, sucking the boy's tongue and pushing his own tongue into the willing mouth. Felipe pulled the boy to him tightly, his hands running over the firm, brown flesh of the eighteen year old, cupping his buttocks, enjoying the crisp texture of his hair, even as the boy reveled in exploring the loose black curls of the man, in feeling the hardness of his man muscles. Felipe's brown dick was fully engorged now, and rubbing against the iron hard midnight black rod of the eighteen year old. Sliding down the boy's frame, kissing, tonguing, nibbling nipples, licking the abdomen, sucking on the navel, Felipe finally nuzzled the boy's small pubic patch and then engulfed the hard dick in his mouth, sucking hard, bobbing his head up and down while Mthobisi writhed in ecstasy, his fingers embedded in the Spaniard's black curls. The eighteen year old had no control and very quickly yelped, tensing, pushing his rod deep into Felipe's throat while he shot ropes of cum, quivering and gasping.

No sooner had Felipe drained the eighteen year old black dick dry than he turned the boy's body in their weightless space and, reaching down to the tube of lubricant, came up with a dollop of goo to oil up the maroon brown anus and his own rampant lighter brown penis. Felipe inserted one, then two fingers into the rectum, and found that the boy relaxed immediately, having been well fucked and well trained by Little Mandla over the last few days. Sliding upward now, Felipe pressed his cockhead to the anus and pushed. It went in easily, and the two were locked together, Mthobisi crying out in passing pain and enduring pleasure. Felipe immediately began a frantic rhythm of fucking the boy, in and out, as he wrapped his arms around the boy's thin chest, sliding his palms over the slick, thin chest and up and down the curved belly. The two slowly rolled in space as Felipe's hips pistoned in and out, in and out of the boy like a locomotive, and then with a roar he, too, came, pushing his penis hard against the boy's rounded bottom, filling the young African with his spunk.

Felipe held the boy to him tightly for a few minutes as he recovered his breath. Then in a flash he pushed the boy away, pivoted to his right, and lunged upward. Thatho had snuck in to watch the proceedings, hoping to remain unobserved while the Spaniard fucked his brother. He was mistaken. In but a moment, Felipe was upon him as the boy giggled and squealed and Mthobisi taunted his brother in derision, shouting at him to "warn" him in between laughs. Thatho gave up the fight quickly and willingly, and was soon being fondled, kissed and sucked just as his brother was a few moments before.

This time, though, Felipe applied the dollop of lubricant to his own anus, and then another to Thatho's straining eighteen year old purple black erection. The boy's eyes grew wide as he understood that he was about to fuck his first white man. Turning in the buoyant space, Felipe pulled the boy up over his own belly, wrapping his legs around the thin brown back, and guided the rigid, slick, midnight velvet shaft toward his waiting anus. Thatho connected and, with the enthusiasm of youth, pushed with all his might, breaking past the anal sphincter and landing himself all the way inside the Spaniard's bottom. Felipe groaned with the momentary pain, and caught the boy's writhing body in a vise made of his legs, keeping him still until the pain passed. Then, as the two floated in space, Felipe cocked his pelvis to push up and down on the boy's dick, and Thatho picked up the rhythm immediately. Clasping himself tightly to the Spaniard's muscled chest, Thatho began pumping in and out as fast as he could. Felipe slipped his hand in between their bellies and grasped his own cock which had now returned to rock hardness, the prostate stimulated by the steady rhythm of the boy's slamming penis. In and out, in and out the African boy went as he clutched the Spaniard tighter, and the man's hand slid on the coating of lubricant, precum, and sweat between their bodies while he pumped his own penis. Thatho had little more control than his brother, and soon he also cried out, his body clenching and twisting as he shot his teen cum into the Spaniard's gut, pumping and shooting, pumping and shooting until he slumped exhausted. A minute later, Felipe came a second time, filling the tight space between his and the African boy's body with his white spunk, then enclosed the thin brown body with both his legs and both his arms, running his cum-slick hand over the boy's back. In a moment he felt Mthobisi slide up alongside him and wrap himself and Thatho in an embrace. The three floated like that in lazy ease, held up in a pool of soft lighting and gentle, cool air, laughing and caressing one another, gathering their strength for the adventures that would follow that afternoon and the next day.

Outside, Little Mandla and Simpson turned, laughing, toward each other and exchanged high fives. From their distance, they could not make out the events inside distinctly, but it was clear enough from the movements of the dark brown and olive colored shapes that the Ball Room was a success.

- CHAPTER 9 -

"Huh?!" muttered Motumbo, startling awake in the early dawn. He pushed himself up on one elbow, which turned Andrew Simpson over. The white man had been sleeping with his head on the African's muscular chest, but was now himself awakened. Motumbo looked around in confusion. Then they heard it again, louder: a knock on their door.

"I'll get it," said Simpson as he staggered out of bed to walk across the floor of the lodge, naked. He didn't know who was at the door at this hour, but if they didn't want to see a naked white man, then they shouldn't be knocking. His morning half-erection bobbed as he walked. Simpson opened the door a crack, then wider, upon finding Big Mandla at the door.

The huge African's eyes widened a bit and he looked the naked white man up and down. It was not the first time he had seen Simpson naked, by any means. Both men had seen all there was to see of the other, and in frantic sexual action as well, when Big Mandla and Strello had shared their conquest of the two blonde Brit twins with the rest of the camp. Still, Big Mandla's eyes lingered for half a second on the white man's incipient erection before he remembered his errand.

"Oh! Boss Andrew, Thabo, he want to know where key to second car. We go get next two sets men in hour from Jo'burg," said the big man.

"Come in, come in," muttered Simpson, stepping back from the door to let the large, muscular black man enter. "Just a second," said Simpson, and darted into the rest room, not bothering to close the door, where he stood at the toilet and relieved himself, a strong steady stream splashing in the bowl. He finished and flushed and re-entered the great room, nodding again at Big Mandla, and nearly colliding with Motumbo who had risen and was hurrying from the bedroom. Motumbo's morning erection was fully realized, his heavy shaft sticking out at nearly a ninety degree angle, seemingly impossible for such a big tube of meat. "Piss," whispered Motumbo urgently to Simpson. The white man headed for the bedroom to search for keys while Motumbo rushed to the bathroom. All the while, Big Mandla looked at the spectacle with a grin on his face.

Simpson poked through trouser pockets and opened drawers to find the keys to his vehicle, which Big Mandla would drive following Thabo to pick up two parties that were arriving that day. He could hear the initial start and stop of Motumbo's piss in the bathroom next door as his large African lover pushed the yellow fluid past his erection, then the strong flow as the stream came on full force. Simpson found the keys in a moment and went back into the great room to hand them to Big Mandla.

There he found Mandla standing just inside the bathroom doorway, watching the last of Motumbo's urination. The two exchanged soft comments in their native tongue and then Big Mandla chuckled and, reaching out his hand, softly slapped Motumbo's naked bottom......and lingered there a moment. Simpson stood in the doorway and watched, in amusement rather than with jealousy. The floor creaked under him and Big Mandla turned with a start, pulling his hand off of Mandla's rounded butt and holding it behind him, his dark skin darkening even more with a blush. Motumbo himself, slowly shaking the piss from the end of his penis, looked at his white lover, then at Big Mandla, then raised his eyebrows and smiled at both.

"Here is the key," Simpson said, handing it to Big Mandla, who murmured a thanks and dropped them into his pocket. "And here is Motumbo's butt again," he said, stepping forward to grasp Big Mandla's arm by the wrist and placing his tan palm against the hard, rounded buttock of Motumbo, who chuckled. Big Mandla's mouth flew open wordlessly.

"It's alright," said Simpson. "You like?" Big Mandla continued to stare open-mouthed, but did not remove his hand from Motumbo's butt. "Motumbo, OK with you?" In answer Motumbo nodded, grinned, and pushed his bottom back into the cupped hand that Big Mandla held against him. Big Mandla grunted and, shifting position, grasped both of Motumbo's buttocks with his big hands, kneading them deeply while Motumbo braced himself against the wall behind the toilet and pushed back. For a moment Big Mandla stepped back to shed his clothes in a flash, then returned to fondling the strong, bubble bottom of the other African. The penises of all three men were now becoming fully erect, one tan and pink, and two deep midnight purple black shafts.

Motumbo pushed off from the wall and spun around, enfolding Big Mandla in an embrace, while their two huge organs slapped and batted each other, two bushes of crinkly pubic hair mashed together. Their strong brown arms now entwined each other, pulling shoulders and buttocks in towards their own bodies as they ground their torsos together, their breath coming more heavily now. Then their lips found each other, two sets of full, moist maroon brown lips locked together as tongues explored tongues and slid along teeth.

Simpson, his own breath coming heavily now, reached out to tug on two elbows. "Come," he said, urging them in the direction of the bedroom. They quickly complied, heading for the bed with huge, engorged poles swaying, strings of precum already flying from the lighter pink-brown tips that were now fully exposed. Motumbo and Big Mandla flung themselves onto the bed, while Simpson stood at its edge, slowly pumping his own organ while he watched the spectacle. The two black men mated like Cape buffalo, like two oak trees coming together. Powerful, meaty chests rubbed against each other as first one and then the other rolled on top, each in a competition of lust to dominate the other. Their heavy penises now lay pointing straight up between their bellies, their dark skins shining with sweat and a sheet of precum as they slid and squirmed on each other.

Big Mandla managed to turn Motumbo onto his belly...perhaps not without some help...and reached quickly for the tube of lubricant on the bedside table. Resigned to the situation, Motumbo cocked his pelvis up and back, waiting to be impaled. Big Mandla's engorged dick, now slick with the lubricant and precum, was positioned at Motumbo's asshole, the head placed up against the wrinkled anus. Squatting on his haunches, Big Mandla pushed. As big a man as Motumbo was, he was unused to being fucked by so large an organ as that on Big Mandla. Motumbo gasped and cried out, but kept his bottom turned up, offering a large, rounded, bubbled bottom to the huge African behind him. Big Mandla pushed again, then in a long, slow slide landed himself entirely within Motumbo. The big black man on the bottom cried out again, closing his eyes in pain, but maintained his position.

Big Mandla now held himself up off of Motumbo's back, his palms flat on the bed on either side of Motumbo, and began swinging his pelvis back and forth, back and forth. Slowly, then in a definite rhythm, the massive Mandla fucked Motumbo, fucked him as Motumbo had never been fucked before, allowed him to learn what it felt like to be fucked by a huge African dick. Moaning and gasping, Motumbo took his punishment willingly, continuing to push back and up into Big Mandla, matching his rhythm with his own cocking of his pelvis. Then faster and faster Big Mandla went, pushing his huge penis all the way into the open hole between Motumbo's rounded buttocks, until Big Mandla roared and pushed forward. He shivered, then pumped back and forth quickly, pushed and cried out again and held that position, gasping and trembling. Then Big Mandla slumped forward on top of Motumbo's back, heaving, fighting for breath.

He did not stay there long. Simpson had not been idle. He had slicked up his own rampant purple pole with lubricant and precum, and now moved quickly onto the bed. He rolled Big Mandla off of Motumbo, the long, still-rigid penis sliding out with a slurp and a pop, the big man lying on his back right next to Motumbo. Simpson quickly positioned himself on his knees between Big Mandla's thighs and lifted both legs up and back. Motumbo raised himself onto his elbows to watch the fun. Simpson placed the pink, swollen head of his rigid cock against Big Mandla's brown anus and pushed hard. Big Mandla cried out, but Simpson landed himself entirely in one push. His penis, of adequate size for a white man, was not as large as what Big Mandla was used to being fucked with, so the African soon smiled and nodded at Simpson. The white man stretched out over the African, holding himself up off the man with his palms on the bed, looking deeply into the dark eyes of the black man beneath him, and began fucking him with long, powerful strokes.

Both men were breathing heavily, into the rhythm of the fucking, Big Mandla's legs pushed back by Simpson's arms. Big Mandla reached up and locked the brown fingers of his hands behind the white man's neck, entwined in his cornsilk hair, while Simpson's purple cock plunged in and out of his butt. Simpson broke his gaze and turned quickly to Motumbo, who had been enjoying the spectacle. "Fuck me," he said simply, then went back to an intense absorption with Big Mandla.

Needing no further encouragement, Motumbo got into position behind Simpson, lubricating his massive pole, while Big Mandla's semen dribbled out of his own asshole and down his inner thighs. The white man's bottom had been stretched in the night by their usual lovemaking, but nevertheless it was still all Simpson could do to take Motumbo's massive pole which he slid bit by bit into Simpson's ass. The white man helped to impale himself as his rocking motion in and out of Big Mandla pushed his own butt farther and farther onto Motumbo's rigid cock. As soon as Motumbo was fully in he pushed forward with all his might. Simpson landed flat on Big Mandla's chest and belly while Motumbo stretched out flat on Simpson's pink and tan back.

Simpson set the pace, a white man sandwich in between two powerfully muscled African men. In and out of Big Mandla he swung, while Motumbo matched his rhythm from behind. Simpson's pale pink lips found Big Mandla's luscious, full maroon brown lips and they kissed deeply and passionately, sharing breath as they moved toward climax. Big Mandla's cock remained rigid between his and Simpson's body. Motumbo's hands grasped first the white man and then Big Mandla, he nuzzled Simpson's neck and chewed on his cornsilk hair as his own strokes became stronger and stronger.

Oddly enough, Big Mandla was the first to come, again. Crying out, arching and twisting his body as much as he could while supporting the weight of two men, his prostate stimulated beyond endurance by the white man's fucking, his dick unloaded a pool of cum that slicked up his dark and Simpson's light chest and belly skins. Then Motumbo came, groaning and swearing under his breath as he pushed forward, crushing both white and black men beneath him as he poured his semen into the white man's rectum. Before he was done, Simpson came, his body straining to buck and push but with no room to do so as electric waves of ecstasy washed over him. All three men gasped and heaved, clutched and groaned, and then one by one they subsided. A moment of quiet descended. Sweat and semen leaked from Motumbo, down Simpson's sides, neck, and bottom, to join with Simpson's own sweat and cum that was leaking down onto Big Mandla. White and black joined into one for a few moments of bliss.

Big Mandla came to his senses first, chuckling and pushing both men off of his powerful body. "Got to drive, Boss!" he said with a grin. Slapping first a white butt and then a black one, Big Mandla rose and went quickly into the shower. Motumbo and Simpson lay in bed a moment longer, smiling and looking into each other's eyes, stroking each other's faces, and then went to join Big Mandla in the shower, the three men steaming up the small room as they cleaned themselves and each other. Then Big Mandla was off on his errand while the other two got dressed.

Simpson and Motumbo led the staff through procedures for the event that would occur the next day. There was to be a paintball hunt, much like the one that first introduced Simpson to Motumbo, but with this new twist: it was to be a battle, a contest between the two visiting parties. Three white men from the States were to compete with three Japanese men, the winner to "own" the other party for the next forty-eight hours. The Africans on the staff, previously used to serving as prey, were now serving as referees and marshalls for the conflict. Grins of excitement were on every dark face as they looked forward to the coming battle, and to its outcome. These preparations, and making sure two lodges were in good order, took up most of the morning.

It was shortly before lunch that Simpson heard the sound of the gate to the enclosure opening in the distance, and the oncoming noise of a vehicle engine. As it got closer it seemed to him only a single vehicle, not the two that had set out for the paying guests. Looking at his watch, Simpson realized it was a little early for Thabo and Big Mandla to return anyway. There was the sound of a truck braking outside. He rose to see what the matter was.

There was an old pickup truck parked in the open area in front of the main lodge. Motumbo was standing by the driver's side door, speaking to someone in the truck. Then the big African turned and saw Simpson, half turned back to the truck, spoke something in a low voice, then turned again and began walking slowly toward Simpson, his face alternating smiles and worried, backward glances. He stepped up to Simpson, who was trying to read his lover's face.

"Chele," said Motumbo.

"Pardon me?"

"Chele," the African repeated, then stepped to the side, his head down, gesturing back at the truck. Looking over Motumbo's shoulder, Simpson caught his breath. It was Motumbo's woman sitting in the driver's seat, a big smile splitting her beautiful face. "Chele," Motumbo said again, "She come for visit. She come to see. She…Boss, she say she stay here this night." Motumbo was looking anywhere but at Simpson.

Simpson tottered for a moment, balanced among several dangerous emotions, looking back and forth between the man and the woman. Yearning, fear, calculation, strategy, despair…and then he spoke.

"Of course, Motumbo," he said softly. "And you must stay with her. Take… " he looked around, "take that lodge over there, it won't be used tonight," he said.

Motumbo's head jerked up, his face a mask of relief but also washed with worry and indecision. "Boss… Andrew… This OK? Really? It just tonight… maybe," he said. Simpson could not speak now, afraid of what he would say, but he nodded and thumped Motumbo on the shoulder. Summoning up courage and speech, Simpson walked over to the truck and extended his hand to the woman.

"My name is Andrew Simpson," he said, "Welcome." The woman smiled broadly, perhaps not understanding a word, and whispered something in another language. Simpson nodded, turned, and walked back to the main lodge, passing Motumbo on the way, winking at him and flashing a forced grin…then continued winking to clear his eyes of the unwanted tear or two that snuck out, unbidden, as he walked into the lodge.

Simpson just picked at his lunch, and could only seem to shuffle papers around for the next hour. Every now and then he would walk to the window; the lodge that Motumbo and Chele would take for the night was just barely in view. Simpson could see little, but imagined much.

In mid-afternoon the gate to the compound opened again and in drove the two vehicles with the new guests. Simpson stepped out to meet them. Thabo drove three Japanese men in his vehicle, all in their twenties or early thirties, slim and handsome with shocks of thick, glossy black hair, all speaking passable English. Big Mandla drove the three Americans, of about the same age, two brown haired and slim, and one blonde, the blonde large and strapping, with beachboy hair. The groups had evidently met at the airport, and as they milled around collecting luggage they covertly eyed each other, sizing up their chances in tomorrow's contest. Simpson introduced them all, greeting them cordially, but his mind was in a fog, and he had to admit as the men were escorted off to their respective lodges that he could hardly remember a name among them.

Simpson caught sight of Motumbo and Chele strolling around the grounds a couple of times that afternoon. Motumbo was gesturing, a proud look on his face, no doubt explaining his role in the renovations and new constructions. A shy smile played on Chele's face as she admired both the facilities and her man, looking up at him proudly from time to time as they walked along. Simpson shook his head as if to clear out cobwebs. He knew she was a presence in his life, he reminded himself...he knew they were not going to be apart permanently...he knew he'd have to share Motumbo...he knew, he knew, he knew...but that didn't make this any better.

Dinner that night was a rollicking affair. Both the Americans and the Japanese flirted shamelessly across the table, inhibitions loosed by the cocktails and wine, by the tasty game dinner, as boasts and frank calculations of each other's sexual prowess were hurled from one side to the other. Simpson sat at the head of the table with a fixed smile, Thabo at the other end. Thabo eye his boss covertly throughout the meal, knowing of the anguish that Simpson was feeling. Simpson rose at the end of the party and bade his guests goodnight, then watched as each party strolled down the path to their respective lodges, still offering humorous challenges to each other as they went. Standing in the quiet moonlight for some time, Simpson thought he heard sounds from Motumbo's lodge. Try as he might he could not tune theme out. Sighing, he turned and headed down the path to his own lodge.

Simpson's head was cast down as he entered, so he heard before he saw: "Hey, Boss Andrew!" It was a low, soft, sexy growl. Startled, Simpson looked up to find Strello stretched out on the couch, smiling, dressed only in shorts. The light from the oil lamp on the table flickered and danced on his shiny, deep chocolate skin. "Boss, you want company? Motumbo, you know, he come back to you Boss, you no worry 'bout that. But tonight, you want company?"

Simpson stared at Strello for a moment, open-mouthed. Then a slow burn and a jerk in his loins answered for him. He chuckled. "Yes, Strello, I would. It's very kind of you to think of me."

"I not kind, Boss, good for me, y'know?" said Strello, bounding up off the sofa, vitality coursing through his short but strong, stocky body. "C'mon, we play like we customer," he said, grabbing Simpson's hand and tugging him toward the door. Now laughing in spite of himself, Simpson followed out into the night and up the path. In a moment it was clear where Strello, still holding his hand, was leading him.

By the foot of the stairs to the high entrance of the Ball Room, Strello flicked on the electricity. Lights shone through the windows one floor up, and a hum indicated that the air system was working at full blast. Strello tugged Simpson up the stairs. On the landing by the entrance, Strello shed his shorts and shoes, his semi-turgid penis flopping against his thigh. Simpson followed suit, soon standing naked in the evening breeze. Strello opened the door to the building.

"You go, Boss," he said. Simpson nodded and ducked inside the air lock. The door behind him closed, he opened the door in front of him, and pushed off into the dimly lit sea of lightweight plastic balls. A few strokes and he was away from the door. Hearing a noise, he looked behind him and could just vaguely make out a dark shape where he had been a moment before. Strello had entered and was pursuing him.

For perhaps fifteen minutes the two men floated, swam, and soared through the balls, enjoying the illusion of weightlessness, enjoying the sexually charged thrill of the chase. A couple of times Strello nearly had Simpson, grazing his ankle with his fingers once, but Simpson lurched, rolled, and escaped. Strello was relentless, however, and eventually cornered Simpson in a top corner of the room. Closer and closer he came, and then Simpson turned the wrong way, making the wrong guess, and Strello was upon him. Simpson did not struggle much. Rolling together, laughing, first one on top and then the other, the two frolicked like naked otters in water. And then Strello got Simpson around the waist, holding on firmly with his arms, his head by the white man's fully erect, pink and purple rod. Twisting, Simpson caught Strello by the hip and pulled, bringing their bodies together.

Slowly turning in the sea of balls, the two sought each other's bodies with their mouths. Simpson swallowed Strello's large nutsack in his mouth, gently sucking, his tongue feeling the gentle scratch of the kinky hairs on the wrinkled skin, while one hand slowly pumped Strello's iron hard purple black cock and the other hand anchored itself on a rounded deep chocolate buttock. Strello grasped Simpson's pink and tan bottom with both his hands, his strong brown fingers kneading the flesh deeply, and took aim for the white man's rigid shaft. Strello enclosed just the pink head of the white man's shaft in his full lips, massaging the knob with his lips and slipping his tongue over and under it. Simpson quivered and pushed involuntarily, sliding his shaft further into Strello's mouth. The black man's broad nose was soon mashed against the white man's heavy ballsack as his mouth sucked the swollen rod. His massaging fingers now probed Simpson's anus as well.

Simpson gently spat out Strello's ballsack and moved his mouth around to the African's brown and purple wrinkled asshole. He tongued it, causing the black man to twist with pleasure. Then he moved his mouth back down, and took the iron hard black cock in his mouth, spewing precum across his chin and chest. Strello began pumping, bucking his hips back and forth as he fucked the white man's mouth, while for his own part he sucked greedily on Simpson's pink and purple dick, sliding his tongue up and down the shaft as he took the penis in as far as he could. Locked together, both of their hips now pumping back and forth, both men loved each other's penises with their mouths, balanced between the pleasure of sucking and of being sucked, until Simpson groaned, arched his back, his thighs quivering, his whole body tense, and shot a load of semen down Strello's throat. Strello pulled back some, grasped the shaft with his fist, and slowly pumped as his full, moist lips enclosed the dickhead and milked it of every drop.

Simpson was still shivering when Strello belt the tingling start in his knees and thighs, felt the movement and shift within his own loins, and with a roar muffled by holding the white man's dick in his mouth, pushed his pelvis forward, filling the white man's mouth with his own spunk. Simpson held on tight and began swallowing greedily, milking the black man's huge, pumping dick as floods of white spunk ran out of it. Both men's chests were heaving, their breath ragged, as each finally let the other's drained dick slide from his mouth. In a moment, Simpson twisted and repositioned himself, turning around so as to lie head to head with Strello. In the soft twilight of the world of balls, Simpson held the African's head, caressing his crispy hair, exchanging kisses. The two came closer, wrapping arms around each other, and held tight as their breathing continued returning to normal.

"Motumbo, he come back, you see tomorrow, Boss," whispered Strello. Simpson chuckled, nuzzled the African's soft broad nose and lips with his own mouth, and looked deep into Strello's dark eyes.

"Thank you, Strello. Perhaps you are right. But for tonight...for tonight it's just us, OK?"

"OK, Boss." and the two remained there until the early morning hours, floating in the sea of balls, awaking, loving, and returning to sleep again and again throughout the night.

A Boner Book

- CHAPTER 10 -

Strello awoke with a start. Always one to be aware of time, and the turning of the earth under the sun, he was suddenly aware of the morning's impending duties. In the dim light of the Ball Room, Andrew Simpson had rolled a foot or two away and was still sound asleep, suspended in the sea of lightweight globes. Strello rolled toward him and put his strong brown arms around him.

"Boss! Andrew! Wake up, we gotta start the games! Boss!" His own morning erection batted against the white man's thigh, and he couldn't resist...his hand slid down to investigate and found Simpson's pole was rigid as well. Strello gave a gentle pump or two up and down and Simpson awoke with a smile, rolling toward the African, pulling him close in to himself. Wordlessly he looked deep intro Strello's dark eyes and smiled, kissing him. "Boss! We gotta go!" repeated Strello, but now giggling as his increasingly rigid midnight black cock slid against Simpson's pink and purple rod. Strello put one and then two fists around both organs, holding the black and white penises together, and began pumping in earnest. Both men began pushing against each other, kissing, sharing breath. They knew they would soon have to be at work, and so relieving the sexual tension of the moment would take focused attention.

Each man pushed and squirmed against the other, Simpson sliding his hands around Strello's strong, dark brown shoulders, Strello pumping both stiff cocks together. Precum began lubricating both dicks, and a quick slurping sound covered the low hum of the air system. Faster and faster Strello pumped, harder and harder each man breathed. And then Simpson bucked and shuddered, pulling Strello into him tightly with his hands while Strello continued pumping for a moment, and then the African came as well, both men shooting ropes of semen that mixed in the space between them, slicking up their bellies and chests. Strello's fists slowed as each penis was milked for all its spunk, and then he also put his hands, slippery with semen, around Simpson and the two snuggled, rolling slowly in the balls for a moment.

Simpson broke away. "Yes, we must go!" he whispered, kissing Strello. For that night and in that place, he forgot Motumbo, who was sleeping with his woman not far away in another lodge. But memory came flooding back as the two men grabbed their clothing, damp with dew, left on the platform outside the door to the Ball Room. Pausing at the bottom of the steps to switch off the controls to the room, they each ran naked down the path to Simpson's lodge. If anyone saw them they were unaware of it, but they heard the unmistakable sounds of stirring from the cabins of the Japanese and of the white Americans who would hunt each other that day.

Simpson and Strello showered together in the lodge, their penises rising again from the soap, the warm water, and the gentle ministrations of the other, but duty called. Half erect, laughing, they bounded from the shower and dressed quickly, Strello borrowing some fresh clothes for the day from Simpson. By the time they emerged, Thabo had the two parties fairly well organized. The judges for the combat would be Big and Little Mandla and Strello. Thabo and Motumbo would wait with vehicles to go out and collect both the victors and their...spoils. Motumbo was still nowhere to be seen, still in the arms of his woman.

The Japanese and Americans were fully clothed for the adventure, protecting their skins against the sun and harsh terrain of southern Africa. Each team of three was armed with the usual paintball guns. By the toss of a coin, the Japanese were designated to leave first. Thabo opened a gate and out they ran into the early dawn dim light. The Americans waited, tense, shuffling their feet and checking their gear, for half an hour. Then they, too, were released and stalked warily out into the growing light. They did not know whether they were walking into a quick ambush or toward a strategic, and sexual, conquest. Close on their heels were both the Mandlas and Strello, armed with radios and, in the case of four legged predators, rifles. They would monitor the contest and call for vehicles when necessary.

Talking softly, Simpson and Thabo walked back up to the main lodge. The unexpected sounds of people stirring, and the smell of cooking, greeted them as they neared the front door. Going in, they found Motumbo sitting at the table.

"Andrew!" he said, smiling shyly, and half rose. He glanced swiftly toward the kitchen, back again at Andrew, stepped quickly to the white man and hugged him. Glancing at the kitchen again, Motumbo slipped back down into his seat. Thabo and Simpson approached the table, puzzled, and were just seating themselves when Chele came bustling out of the kitchen, a large serving dish in hand.

She smiled a broad smile at the men and put the dishes on the table. Then she deliberately came around to where Simpson was sitting and, nodding to him, spoke a few soft words in her language, smiling broadly. She put a soft hand on his shoulder, nodded again, then returned to the kitchen. Motumbo's eyes watched her go but his head was slightly lowered, and a smile played about his lips.

"Motumbo...what did she say?" asked Simpson.

"Uh...she say she give us breakfast, Andrew," said Motumbo, his head still lowered, looking steadily at the table. A puzzled look came into Thabo's eyes but he said nothing. Simpson thought for a moment. He didn't believe a word of it.

"Motumbo," said Simpson, "does Chele know what kind of place this is...what kind of business we do here?"

Motumbo perked up. "Yah, sure Boss, she know. It OK, Andrew, she not mind, she know we OK 'bout health...she OK, true." Simpson nodded and thought for a moment. Chele came back out and put two more dishes on the table, then bade the men eat with waves of her hands. The men tucked into the food in silence. After some steady munching, Simpson spoke again.

"Motumbo...does Chele know about us? You and me?"

There was a moment of silence. "Yes, Andrew, she know."

"And...is she OK with that?"

"Yes, Andrew, she OK." Motumbo looked up shyly at Simpson. "Before, Boss... she not say about breakfast. Chele say...she say thank you, to you. For me... for being good to me..." Motumbo broke off in confusion and concentrated on his breakfast. Simpson stared at him, then in the direction of the kitchen. He rose, and Thabo and Motumbo both stopped eating and watched him walk into the kitchen.

There Andrew found Chele preparing one more dish. She stopped in surprise. Simpson walked up to her and took her hands in his. "Thank you, Chele, for being good to Motumbo," he said. They looked deeply into each other's eyes, and for a miracle, Simpson was sure that Chele, who spoke not a word of English, understood. She nodded gravely, then smiled brilliantly again and withdrew her hands to shoo Simpson before her back to the dining room, where she carried the last dish. Sitting at the table with the men, she smiled all around, and the men, boyish in their unaccustomed shyness, looked to the left and right and to the far wall, and then smiled as well.

Small talk occupied the rest of the meal, with Motumbo or Thabo translating back and forth for the benefit of Chele and Simpson. When they finished, Simpson went into the office to work while Thabo and Motumbo went to prepare the vehicles for picking up the guests. Chele cleaned up the breakfast things and then slipped out to return to the lodge she was sharing with Motumbo.

Stopping by the main lodge later in the morning, Thabo found Simpson frowning, holding a hard copy of an email that he had printed. Simpson looked up and wordlessly handed the paper to Thabo. The African man read it, his eyebrows rising as he went along. Finished, he looked into the middle distance, then again at the paper, and handed it back to Simpson.

"I can't do it, Thabo," said Simpson, "I draw the line." Thabo shrugged.

"Boss Andrew, see what they offer to pay," he said, pointing at a figure near the bottom of the page. "That good money."

"Oh I know, but really Thabo, I can't do this!"

Thabo shrugged again. "It what they want, Boss, nothing real. Nobody think it real. Who knows why people want what they do, but it just play, like.

112

Good money, Boss, nobody hurt" he concluded, returning to the main point. Simpson shook his head again and muttered something about thinking it over. At that point, Thabo's radio crackled. The contest was over, it was time for him and Motumbo to drive out and bring in the two teams.

Thabo drove back with the American team, whooping and shouting. One of their number had a paintball splat on his chest. Motumbo drove the Japanese team back, the black haired men grinning broadly but not as boisterously. All three had paintball marks on them. It was clear who had won. The Japanese men would be "owned" for the next two nights by the victorious Americans. Simpson congratulated the winners and joked with the losers, who seemed happily resigned to their fates. Both teams went off to their respective lodges to rest. The evening's activities would begin later on.

Lunch was a repeat of breakfast, with Chele cooking and serving, her skills in the kitchen being evident and appreciated by the men. As they finished, Simpson asked Motumbo to walk into the office with him. Chele cleaned up again, and Thabo went to make sure preparations were complete for the evening's activities.

In the office, Simpson handed the email hard copy to Motumbo, who labored for a minute over the printed English. At the end his handsome dark face split into a brilliant smile. "Boss, we be rich, look what they pay!"

Simpson groaned. "Look what they want to DO, Motumbo," he said. "I can't."

Motumbo shrugged. "Andrew, it not about you or me, they want it, they pay good, why not? Maybe we have fun also, eh?" He winked broadly. Simpson shrugged in turn and thought for a moment.

"You really think so?"

"Sure."

"They want to come next week. Let me see...we have a Ball Room party, that's all. We could...we could do it." He sighed deeply. "Alright."

Motumbo smiled again and reached out to squeeze Simpson's arm, letting his hand rest there. Simpson smiled back at him.

"So, Motumbo...is Chele happy here? She cooks well, she..." he broke off and cleared his throat. "Motumbo, what is going to happen?"

Motumbo looked at him for a long moment, then took a step forward and took Simpson into his strong brown arms. "It be OK, Andrew. Chele and me, we good. You and me, we good. Nobody have to choose. You got Strello, the boys, eh, for a while? You know, Andrew, we here in Africa...maybe we do things not like you do back there, eh? Can we all share?"

Simpson felt a wash of relief over his riverbed of anxiety. He knew his jealousy and insecurity was probably coming from another place foreign to his new land, but it had been a struggle for him. He nodded and returned Motumbo's tight embrace, resigned to the situation but still, in his heart of hearts, fearful and unsettled. The truth was that he wanted Motumbo and wasn't sure how sharing him would work in the long term. A soft female voice in the hallway broke their embrace; had Chele passed by the door and seen them? If so, she had the grace to withdraw down the hallway. Motumbo kissed Simpson quickly and stepped out to talk softly, quickly with her. He stuck his head back in the office. "We go to work now, Andrew. You tell 'em yes, OK?" he said, nodding at the paper. Simpson nodded and smiled, and the couple departed.

The two parties had light, early dinners in their respective lodges while the staff ate in the main lodge, Chele cooking once again to applause all around. Then Thabo and Big Mandla went to lead the two parties to a specially prepared building consisting of one large room, empty except for the wall to wall mattress that covered the floor, and an ample bathroom. Towels and tubes of lubricant, drinks, and piles of pillows, were distributed here and there on the floor mattress. Best of all, from the point of view of the staff, were two one-way mirror/windows along one side of the room. From a small room on the other side of what seemed from the big room to be mirrors, the staff could secretly watch the proceedings. Here Simpson, the two young teenage boys, Thatho and Mthobisi, and eventually Thabo gathered to watch the festivities. The rest of the staff was occupied with other work or leisure that evening.

Thabo led the Americans to the room first. One was large but fit, looking the very stereotype of the blonde surfer beachbum. The other two were lean but muscular, with brown hair, and one sported a scruffy goatee. The three men left their shoes outside the door, but remained dressed in slacks and shirts. They poured themselves drinks and toasted their success, plus the imminent

114

sexual blowout. Thabo slipped into the viewing room. Soon there was a knock on the door and Big Mandla entered, leading the three Japanese men into the room. They were naked, their apricot skin flawless and smooth in the soft light, with soft cords binding their hands from behind. Two were slim and muscular, but not exceptionally tall. The third was the slightest bit stocky, but not fat by any means. Their penises, in anticipation of the moment, were semi-erect and swinging like pendulums. The two slim men sported thin, relatively long organs, although nothing by African standards. The chunky man's penis was not so long but was unusually thick. Sprays of black pubic hair curved out from the base of each shaft, and hairless ballsacks dangled beneath each bobbing cock. Big Mandla nodded at the white men and left the room with the Japanese men still lightly bound. In the viewing room, the boys, Thatho and Mthobisi, giggled with excitement and anticipation, while Simpson and Thabo winked at each other and smiled.

The three white men in the room lined up opposite the three Japanese and ordered them to their knees. Each Japanese man had his hands tied behind his back with a soft cord, held in place over their firm, rounded buttocks. The white men lost no time in pulling off their own clothes and stepping forward with bobbing cocks to stand close to the three Japanese. Their increasingly hard pink and red dicks began batting the Japanese men's faces, leaving streaks of precum on their cheeks, rosebud lips, and button noses, although the three men on their knees kept their heads held down submissively. As they kneeled there, their own deep red and purple cocks began to rise until they were straight up, perfectly aligned with the two slim and hard abdomens and the one slightly rounded apricot colored belly. The whites then lifted the chin of each Japanese man with one hand while the other hand sank into their thick, glossy black hair. Three cockheads were pressed against three mouths, and as the Japanese men opened the white men thrust forward, gagging one of the kneeling men, sinking their rigid dicks into the waiting mouths. Slowly, they began swinging their hips back and forth, face fucking the men in front of them.

In the viewing room, Thatho and Mthobisi, the eighteen year old twin African boys from Motumbo's village, were breathing heavily, their beautiful trumpet lipped mouths slightly open. First Thabo and then Simpson slid up right behind the boys, and then each pulled the boys' shirts up and off of their slim, tubelike torsos. The boys giggled but would not be distracted from the spectacle on the other side of the glass. The adults reached down and unfastened the boys' trousers and underwear, sliding both to the floor. Quickly, Simpson and

Thabo likewise shed their clothing and again took their positions behind each boy, pressing their growing erections in the middle of each boy's back while their hands slid down over the thin pads of muscle on the chests and bellies of the young teens. The boys stared intently at the proceedings in the room, their young cocks now rising straight out in front of them. From time to time they looked sideways to their brother and to the two men who were fondling them, giggled, and returned to the window.

In the room, the whites nodded at each other and withdrew their dicks from the wet Asian mouths with plopping sounds; it was clear they had planned their every move. The soft cords were removed from the Japanese men's hands, and then they were made to lie flat on the mattress. Each white man covered an Asian and humped him slowly and thoroughly, sliding their slick, leaking dicks up and down between ass cracks, or alongside a deep purple Asian cock that lay on a belly, mixing white and Asian precum in sheets on the golden brown skin of the conquered men. Lips sought lips, tongues ran along tongues and along teeth. Then one white man would trade with another to taste the pleasures of another captive, and so for a while as passion mounted slowly but inexorably.

With a soft word spoken by the big blonde, the white men reached for tubes of lubricant and greased each pink Asian asshole thoroughly, inserting one, then two, then three fingers as the Japanese men lay on their bellies, their rounded butts thrust up, grunting but wordless at each invasion of their innermost parts. When thoroughly greased and relaxed, the Asians assumed they would be ravaged by the bigger white men, but that pleasure was yet to be. The whites positioned the Asians so that they would fuck each other in a line, all on their hands and knees. Willingly, the chubby Asian took his place in front, while his thinner companions positioned themselves in line behind him and first one, then another, slid a steel hard cock into the gaping asshole in front of him. A few gasps and sighs, and they fell to pumping rhythmically, the pace set by the Japanese beauty in the middle. Soon their muscular, firm butts were fanning back and forth quickly, as Asians often prefer, to both give and receive dick. The whites gathered round on their knees, slapping butts, rubbing heaving chests and rippling bellies, or grasping the cock of the chubby man in front, touching and fondling their "property" as the vanquished Asians fucked each other ferociously.

In the control room, Simpson slipped a little to the left behind Thatho, then ran his right hand down over the boy's chest and abdomen to clutch his dripping, rampant eighteen year old midnight black cock. Thatho gasped and, glancing down, saw Simpson's pink and red cock bobbing along his left side. Thatho grasped the organ with one hand, steadying himself against the wall beneath the window with his other. He pumped the white man while Simpson began fondling and pumping his own teenage organ.

Thabo, seeing this, decided to try something different. Remaining directly behind beautiful Mthobisi, he picked the boy up and held him tight against his chest and belly. Thabo's organ, middle-aged but large and full, now rose up between Mthobisi's dark brown legs, lifting his young ballsack, and aligning itself with the boy's rigid cock. Thabo's dick was so long that his flared light brown cockhead was now directly under Mthobisi's own knob. Mthobisi, seeing what was wanted, hooked his legs back around behind the older man's thighs, grasped both the older adult's ponderous dick and his own rampant cocky with both hands, and began pumping.

In the main room, the Japanese man at the back end threw his head back, crying out, shuddering and pushing, gulping for air. Before he finished filling the rectum of the man in the middle, that one also came, bucking and twisting so hard he nearly disconnected the line. The chubby man in front pushed back hard, receiving his friend's copious cum. The two in the middle and the end had scarcely recovered breathing when the whites pulled the chubby man in front away, while keeping the other two locked together. The chubby Asian was put at the back and made to push his short, fat, hard dick into the ass of the man who had been at the back. The dark red cock slid in with no trouble, its target gasping, but still he held on to the hips of the man in front of him who kept the middle man's dick still inside his asshole. The chubby man now began fanning his hips back and forth very quickly, taking short, quick strokes, as the white men laughed, slapped his exposed buttocks, and fingered the cum drooling from his gaping asshole. His prostate was so stimulated by being fucked, it took but a moment and he curled forward, grunting like a pig.

In the viewing room, Thabo and Mthobisi came first, the black teenager's combined fists bringing both of them to climax at the same time. Heavy shots of cum came from the older man's thick dick and splattered the wall in front of them below the glass, while Mthobisi shot one load right at the wall and then leaked a heavy drool of white fluid down over Thabo's wide cockhead that was still held just below his. Both boy and man grunted and moaned, Thabo nuzzling and biting the boy's neck, and then they stood there shuddering and gasping.

Next to them, Thatho looked back and forth from his brother and Thabo to the white cock of Andrew Simpson that he held tight in his left hand, pumping vigorously, then straight ahead to the Asian ass fucking going on in the main room. It was too much to resist and he cried out, arching his body, pushing his pelvis out, and Simpson slowed the sliding of his white hand up and down the coal black penis as it sprayed out white droplets onto the wall. Then as Simpson began to moan and shudder, Thatho, sensing the white man's moment of crisis, pivoted around onto his knees in front of him, his leaking dick bobbing about, and took the red cock into his mouth. Simpson quickly grasped the boy's kinky head with both hands, one dripping with the boy's own semen, and held on for dear life as he filled the black boy's mouth with spunk. Thatho gurgled and choked but swallowed every bit, his large dark eyes looking up as the white man shuddered and spasmed above him.

Back in the main room, the whites now pulled apart the well fucked Asians, each rosy brown asshole winking and oozing cum, and each American now took possession of one of the captives. The blonde laid the chubby Asian on his back, his legs spread apart, and rammed his long, rigid, pink dick right up to the base, mashing his dirty blonde pubic hair against the man's thighs. Arcing out over the Asian, the blonde began fucking him with powerful strokes. Each of the other two brown haired white man put their victim on the mattress floor with butts raised and, covering them, slid their hard cocks inside their gaping assholes with single pushes. Clutching the Asians' shoulders and glossy black hair, the two brown hair whites now rode them unmercifully, pounding their upturned asses hard, as the Asians pushed back willingly to receive their punishment.

The two men in the viewing room held their teenage boys in front of them, cuddling and fondling them in their afterglow, as four dicks, three black and one white, slowly subsided. The four of them looked on intently as first one of the brown haired Americans, then the blonde, then the last American came, each one groaning or squealing and pushing hard, digging into the thin but muscular shoulders, raising deep blushes in the apricot skin, pushing and trembling into each Asian asshole to fill it with their victors' semen. Then the Americans collapsed, heaving and gasping, on top of their conquests. The "victims" smiled and, where they could, winked at one another; it was not such a bad contest to lose.

Nor would that be the end of what the Japanese men owed to their white masters for the next twenty four hours. But they would do that in private. The two men and two boys in the viewing room quietly dressed, whispering jokes and speculations as to what would follow in the main room, and then slipped out into the night. They bade each other goodnight as they parted on the path, and as Simpson came to the door of his own lodge he could not resist a glance in the direction of the lodge where he knew Motumbo and Chele were staying. But one light was on, and it was low, and in a bedroom.

- CHAPTER 11 -

Andrew Simpson stepped out into the bright morning and breathed the fresh air. He had just passed one of the few nights he had spent alone at DeGroot's. This was not a problem for him, other than the fact that Motumbo was still occupying a guest lodge with Chele, and although Andrew was having a serious talk with himself about letting go and sharing, the talk was barely working. Strolling around the compound, he passed Thabo wheeling a cart with breakfast in it toward the guest lodge that was one large room with a mattress floor. Andrew nodded at Thabo and they exchanged smiles; even at this early hour there were groans coming from the lodge; no doubt the Americans were pounding some Japanese butt as soon as the sun came up.

Entering the main lodge, Simpson found Motumbo there already, while Chele bustled about in the kitchen. She had again prepared a marvelous breakfast, and was bringing out serving dishes to the table. Motumbo's eyes darted back and forth between Chele and Simpson, a shy and uncertain smile on his face. Chele greeted Simpson, smiling broadly at him and giving him a quick, gentle hug before she scurried back into the kitchen for more food. Simpson watched her go, his heart twisting. She really was very beautiful, and a kind and lovely person to boot; how could he compete with such a one? But when he sat down next to Motumbo at the table, the African quickly covered Simpson's hand with his large brown one and squeezed it quickly, smiling brightly at him.

Thabo returned for breakfast and Chele joined them. Thabo reported, to laughter all around, how his knock on the door had brought a yelp of "leave it outside" from within, amidst moaning and banging sounds. Simpson marveled at Chele's laughter, at her evident acceptance of the business done by DeGroot's. As they finished their meal they heard the sounds of footsteps from outside as the staff gathered for a briefing, as Simpson had requested.

Both Mandlas and Strello, plus the teen twin boys Thatho and Mthobisi were there. Simpson gathered them in the great room of the main lodge and cleared his throat.

"As you know, we have a party of two from Sweden arriving next weekend, requesting a Ball Room adventure. Little Mandla, and Thatho and Mthobisi, I think that will be you, either taking turns or all at once as they request when they get here." Little Mandla and the twins nodded, beaming, as they thought ahead to their role in the weekend's adventures.

"Now we have another party, and I have just confirmed that they will be here, and have received payment, so it's a 'go.'" Simpson paused, cleared his throat, and continued, avoiding eye contact. "It is a party of three African Americans, from two cities in the States. They..." He paused. "They want to reenact a slave march and sale." He paused and looked around. He might as well have announced the day's weather forecast for all the reaction this drew from the staff, who nodded and maintained their attention. Simpson decided to elaborate. "They want to be bound and marched a day out, to sleep as if captive under the stars, as if on a march to the slave castles on the west coast. Then they want to march back, and the day following be 'sold.' Of course, they expect, uh...they expect sexual activity connected with all of this." Simpson looked searchingly at the the staff, who returned his look passively.

Simpson burst out in a bit of pique: "Look, Thabo and Motumbo both thought this was a good idea, and I suppose the clients are coming since they've paid and I've approved it, but... Come on, this is a slave reenactment! How can we do this? How can...." his voice trailed off and he stood there shaking his head and looking down. Thabo looked at him thoughtfully and with kindness and then spoke.

"Boss Andrew, we see here lots of strange things the people want." The rest of the staff murmured assent and exchanged looks, some of them rolling their eyes and some chuckling at the memories they had. "Some guests, they want we should tie them up and beat them. Some, they ask real blood to be drawn. Stranger than that! We do that Boss, if they like. Who know why people want what they want?" Thabo shrugged hugely. Another murmur of assent all around. Simpson looked doubtful.

Motumbo spoke up. "Andrew, you never own slave, eh?" Simpson's eyes widened and he shook his head vigorously. "These men, they never been slave, eh?" Simpson shook his head again. "Well, it all a game. We, we never ran no slave march, but can act like we do, eh? Some people come here, they want be little boy, some want be girl...it all a game, Andrew."

"Are you all sure you are OK with this?" asked Simpson. Every man and boy murmured agreement and then, without his prompting, began brainstorming about ways to make the experience as authentic as possible without actually harming the clients in any permanent way. Simpson sat down open mouthed, still aghast but resigning himself to the creative enthusiasm of his staff. After an hour they had it all planned out among themselves, including the assignment of Simpson as the "purchaser" of the "slaves" at the end of the march. Simpson had to admit that the idea was beginning to intrigue him, which warred with his sense of propriety, justice...and perhaps guilt? He resolved to himself to discuss the matter with the clients once they arrived.

As the meeting broke up, Motumbo took Simpson aside. "Andrew," he said softly, "Chele go back to home today, I go with her, just a few day. I be back by weekend for guests." Simpson looked at him and nodded, forcing a smile. It seemed like another step Motumbo was taking away from him, despite Motumbo's reassurances and promise to return on the weekend.

"I will miss you, Motumbo. I will miss Chele's cooking." Both men smiled broadly at that, and Motumbo nodded.

"She good cook, eh Andrew? Maybe she come work here, help Thabo?" Simpson thought quickly; that would mean Motumbo would leave less often; it would also mean that Chele would be around all the time. Would Motumbo really leave her bed to come to his? Treading carefully, Simpson smiled again and replied, "Maybe so, let me know." The two men embraced tightly, and then Motumbo slipped away. Simpson occupied himself with paperwork in the office so that, half an hour later, he heard rather than saw Motumbo and Chele's old truck start up and rumble out of the compound.

The week flew by for Simpson since its end would bring the dubious slave march; but also it dragged its heels, since its end meant the return of Motumbo. The time was put to good use, however, in preparation for the two parties that would arrive soon. Big Mandla and Thabo were just pulling out of the compound at the end of the week to fetch the guests arriving that day when Motumbo and Chele drove their old pickup truck into the area. The couple emerged with beaming faces, Chele stepping quickly ahead to embrace Simpson lightly and say something cheery in her language. Simpson smiled back, and then caught the sight of an unusually large number of parcels in the back of the truck. Motumbo came up from the other side of the vehicle and also hugged Simpson, murmuring "Good to be back, Andrew" in his ear. Simpson stood between them, feeling awkward, for but a moment and then Motumbo cleared his throat and jerked his chin in the direction of the truck.

"Chele, she come to cook, Andrew. You say we can try hire her?" All was clear to Simpson, and it was also clear that Chele was now intending to stay for some time. He swallowed hard, forced a smile, and said "Of course." Motumbo and Chele, the latter needing no translation, smiled broadly and immediately began carrying packages and luggage from the truck to the lodge they had used. Simpson grabbed a bundle or two himself, and three times in passing Motumbo paused to squeeze his arm or shoulder and smile a wordless thanks.

Hours later, after another wonderful lunch prepared by Chele, the first vehicle came back into the compound. Big Mandla had the two Swedes, tall, lean and good looking in their early middle age. Simpson greeted them warmly and directed them to their lodge, inviting them to the main lodge for drinks and dinner later on. An hour later Thabo rolled in and parked his vehicle. From it emerged three black men.

Walking up to greet them, Simpson recognized two of them as NBA players. He was trying with difficulty to place them, having not been that much of a sports fan. They introduced themselves as Jim and John, obviously aliases but Simpson was willing to accept that. Each was a tower of iron muscle, not overly tall but more so than the normal range. It was clear they had developed powerful physiques, the better for slamming opponents with. The third man Simpson did not recognize, and introduced himself as Antoine.

He was slim and of average physique; no doubt a professional of some sort. Simpson thought for a moment about how different most African Americans, intermixed with white and Indian blood as they are, look from native Africans. These guests were nearly as dark as DeGroot's staff, but their facial features and a certain tone of skin distinguished them from those born in the mother continent. Which was not to say they were not attractive men; Simpson felt his dick twitch as he welcome the three to the camp.

Simpson hosted both of the client parties for cocktails and dinner at the main lodge. The African Americans arrived first, and Simpson poured drinks all around. Once they had all settled comfortably into chairs and sofas, Simpson proposed a toast. Then, looking all around, he began: "Well...." and could not think what to say. There were some awkward chuckles, and the three men eyed him with interest. He decided to plunge right in.

"Look, I just have to say, this makes me uncomfortable. I mean, we'll do our best, I don't think you'll be unhappy, but..." He trailed off.

Jim, a powerfully built man with short twisted tufts of hair, stepped in. "Makes you feel guilty, huh?" Simpson shrugged and nodded, silently. "Maybe, not the right thing to do?" Simpson nodded again. And then Simpson asked one question: "Why?"

The three men looked at one another and shrugged. "I dunno man," said John, "kinda turns me on, y'know? Like when I see a white man, I wonder, what would he do back in the day? And more important, I guess, I wonder what I would do. I want to find out."

"For me, yeah, it's something I have to sort of get out of my system, you know? Maybe kind of come to terms with the ancestors? A rite of passage? My ancestors were on the boats, but they were also running the slave coffles," said Antoine.

Jim looked around, put back his head, and laughed. "Man, me, I like the idea of getting fucked hard by a homegrown African, and then getting felt up by a white man!" All three of his companions roared with laughter at that, and if Simpson said his penis lay still at that point, he was lying. Jim continued: "Look, Andrew, it's just a game. You feel me up without my asking on the streets, you're dead. But here? That's why we paid so much to come. It's different, y'know?" Simpson nodded. He refilled drinks, feeling better about the adventure to come. At that point the Swedes entered the lodge. There was much friendly talk and sexual banter, even though the two groups were not interacting by way of their games, and the play continued throughout the dinner. At the end of the evening, Simpson bade all parties a good night and wished them well in their adventures to begin the next day.

It was early the next morning that Simpson went to observe the start of the march. Thabo was dressed as a chieftain, and accompanied by Motumbo, Strello, and Big Mandla. Simpson stood some distance away, but close enough to see and hear. Without knocking, Thabo flung open the lodge door and was followed by his three "soldiers." Thabo began shouting at them in his language, echoed by the three staff members who invaded the lodge. Roughly, but not so roughly as to harm the clients, Motumbo and his crew turned the three African Americans out of bed. Surprised exclamations and muffled protests were evidence that the clients forgot for a moment what they had arranged for themselves, but then the objections subsided into mutterings. Simpson could see that each man was dragged from the lodge with his hands tied behind his back. Tied by soft cords, but securely tied. The three men were hussled into the dawn light, genuinely looking none too happy.

Jim was wearing some expensive looking pajamas. Big Mandla stepped up to him and, drawing a knife, simply cut the garments from his body. "Ah, man, that's Armani!" Jim protested, and was rewarded with a slap from Big Mandla. Rip and rip, and the powerful athlete stood naked, his hands tied behind his back. His penis was a dark hose hanging down over a heavy ballsack, under a dense thatch of pubic hair. His body was milk chocolate muscle, flesh rolling in hills and valleys of strength. His butt was the high, upward rolling, rounded butt of Africa, no mistaking that. John stumbled after him wearing only briefs, which Motumbo likewise cut off with a knife. He had seen Jim's treatment, and kept his head lowered, a sullen look on his face. John's body was similar to Jim's, a shade darker, the perfection of muscled black manhood, a heavy penis angled down and to the left. Finally, Strello pushed Antoine out of the lodge ahead of him, already naked. Antoine was slim, a tube of thin pads of muscle but again, the high bubble butt of African men. His long but slim penis was half erect, and Simpson wondered whether Strello had fondled him while in the lodge. Antoine's head was up and his eyes defiant, but he kept silent.

The three men all had their hands tied behind their backs, and they were then joined together by soft rope tied around their necks. The crew of Africans pulled out simple lengths of white cloth and swiftly fashioned loincloths, wrapping the fabric around the captives' loins to hold and protect their heavy

126

genitals on the march. At the last minute their captors discretely bent down and slipped heavy sandals over the captives' feet; not historically accurate, but their tender American feet would need the protection. Simpson noted with relief that the day was overcast, and so sunstroke dangers would be reduced. Down the path to the gate and out of the compound Big Mandla, Motumbo, and Strello now led their captors, winking behind them at Simpson, while Thabo continued to intone something in his language. He was "selling" his countryman off to a distant bondage.

Throughout that day the captives were marched through the African bush. The crew from DeGroot's had "whips" of soft fabric that would smart but not tear skin, and they used these every time one of the slaves slowed down or would trip. Although the sun was behind clouds, sweat began running down the bodies of the captives, making their dark chocolate skin glisten. At one point Antoine, who was in the middle, begged to stop so as to urinate. Motumbo stepped up to him and stripped his loincloth off at once and said, "Do it." Antoine looked bewildered and asked "Where?" Motumbo slapped him, saying "Right here, now do it." Antoine looked dazed, then concentrated for a moment and began urinating, the yellow stream splashing around the legs of Jim, in front. Big Mandla pulled off the loincloths from Jim and John and commanded, "You, too!" John, behind, wordlessly began peeing on Antoine's legs, while Jim, in the front, grunted once or twice and sent his spray of urine out onto the dust. As soon as they were done, yellow drops falling from their pendulous cocks, the loincloths were quickly wrapped around them again and the march continued.

There were three breaks for water, but no real lunch. The captives sat in a huddle under a tree, beginning to feel miserable, while the African crew ate well and joked among themselves. At the end of their meal each of them brought a crust of bread to a captive and pushed it into their mouths; the African Americans seemed grateful for it. Then it was back on their feet to march on.

The day was not as long as it would have been in history. Simpson did not want to kill off his paying customers, of course. Toward the end of the afternoon the slave coffle approached a camp that had already been set up; not historically accurate, but some compromises had to be taken. There was a large tent, for use by the African captors, and some straw spread under a tree, which was evidently where the captives were to lie. They flopped down on the straw, hands still bound, and were given water. Then their hands were unbound but ropes still ran from one neck to another. And in truth, where would they run to if they did want to escape? Strello brought bowls of a sort of thin porridge to each captive slave, which they consumed greedily, slurping the stuff directly from the bowls. At a makeshift table nearby, the African slave masters enjoyed a tasty and more substantial meal as the sun dipped below the horizon.

As the light was waning, Jim called out, "I gotta shit." Their captors walked over and made all three rise, leading them several yards away. Loincloths from all three were stripped away. "Do it here," Strello commanded. Jim and the others looked at him in disbelief. Strello shoved the big man down, bringing the rest of the party with him. A look of anger flashed in Jim's eyes, but the "reality" of the whole exercise was beginning to take hold of him. "Here!" commanded Strello again. Jim, his eyes cast down, squatted on his haunches, concentrated for a moment, and then with a grunt and a gasp expelled a long, brown tube of shit down from his ass and onto the dusty ground. Realizing this might be their only chance, Antoine and John assumed the same position and, in a few moments, each was dropping turds onto the ground. "What do I wipe with?" asked Antoine, and was rewarded with a slap from Big Mandla. The three captives were jerked to their feet and led back to their straw. Their loincloths were not returned.

Night had now fallen, broken only by the stars and the flickering oil lamps of the camp. The captives sat in silence, deep in thought or exhaustion. And then their masters came to them and jerked them to their feet again, leading them to the big tent some yards away. Some hope for more comfortable accommodations grew in their minds, maybe some cover or a blanket for the night. It was not to be. The three captives were thrown to the dirt floor of the tent, and then Motumbo and Big Mandla untied Antoine from the other slaves and led him to a mat a few feet away in the center of the tent. There Antoine stood, his head down but his eyes watchful, as Strello walked slowly around him, appraising his body. Antoine's tub of slim muscle shone in the lamplight, a flawless milk chocolate. As he walked around the slave, Strello reached out to tweak a nipple or slap a rounded butt cheek. Slowly, Antoine's penis began to rise, a long, heavy hood on a long but slim shaft, like a tulip, with heavy balls tucked in close beneath, below a short bush of thick black hair. Strello's own trousers were tenting ominously in front.

Then suddenly Strello pushed the slave Antoine to his knees, and with his hand on Antoine's shoulders pushed him to his hands and knees. In a flash,

Strello's trousers were off, revealing his ponderous penis thick and erect. Scooping up a nearby tube of lubricant, Strello put only a dab on the tip of his organ. He spread Antoine's legs and positioned himself behind the slave, then leaned forward and pushed again on his shoulder. Antoine gasped and went down, his arms splayed, while his pelvis remained up, his now erect penis stretched out behind him, his bubble butt poised and waiting. Strello put the lighter brown dickhead of his midnight dark shaft to Antoine's asshole, still smudged from his earlier shit, and pushed with one might shove. Antoine cried out and struggled to rise, but Strello was on top of him, pinning him. Now Antoine moaned, gasped, and cried "stop! stop!" but to no avail. Holding himself up off of Antoine's caramel brown, thin back with his palms flat on the ground, Strello began pounding the slave's ass, Africa fucking African America hard and fast. Antoine writhed and wept, but Strello was without mercy. His butt cheeks clenching and unclenching as he slammed in and out, in and out, Strello soon came, slamming hard, pushing his iron dick hard into Antoine as he pumped his semen into him. Strello pushed, shuddered, held his position, and then in an instant pulled out of the captive with a plop and rose, his dick still hard, leaking and dirty, and roughly grabbed Antoine up off the ground. The milk chocolate slave's dick was still hard as he was dragged to the other two captives and tied up again.

Jim and John had been sitting, staring, their mouths half open in disbelief... but their penises also slowly hardening at the spectacle. Now Motumbo walked over and untied Jim, jerking him to his feet long enough to bring him to the mat, then pushing him down onto his back. As did Strello, Motumbo put but a dab of lubricant on his huge cock, then pushed Jim's legs up toward his chest and, positioning his iron rod at Jim's unwiped asshole, pushed. Jim gasped and his torso curled up, his hands pushing at Motumbo. His erect cock wagged and flopped on his lower belly, his heavy ballsack swaying left and right. "Naw, bro, wait a minute!" Jim cried, pushing his attacker away. But Strello and Big Mandla rushed forward to grabbed the athlete's arms, pinning him back to the mat, as Motumbo impaled the slave completely on his enormous dick. Jim cried out, but Motumbo immediately set up a powerful rhythm of fucking. Back and forth, in and out, holding himself up off of the captive, staring down and laughing in derision at him, Motumbo fucked him hard as Jim's arms remained pinned by his African captors. Motumbo took longer than Strello, but eventually grunted hard, bucked twice, and clenched his buttocks, pushing forward with all his might into the slave's bottom as he shot ropes of semen into the black man's gut. As soon as he was done he rose, his iron dick still hard, and Big Mandla and Strello immediately pulled Jim back to the captives, securing him once again.

They returned with John, who now struggled a bit even though his erect penis betrayed his excitement. With Motumbo's help they pushed John flat onto the ground, where he landed with a huff. Big Mandla wasted no time with lubricant. Scrambling around behind the slave, he entered him, his way eased only by the stuff left over from John's earlier shit. John cried and cursed, squirming and struggling to escape, but Motumbo and Strello held him tight as Big Mandla banged him hard, African muscle pistoning a purple black dick as hard as steel in and out, in and out. Big Mandla came faster than either of his friends, mercifully, finally lubricating John's manhole with gouts of his semen as Big Mandla pushed hard, ejaculating into the slave's ass.

With John jerked to his feet, the other captives were treated likewise and were led back outside beneath the tree, where they were securely tied. Their captors returned to the tent, where the sounds of laughter and drinking could be heard late into the night. The three slaves huddled beneath the tree, cuddling together for warmth, but each felt the still-erect dicks of his friends poking or slapping at his thigh as they took what rest they could during the short night.

The next day the African captors rose with the dawn light, roughly shaking their slaves awake, feeding them another bowl of the porridge and some water. Then they pulled the slaves to their feet again, affixed the loincloths loosely about their genitals and hips, and began the return march. A shorter way was taken this time, so as to return to the compound by mid-afternoon. The slave coffle was made to wade through a waist high creek halfway through, and they emerged wet and dripping on the other side, water running off their dark skins in rivulets that soon dried in the sun that was beginning to emerge from behind the clouds. The slaves were tired and subdued by the time the compound came into sight. Thabo was there to greet them, once again in tribal garb. He showed the way to a hut, where the captives were stripped entirely naked and untied. Buckets of water were brought in and soap, and the teenage boys, Thatho and Mthobisi, gleefully took on the task of washing the captives, scrubbing their skin with brushes, pushing back their foreskins to clean their swelling cocks, sticking soapy fingers into their stinking assholes to scour them. Exhausted but clean, the three slaves were given some porridge, this time with a little meat in it, and then shut, naked, into the hut. There they would await their inspections by the white master who would purchase them.

- CHAPTER 12 -

As Motumbo, Strello, and Big Mandla led their captives away that morning, the rest of the staff at DeGroot's turned their attention to the two Swedes who had chosen to experience a Ball Room adventure. Eager for the fun to begin, they had asked for their session to start promptly after lunch. The two twin boys, Thatho and Mthobisi, and the other eighteen year old, Little Mandla, shared lunch with the two middle aged Swedes, the five of them laughing and joking through the meal, but the two Swedes also quietly appraising which boy they would begin with. A brief, whispered consultation after lunch produced the decision that Little Mandla would be their prey in the Ball Room that day, the twin boys would work tomorrow. The arrangement was satisfactory to all concerned, and Little Mandla prepared himself to enter the Ball Room.

Simpson, Thatho and Mthobisi escorted Little Mandla and the Swedes up the outside stairs to the entrance to the Ball Room. Little Mandla quickly shed his clothes, the Swedes pausing in their own disrobing to assess his slim, muscular figure, the cap of peppercorn curls, the full, ripe lips and broad nose, the deep caramel color. Broad grins creased their faces and they whispered to each other in their own language as Little Mandla, his long, slim penis bobbing with the beginnings of an erection, smiled at them and then entered the Ball Room. A minute passed and then the Swedes, their bodies tanned and toned in their early middle age, entered the chamber as well. Sealing the door, Simpson and the boys stepped quickly to the observation port and looked in.

The lightweight plastic balls filling the room distorted the low light. Simpson and the boys could indistinctly see Little Mandla's lithe, brown body swimming through the balls, the outline and contour of his strong, slim form blurring and wavering. In a moment the lighter tan bodies of the Swedes were evident, moving in two different directions so as to outflank and corner the African boy. Little Mandla seemed determined to make a contest of it, and muffled laughs and shouts could be heard from within as the two men slipped and slid, nearly catching him twice as he wriggled out of the way with dexterous turns. But the end was inevitable. One Swede caught Little Mandla's ankle and held on for only a moment, but it was long enough to slow him down and then the other Swede was on him, enfolding the brown body in his tan arms like an eagle taking its prey.

Giggling, breathless from the chase, Little Mandla surrendered. Floating in space, an illusion of weightlessness created by the magic of the balls, lighting, and air system, the three snuggled in close, Little Mandla stretched out between their bodies. The Swedes ran their hands up and down Little Mandla's dark caramel skin, nuzzled his peppercorn hair, kissed and sucked his wide, luscious lips, rubbed their long noses against his broad, rounded one. Hands grasped cocks now as they rolled in space, arms and legs entwined. Reaching for the tube of lubricant strapped to his ankle, one Swede oiled his rampant, pink dick and quickly entered Little Mandla from behind with no further ceremony, the African crying out and gasping. The pain soon subsided, though, as the second Swede slid down to engulf the boy's iron hard, leaking purple black dick, running his tongue up and down the shaft, swallowing precum and flicking his lips over the exposed, flared cockhead. Now Little Mandla began moaning in pleasure, a sound echoed by the Swede behind him who was fucking him very slowly, pulling back almost all the way out, then sliding forward to press firmly in as far as he could, then back out again. The cycle was slowly, slowly repeated, as the stimulation on Little Mandla's prostate and the expert sucking he was receiving soon became unbearable. The African boy entwined his dark brown fingers in the dark blonde hair of the man who was sucking him and cried out, squeezing his tight rounded buttocks together and pushing out a long rope of semen into the waiting mouth that engulfed his dick. The tightening of his muscular bottom as he clenched and ejaculated was what the patient Swede behind him needed, and he instantly moaned loudly and exploded into the African boy's asshole, filling his rectum with white cum.

Little Mandla had only just finished squirting the last of his boyjuice into the Swede in front of him, trembling and gasping, when the man, swallowing the last drop, pulled away and slid halfway up his brown torso. Little Mandla was expecting the Swede to bring his own rigid pink cock up to his full maroon and brown lips, but that did not happen. The Swede stopped halfway up and pivoted the African boy's legs up to his chest. Then the Swede pushed his own groin up under Little Mandla's rounded buttocks. It became clear what was going to happen, and Little Mandla gasped in fear. One Swede still had a rampant dick inside Little Mandla's asshole, holding him tight by the arms, fully landed inside his gut. Now the second Swede who had just sucked Little Mandla dry put his own swollen cockhead to the African boy's cock-filled anus and pushed. The rectum stretched, loosened as it had been by the slow fuck he had received, but it could not stretch enough to make it entirely comfortable. Little Mandla cried out in pain and surprise as the Swede pushed his dick up alongside the rod of the other Swede, both rigid cocks now fully inside the African boy. Little Mandla struggled a bit but his arms were held tight from behind by the man who had just fucked him. Now his new assailant began sliding in and out, slowly, and pulled Little Mandla's heaving torso tight against his chest as he held him from in front. Little Mandla was breathing heavily in evident discomfort, but no longer crying out. The first Swede stayed anchored—in fact, his dick was trapped inside the boy's rectum by the pressure of the second penis—while the second Swede fucked him slowly, slowly, in and out, up and down.

Simpson and the boys outside exchanged looks of concern mixed with lust, but they could not ultimately tear themselves away from the spectacle. The three males remained locked together as the second Swede moved in a slow, deliberate cycle, in and out, in and out, until he too cried out and pushed up, squeezing his hips together to send a spray of cum inside the African boy's gut. Trembling and bucking, the three held tight together for a while and then a while longer, the African boy held captive between the two men who were fucking his butt simultaneously. After long moments both Swedes pulled out at the same time, a stream of cum following them from Little Mandla's gaping bottom. The three rolled together as they recovered, each in his own way, and it was clear from Little Mandla's caresses and fondling of his two captors that he had fully recovered from, and had even enjoyed, being ravaged in that way. Simpson and the boys knew there would be much more of that sort of thing, both in the Ball Room and back in the Swedes' lodge, for the rest of the night, but they withdrew, having other duties to attend to.

Simpson worked in the main lodge office the rest of the afternoon, processing applications and doing other paperwork. Business was beginning to look up; requests were coming in more frequently, including some really novel suggestions for sexual adventures that Simpson wished he had thought of. A couple of requests he rejected out of hand, involving violence or degradation beyond what he could possibly stomach, but for the most part he smiled in anticipation at some of what was proposed.

Chele came over in the late afternoon and began preparing the evening meal. Thabo pushed a cart down to the lodge where the Swedes were enjoying Little Mandla, and he was enjoying them, in new and interesting ways. He returned with Thatho and Mthobisi and joined Simpson and Chele, who kept rising up to fetch food from the kitchen, at the table. Conversation was light and cheerful, with Thabo and the boys translating between Chele and Simpson. Twice during the conversation she softly laid her hand on Simpson's forearm as it lay on the table, and he could not help but think that the same hand had caressed Motumbo within the last twenty-four hours. After the meal, Simpson returned to the office nearby to finish his work while Thabo went to check on the Swedes and the boys scattered to amuse themselves at play. Chele bustled about cleaning and making preparations for the next day.

Simpson worked steadily and as he finished realized that the lodge was utterly quiet; he surmised he was alone. He was mistaken. Having made his work space tidy and shut off the light, he stepped into the hallway to find Chele sitting there in a chair; she had been placed so she could observe him, but for how long? Simpson smiled at her, nodded and bade her good night. But she rose to walk with him as he went out the door, smiling at him and speaking softly in her language. As they stepped out into the night air Simpson nodded at her again and half turned to head for his cabin. She put her hand on his forearm again and spoke, looking into his eyes. Uncomprehending, he nodded, smiled, wished her good evening again, and made as if to step away—but she would not release his arm.

Then it hit him. Although equipped with a well functioning gaydar, and often oblivious to the advances and hints of women, a man as attractive as Andrew Simpson had not gone through life without receiving the sexual advances of females. He saw in a flash that it was happening here. He stared at Chele open-mouthed for a moment, the two frozen in time. Then she took half a step toward her own lodge and tugged gently on his arm. Almost stumbling, he followed, his mind racing. As they neared Chele and Motumbo's lodge, her hand slid down his forearm to his hand, grasping it lightly, and she led him in the door. Simpson couldn't think, he could only float along in the moment.

They slipped inside and Chele closed the door. She turned to him, holding both his hands playfully and speaking softly, coyly to him in her own language. He could only stare; his lover's lover was seducing him, that much was clear. Women were not really his interest, although Chele was undeniably beautiful. And yet, and yet there was also an attraction in fucking the one his own lover fucked. What should he do? Simpson's rational mind seemed absolutely locked, and he could only go with his feelings in the ongoing rush of events. He smiled at her.

Chele dropped his hands and, still smiling seductively up at him, reached up to run her hands through his silken hair. It was clear she had not done this with a white person, with a white man, before. She looked and felt appraisingly. Then she moved her fingers to his shirt and unbuttoned it quickly, reaching down to unfasten his trousers as she neared the bottom of his shirt. Helpless, Simpson stood in an instant in only his underwear and boots, his trousers bunched around his ankles, his shirt on the floor. Chele stepped back to appraise his muscular, light skinned body, nodded, and then in one smooth motion removed her own one piece garment, which fell on the floor. It was all she wore. Her body was unmistakably feminine, with a thin waist, full rounded pelvis, and high, firm breasts, with her skin a lovely dark chocolate. She reached forward and tugged down Simpson's underwear and, to his surprise, his penis bounced out in an erection. She gasped, seeing her first white cock. Simpson kicked off his boots as he stood, his bunched trousers with them and then tentatively reached to cup her breasts, to pull her toward him, hands sliding over her smooth shoulders and back.

The two now embraced in a flash, grinding against each other, now falling to the antelope skin rug on the floor. Their passion was intense and physical, Chele giving as good as she got. They kissed hard and passionately, sucking and gently biting, licking, sharing breath, squeezing and kneading skin and muscle. When he impaled her, Simpson's mind flipped back and forth between the immediate and unaccustomed pleasure of fucking her and the realization that his iron hard pink rod was sliding in and out of Chele just where Motumbo's own midnight purple staff had been so often, so recently.

He fucked her hard, slamming back and forth, conquering her with his rigid cock. Maybe Motumbo's pumping dick was the image that helped sustain this unaccustomed intercourse to the end, for he remained hard until he cried out, arching his back, squeezing his hips and bucking as he slammed down into the woman who cried out in her own ecstasy, filling her with his white man's cum, and the two clutched each other, thrashing and bucking as the passion subsided. Simpson slumped forward and lay on top of her, her dark brown arms entwined over his heaving white back as she held him tight.

An hour later Simpson awoke with a start, his flaccid penis still held just inside Chele, who lay beneath him gently snoring. He shifted and she awoke, looking directly into his eyes. They held the gaze for a moment and then kissed. But the unaccustomed passion did not return to Simpson, and Chele seemed to understand that, seemed not to demand what he could not give again, contrary to his nature. They kissed again, this time in affection, and he rose, then pulled her to her own feet. They embraced once more and then dressed. Smiling at each other, Chele opened the door and waved shyly as Simpson slipped out and walked down the moonlit path to his own lodge, where he collapsed onto the bed in a deep and dreamless sleep.

Simpson stared long and hard at the ceiling the next morning as it gradually lightened in the dawning light. He ran through a list of possible feelings he had, might have, felt he should have. Should he feel attracted toward Chele? Should he feel guilty about fucking Motumbo's woman? Should he use that to split the two up, to keep Motumbo with him? Should he slip out of bed and go back up the path to Chele's lodge and enter her bed, leaving his own sweat and cum on Motumbo's sheets? Some deep breaths and quiet reflection led to none of those things, nor to their rejection. What had happened, happened. He had acted in the moment, and as far as he knew, so had Chele. Why plan? He rose and showered, then dressed and headed out into the day.

In the main lodge were Thabo and the boys, Little Mandla still serving as the toy of the Swedes who had won him in the Ball Room. The smell of breakfast cooking filled the room and then Chele entered. She squeezed Simpson's arm and smiled broadly at him as she passed, and he returned a smile, but nothing passed between them to betray last night's intimacies or to alert Thabo to anything unusual. When she joined the men and boys at the table, conversation was light and general—except that the boys' role in the Ball Room later that day, when they took over from Little Mandla, was discussed, advice and encouragement being given. It was clear, though, that the twin teens were eagerly awaiting the adventure.

More preparations and work occupied the rest of the day, until mid afternoon, when a sound of distant singing alerted everyone to the arrival of the "slave coffle." Thabo quickly slipped back into his tribal chieftain clothing, and the boys eagerly went with him to perform their duties in this fantasy. The three captives were fed and then washed, by the boys, and put into a makeshift hut at Thabo's direction. While those preparations were being made, Simpson consulted with Motumbo, Big Mandla, and Strello as to how the adventure went. All agreed that so far it was going well and seemed to be what the captives had asked for. Simpson and Motumbo interacted easily and naturally, as before—the previous night might never have happened in that space.

In the late afternoon Simpson went to change into some clothing they had found that might be seen as nineteenth century garb. A few rocking chairs had been put on the verandah of the main lodge, so insofar as possible some attempts to recreate a look of the antebellum American South had been made. Simpson was nervous at the role he was to play in this drama but also a little excited, anticipating the enactment of a new and forbidden fantasy. He stepped out onto the verandah and waited. Thabo, back into his chieftain costume, went to the hut and brought out the captives, naked and loosely tied. They were marched up to the verandah and there they waited, eyeing Simpson curiously even as they kept their heads down.

The three captives stood, their hands loosely tied behind them, and Simpson stepped down off the verandah and walked around them slowly, looking at them, inspecting them. He stopped eight feet in front of Jim. Nodding to Thabo, he said, "I'll examine this one first." Thabo said something in his language and dragged Jim forward. He stood in front of Simpson, head down, eyes furtively glancing at him. Simpson took a deep breath and launched into his role in earnest. He grasped Jim's head in his hands, his fingers in the crisp, crinkly hair, his thumbs on the dark skin of his cheeks. Simpson tilted Jim's head up to look in his eyes; the black man looked aside, avoiding his gaze. Simpson tilted the head back farther and then inserted his fingers through the full, moist lips and into the mouth. Jim gasped, but he was fully into the experience. Simpson pried his mouth open and Jim complied so the white man could see the condition of his teeth.

Was it then that some ancient, ancestral experience began to take hold of Simpson? Or would Jim have done the same out of human nature regardless of history, had their roles been reversed? A spirit of dominance and ownership began to wash over Simpson like a drug. This black man before him became a body, a mass of warm, animated flesh, to be owned and dominated. On that spirit was slavery based, and it began to take hold of Simpson; but submission to it was taking hold of Jim as well.

The white man slid his hands down Jim's thick, athlete's neck, slid along the strong, corded shoulders, thumbs and fingers digging into the muscle to test their strength. Fingers splayed, his palms slid down the massive, rounded curve of the chest, sliding along dark chocolate skin that glistened with sweat, with tiny rivulets of sweat that ran down the rich skin in the hot sun. Simpson slid his white hands down around the slim waist and around the pelvis and tops of the hips of the man, feeling, probing, testing the firm meaty feel of his muscles. Simpson walked behind and ran his palms over the two long hills of muscle on each side of his back, down the narrow valley of the spine that opened up into the high, firm, rounded bubble butt of Africa. Simpson pushed lightly on the back and the man bent forward, his hands still bound behind him, hands riding on the high curve of his buttocks. Simpson spread his butt cheeks, exposing the reddish brown starfish anus, checking for piles.

The slave straightened up as Simpson walked back in front, the lust of slavery now fully on him. Thabo brought forward a simple stool, which Simpson sat on in front of the black man's heavy penis which was now half erect above a heavy, dangling ballsack. Simpson sat on the stool and slid his hands up and down the thick trunks of the slave's muscular thighs, kneading and probing. Now there was but one thing left to inspect. He cupped the heavy ballsack, feeling the warmth and the slight scratchiness of the tiny hairs. His hands slid through the peppercorn patch of hair above his penis and then grasped the organ, which sprang into a full erection, a heavy tube of midnight purple with the lighter brown hood now escaping from the foreskin. Simpson grasped the organ with one hand and began pumping, slowly, squeezing as he pumped, sliding his hand up and down.

The slave's breathing became heavier and his hips began to rock ever so slightly in time to the rhythm of the white man's manipulation of his manhood. Simpson's tanned white fist slid up and down, up and down, faster now. The slave's breathing came faster, heavier, his full lips parted, and then he cried out and thrust his pelvis and shoulders forward, his engorged penis shooting ropes of semen straight up as it was gripped in the white man's hand. Again and then again he bucked forward and pushed, gasping, and then stopped, shuddering, as Simpson's hand slowed, milking the last of the cum which ran down the shaft of the penis, down his white hand, dripping onto the dust.

Simpson rose and wiped his hand on the slave's butt, then nodded at Thabo. Thabo pushed Jim away roughly by the shoulder and, at Simpson's nod, brought John forward. The white man was in a fever of lust now, his own trousers tenting out in front and a wet spot of precum beginning to form. John received the same treatment, at the last his semen shooting out even higher than Jim's and adding to the wet spots in the dust. Finally, Antoine was brought forward, his thin, lightly muscled tube of a body a contrast to the professional athletes before him, his shaft lighter in color and thinner, although as long. When Simpson finished probing and prodding, violating the black man's private spaces with his white hands, he once again grasped the erect cock and pumped it until Antoine spurted. This time, the slave cried out in an ecstasy, shivering beyond his own control, nearly weeping with the power of the orgasm that carried him away. Fully sated, Simpson rose and wiped his hands this time by sliding them up and down the crack of Antoine's butt, then pushed him away as well.

"I'll take all of them," he said, as prearranged, to Thabo. The three men, dicks dangling and still leaking silvery threads of cum, were led back to the hut. There, Simpson knew, the fantasy would end. They would be released and would return to their own modern lodge which stood nearby, there to bathe and get dressed and, after that, come to the main lodge for a celebratory dinner.

Simpson took a deep breath, his own passion subsiding, thinking hard about what had just happened. Would he have done this thing, in fact, two hundred years earlier? Would anyone, or was this peculiarly his heritage as a white American? Did the answers matter if everyone was caught up in the passion of the fantasy and adventure?

Thinking these things, he greeted Thatho and Mthobisi as they crossed the compound, gleefully heading toward the Ball Room. The Swedes were finished with Little Mandla, and had asked for the twins to be ready early; they might even forego the evening meal in their eagerness to catch and fuck the two teen African teen boys in the unworldly atmosphere of that Room. Simpson knew the staff would manage that adventure. He changed his clothing and showered, his underwear a sticky wad of precum, and sat in reflection as the evening shadows came on. Chele came in and greeted him with a squeeze on his shoulder and friendly sounding words, then she began preparing the evening meal.

Thabo came in to report that the slave fantasy was ending and the next Ball Room fantasy well underway. And then there was a knock on the door and in came the three African Americans, fully dressed and, to Simpson's surprise and relief, beaming broadly.

"Man!" said Jim, and then repeated it over and over. "Man, man, man...What a trip! Man that will stay with me a long time. Something to think about, eh?" Simpson looked hard at him and nodded, standing up. "Yes," Simpson replied, "something to think about."

John came up and shook his hand. "You and your staff did it just right, Andrew. Thanks. Now, isn't it happy hour?"

Simpson chuckled and led the men to the bar, Antoine following him with a friendly hand on his shoulder. The men were given full doubles and sat down with looks of tired satisfaction on nearby sofas. Motumbo and Thabo came in and were greeted with friendly cries, drinks were poured for them, and the conversation ran lightly over the high points of the last two days. Simpson still couldn't believe it, but who was he to question?

Over dinner Antoine leaned toward Simpson and said, "Andrew, I think I have a business proposition for you." Simpson looked inquiringly at him. Antoine went on. "This thing we did, it wouldn't be for everybody, but I know, and I'll bet you do also, plenty of guys both black and white back in the States who would want something similar. And what I'm thinking of," he said, and then paused: "What I'm thinking of is going into partnership with you on a subsidiary attraction here: a plantation. Wouldn't be too hard to build one, you have the room, it doesn't have to be complete or authentic, just enough to create the fantasy. I can help finance it. White guys come here to have slaves, black guys come here who want to be a slave for a couple of days. It would draw business. We split the proceeds. What do you think?" Simpson laughed and shook his head; he just couldn't believe it. But he agreed with Antoine, and the two began to lay plans during the rest of the dinner.

At the end of the evening everyone stepped out into the evening air, bidding each other good night and going their separate ways. Motumbo stayed behind, standing by Simpson as they enjoyed the evening air. The big African turned to Simpson and spoke softly.

"Andrew, so, I stay with Chele tonight but—" he paused. "Tomorrow, maybe I come stay with you, huh? Chele know about it, OK with her. Maybe—maybe I miss you, eh Andrew?"

Simpson looked in astonishment at the tall dark man who stood beside him in the moonlight. He smiled and nodded. What was Chele up to? And did it matter? He smiled again.

"Alright, Motumbo. You go make Chele happy. Until tomorrow." They embraced briefly, and then went their separate ways in the night.

- CHAPTER 13 -

At breakfast the next morning, when Simpson walked into the main lodge, Chele smiled with extra brightness at him, it seemed. Passing behind him as she served the dishes, she gave his shoulder a surreptitious squeeze when Thabo wasn't looking. Simpson smiled back, but could not help but wonder what it meant. He had to check his own inclinations: no, still gay, but he had felt unexpected passion for Chele in their frantic bout of sex yesterday. Might he again? Or was his passion connected to the fact that Motumbo had possessed Chele many times, that Simpson's white dick was sliding in and out of the very place where Motumbo's meaty organ had been so many times? Was that a stirring that Simpson felt now in his groin as Chele brushed against him when she passed, as she always took a route that would bring her behind his chair and in contact with him?

After a few moments of this drama Motumbo entered, stretching and yawning, grinning widely. He also embraced Simpson, squeezing him tightly, and sat next to him. Now an erection really did spring up inside the white man's trousers. It did not go away when Chele, passing by again, reached down and meaningfully placed Motumbo's hand on top of Simpson's as it lay on the table. The rest of the meal went in that fashion, Simpson feeling as if he were part of a play, he hoped a comedy, but one that he did not fully understand.

Going out into the morning air, Simpson and Motumbo noted the gathering of heavy clouds on the horizon; it appeared as if a storm were brewing. Fortunately, the Swedes were the only guests for that day. At that moment the door to their lodge opened and Little Mandla stumbled out into the morning, blinking and, it appeared, walking gingerly. Simpson and Motumbo walked up to him and inquired of his health, with some concern. The teenager blushed even through his dark skin and grinned broadly.

"Oh, I OK, yeah. Those two, they make fuck a lot, you know? One at a time, two at a time, all three, all night!" The three men laughed, imagining the orgy that Little Mandla must have been put through; Simpson had seen the start of it the night before as the two Swedes had gotten both their hard dicks inside Little Mandla's aching bottom at the same time inside the Ball Room. But Little Mandla assured them again that he was doing well, and that he had been excused from further service as the Swedes wanted to rest and recuperate their strength for that evening's planned session with the twin teenage boys, Thatho and Mthobisi.

Plans and preparations for future guests occupied the rest of the day. Simpson consulted with his staff over Antoine's offer to build a replica of a Southern U.S. plantation for the more realistic enacting of slave fantasies in the future. Simpson's ingrained squeamishness and distaste for the whole thing was gradually fading in the face of Antoine's promised financial support and the encouragement of both the Africans and African Americans.

The Swedes joined Simpson and the senior staff for dinner, and then prepared for the evening's entertainment. Twilight was deepening as they approached the Ball Room structure, where the twin teenage boys, Thatho and Mthobisi, awaited them with visible excitement and enthusiasm. The Swedes gently embraced the boys, running their hands over their crisp hair as they mounted the steps to the platform outside the door. The boys were out of their clothes in a flash of eagerness, semi-erect brown penises bouncing, and flashing smiles and waves at the Swedes, they were through the door and swimming off into the floating space of the Ball Room. The Swedes slowly disrobed and by the time they were naked it was time for them to go through the door in pursuit of their prey. Simpson and Motumbo, who had escorted the party to the structure, shut the door after them and then slipped around to the observation porthole to watch the fun.

The eighteen year old black twin boys swam through the universe of lightweight plastic balls, brown smudges in the distorted light of the room. After them wallowed the larger cream colored shapes of the adult Swedes. To tell the truth, the boys did not look as if they were especially concerned to escape. They did not split up, but stayed within a couple of yards of each other, and headed toward an upper corner of the room, as if asking to be trapped. The men in pursuit came closer and closer, and when the boys, squealing with glee, wriggled off to one side of the room the men quickly changed course and closed in on them. In a few minutes strong white hands closed around thin brown ankles and the boys, giggling, were hauled in.

Then a scene of exploration, seduction, and passion was played out in duplicate, as Simpson and Motumbo watched from the observation port, their arms hanging around each other's waists. Inside the room, adult white bodies covered slender black teen bodies, softly floating and rolling in the balls. In each pair, a black boy explored again the still unfamiliar colors of the white man who covered him, pushing with their tan palms against hairy chests, tweaking pink nipples with their brown fingers, running those fingers through blonde and brown silky straight hair. Young brown fingers luxuriated in the soft, silky patches of pubic hair and grasped the reddening shafts of the men, so much larger than theirs but still not as large as the boys knew their own rigid black shafts would become in just a few years.

The white men ran their fingers across and through the crisp, crackly caps of wiry hair, enjoying the different texture from their own. Hands ran over smooth deep chocolate skin, hairless except for small tufts of kinky pubic hair, hands running over shiny dark skin, cupping firm, round, protuberant bottoms and sliding along thin but strong thighs. White hands slid over chests with thin pads of muscle, pinching dark maroon brown copper disks of nipples. Thin pink lips closed over luscious full trumpet shaped lips, tongues invaded mouths and ran along teeth, slipped along other tongues, black boy and white man breathing into each other's nostrils as their mouths locked. Rigid pink and rose cocks leaked precum onto slim but slightly rounded black bellies, dribbled precum onto the thin but hard midnight black dicks that pointed straight up from the black boys' loins.

Then each man reached for the tube of lubricant strapped to his ankle, slathering the substance on fingers and over assholes. One, then two fingers pushed into the tight brown starfish as each boy gasped and instinctively pulled his legs apart and up, opening up for the invasion that was to come. Slick fingers slid in and out, the boys moaning now in expectation, and then the fingers were quickly withdrawn and replaced with the swollen head of a pink and rose white cock which was pushed just inside the rectum. The boys gasped and pushed again, up against the heaving white chests above them, tan palms splayed on the hairy chests that hovered over them, but to no avail. The men pushed again, the boys gasped, pushed again, and each boy was completely impaled, his white lover fully inside of him. A moment passed, then the boys looked deeply into the blue eyes above them, smiled, and nodded.

Slowly each man began swinging his hips, in and out, in and out, hands now caressing thin brown shoulders, now sliding around to the back and pulling thin brown bodies close. Teenage arms clasped around broad white backs now as the men pumped harder, harder, faster and faster. Breath now came in rhythm, men and boys breathing together, gasping, men biting shoulders, boys pulling their ravishers down into them, their legs crossed over white backs, brown ankles locked together behind white buttocks that flexed and unflexed as the white men fucked the teenage black boys like pistons. From deep inside their thighs came the tingling, from the base of their guts came the warning wave of sensation, and then each man bucked hard, his abdomen curling as he pushed his penis hard into the black boy's butt and filled it with shot after shot of semen. Groaning and seething, each white man shuddered and bucked, squirting again and again, while each boy held on tight to keep every drop of the precious white fluid within him. Then the crisis passed and each man slumped down onto the boy beneath him, laughing, kissing brown ears and necks and shoulders, catching breath.

The men stayed that way for a few moments and then withdrew, making way to the exit, each one pulling a black boy behind him. They would give the boys pleasure, there was no doubt, but that would come in their own lodge. The four emerged from the door to the Ball Room laughing, the men's penises trailing strings of spent cum, the boys fully erect and giggling. Simpson and Motumbo, sporting full erections beneath their trousers, draped arms around each other's shoulders as they watched the four gather clothes and run off toward their lodge to resume their fucking.

Just in time. For the gathering storm reached the breaking point just as the four reached the door of the lodge, and just as Simpson and Motumbo, who could see the crisis coming, were within a few steps of their own lodge where Motumbo was now to stay for a while, as arranged with Chele. The lightning flashed and the thunder broke, and then the rain came down with appalling force. The men were nearly soaked in just a few steps. Despite the arousal both felt from the scene in the Ball Room, they did not rush right in to bed. They stood on the verandah for a moment watching the heavy rain. Then a wind picked up to drive the rain sideways, and they were forced to duck inside. Still they watched through a window as waves of water splashed against the glass, and the sound of drumming on the roof intensified.

After some minutes of this they decided there was nothing to be done but to go to bed and enjoy their time together while the storm raged. They helped each other off with their soaking clothing which they draped over chairs to dry. They laid a fire in the fireplace and lit it, although the storm was forcing drops down the chimney even past the chimney cap up on the roof. Lighting candles against the likelihood of a power failure, hand in hand they went into the bedroom.

Motumbo and Simpson lay happily on top of the sheets, exploring, kissing, taking their time. Several minutes passed and their arousal had increased when, to their utter annoyance, they heard a heavy pounding on their door. It was a strong enough knocking to be heard over the force of the storm, which was not diminished one bit. Looking at each other in surprise and dismay, they shrugged and Simpson rose, wrapping a towel around his loins, which did nothing to cover his rampant erection which tented out in front of him. He opened the door a crack, admitting water even through so small an opening, to see who it was.

It was Zama, well protected against the weather with rain gear, his well oiled shotgun over his shoulder. In a flash of lightning Simpson caught a sight of Thabo, also wearing rain gear, running down the path behind Zama. Simpson opened the door a bit wider to see what was the mater.

"Boss," rumbled Zama, "visitors, come. Bus. Trouble." Then the big man stepped away and to the edge of the verandah, but stopped looking back at Simpson, gesturing urgently. Utterly at a loss to understand, but sure he was needed, Simpson looked around quickly. He had no adequate rain gear in the lodge. Nevertheless he quickly put on his wet clothes and boots, as did Motumbo who had come up behind him to hear the news, and the two stepped out into the torrential rain in but a moment.

Zama led the way toward a bulky white shape that loomed out of the darkness and veil of rain. It was a small bus, perhaps seating twelve or thirteen, and it stood in the middle of the compound. Its door was opened and Thabo emerged; he had evidently been interviewing its occupants. Seeing Simpson he pushed against the wind and rain to bring the news.

"Boss Andrew, this bus, they be from the Catholic mission, the, uh, the school. They kids, some no parents, eh? And two sisters, how you say, two nuns, one drive. Nine students."

"Why are they here?" bellowed Simpson over the storm. He had never been so wet, he was so wet he could not have been any wetter.

"Storm wash bridge out, road gone maybe quarter of mile on down, Boss. We must call government, tell them to come fix, but they can't go on or back, Boss."

The situation was clear. A bus with young people from the mission orphanage not far from Motumbo and Chele's, Thatho and Mthobisi's village, had been caught in the storm, and the tempest had evidently damaged roads enough so that they were forced to find the nearest shelter they could. Thabo led Simpson back to the bus. Stepping into it and up the few steps seemed like entering a cave of calm and peace compared to the storm outside. Simpson was brought up short by the sight of a stern looking nun sitting behind the wheel, and another stern nun standing in the aisle. Simpson was aware of bright eyes looking out of dark faces behind her.

"Welcome, sister," he said. "You are welcome here. If you and the young people will come out, we will find places for you to stay for the night, or as long as you need."

The grim face of the nun cracked into a smile, and she thanked Simpson in her adequate, accented English. She began issuing instructions to the children behind her in her own language.

"Sister, do you, do they, have luggage, or rain gear?" She shook her head no and explained that they had been on a day trip and were expected to return that night. "Well, you must run for it, then," said Simpson. "How many girls and how many boys do you have, sister?" She replied six girls, three big boys.

He turned to address Thabo and Motumbo. "Motumbo, will you please lead the sisters and the six girls to Chele's lodge? I suppose we can put the boys with us. Thabo, please go with Motumbo and help the sisters to call their orphanage afterwards to say they are safe." Thabo and Motumbo nodded, and at that moment Zama came up with some canvas tarpaulins, all they could find to ward off the storm for so many.

The children were quickly organized and in a rush everyone exited the bus. Tarps were spread, but with children confusion was inevitable. As the sisters and girls headed off toward Chele's beneath one flapping tarp, Simpson corralled the boys under another tarp and headed toward his lodge. Between boyish confusion and the sideways-driving rain, everyone was nearly as soaked when they reached the verandah as they would have been without the tarp. Casting the canvas aside onto the verandah, Simpson opened the door and pushed the boys through, shutting the door behind him against the storm.

Once inside, everyone stopped and caught their breaths. Simpson and the boys looked at one another with curiosity, wonder, or awe. The boys were older than he had thought, about eighteen with the dark healthy skin of youth, two of them rail thin and one a little plump. The boys looked around and then at Simpson in awe, open-mouthed. Although they had surely seen a white man before, they had not seen such a creature this close nor been in his house. The three boys and Simpson stood but a moment and then Simpson noticed that the boys had begun to shiver on account of being soaking wet.

Quickly, Simpson moved toward the bathroom, which contained a tub. He began running a hot bath, testing the water to make sure it would warm without burning. As the tub filled, he returned to the main room where the boys still stood, now with their arms clasped around their chests, all three now shivering from the wet.

"Do you speak English? English?" he asked. The boys looked blankly at him, and then recognition stirred in one of the thin boys. He stepped forward and extended his hand, although it shook from the chill.

"Hello. My name...is Bongani," he said. Clearly, his best Introductory English first lesson. The other boys brightened despite their shivering and each now stepped forward to repeat the ritual. "Hello. My name is Khulekani" said the other thin boy. "Hello. My name is Bheka" said the chunky boy. Simpson was charmed and, bowing deeply, said, "Hello. My name is Andrew." The boys whispered his name in response, shy smiles breaking their handsome dark faces, their eyes shifting between this strange man and their fellows.

Then it occurred to Simpson: Thatho and Mthobisi had attended this school. He asked the boys whether they knew the twins. Three brown faces lit up in astonishment. Yes, they had attended and had just graduated, leaving to rejoin their families.

At that point Simpson shook himself and gestured toward the bathroom. "Come, take a bath, warm up, get out of those wet clothes." He had no hope that he was precisely understood, the boys obviously having learned only the most rudimentary English phrases, but he managed to convey his meaning. The first boy peeked inside the bathroom and saw what was planned. He spoke quickly to the other boys in their language and then began taking off his clothes. The others followed his lead, looking embarrassed in Simpson's presence for but a moment, and in a flash all three boys were in the bathroom, taking turns stepping into the steaming tub. Simpson let the water run a bit more as he gathered the boys' soaking wet clothing and spread it out on furniture to dry. He stepped into the bathroom and turned the water off, then paused for a moment to survey the scene. The three boys were small by American standards, seeming younger than their eighteen years, as did Thatho and Mthobisi, their skin dark and flawless and completely hairless except for the thin tight caps of kinky hair on their heads and tufts above their penises. Thin, long penises with tassels of foreskin bobbed above full ballsacks holding ripening testicles that now relaxed somewhat in the warm water. The boys sank down gratefully into the warmth first one and then two at a time, for once curbing their youthful rambunctiousness in favor of warming up, slithering naked together in the water. Simpson nodded and stepped out, in time to greet Motumbo who was coming through the door ahead of a wave or rain, as wet as he could possibly be.

Motumbo brought news that the female visitors were settled in Chele's cabin, that the school had been notified, and that there was nothing to do until the storm abated and the roads could be assessed and repaired. Simpson nodded and took Motumbo to the bathroom, where he chuckled at the sight of a bathroom full of naked brown boys. But youthful energy could not long be contained, and horseplay had begun. Motumbo spoke softly to them in their own language and the boys began coming out of the bathroom. Motumbo tossed a towel quickly to Simpson and grabbed one himself. The chubby boy, Bheka, came into the room and presented himself to be wrapped in a towel held by Simpson. The man quickly patted the boy dry but kept the towel around him like a cape. Bongani came into the main room with a towel similarly draped around him, as Motumbo was finishing up with Khulekani. The whole process had taken but a moment.

For a few seconds everyone stood around in the main room, and then Simpson noticed Bongani eyeing the bowl of fruit that stood on a table. Realizing that they may not have eaten for some hours, Simpson offered the bowl to the boys, who fell on it like locusts on the wheat, greedily consuming every piece there was to the satisfaction of the men.

As the boys were eating, Motumbo and Simpson suddenly realized that they were soaked through, and were beginning to feel chilled. Wordlessly, with a nod, they each began disrobing and hanging up their clothing on remaining pieces of furniture to dry. The three teen boys stopped in mid-bite, each holding a piece of fruit, their eyes wide as they observed the spectacle. Every eye turned to Simpson as he removed his last piece of clothing and stood naked before them. If they had seen few white men so close up before, the boys had surely never seen a naked white man in person before. Wide eyes traveled up and down his body, stopping in fascination as they viewed his genitals. Motumbo, now fully naked as well, chuckled in amusement at the spectacle. Simpson could not repress a blush at being the object of inspection, but decided that the only thing to do was to press ahead naturally. At Motumbo's chuckle the boys' attention was diverted and they now stared at him as well, an image of the powerful African men they would become soon, and his heavy genitalia now received its share of attention. Now openly laughing, Motumbo spoke to them in their own language, translating for Simpson: "I say, time for sleep."

Two of the boys returned quickly to the bathroom to urinate. Motumbo and Simpson consulted quickly and decided that putting the boys on the two sofas in the living room was the only option. Extra blankets were spread. Each boy handed his towel to one of the men and, long penises bobbing, squirmed in naked together on the sofa, chunky Bheka taking one, Bongani and Khulekani taking the other. The eighteen year old boys looked extra hard at the naked adults as the men came close to tuck them in, Motumbo wishing them good night and instructing them to fall right asleep. Lights were lowered, towels hung to dry, and the men slipped into the bedroom.

Snuggling together beneath the sheets to keep warm, the men simply held each other for a few minutes, relaxing from the evening's drama. Snuggles gave way to caresses, and then kisses, each enjoying this reunion and anticipating the sexual passion that was in store for the evening. Slowly the momentum built and the sexual tension grew. Warm enough now, Motumbo threw off the sheets and blanket and rolled over on top of Simpson, grinding his massive cock down into the white man's groin, enveloping Simpson's mouth with his full, rounded lips. Then he switched directions and lying head to toe on top of Simpson he took the white man's rigid purple rod into his mouth while dangling his heavy, meaty, midnight black cock down into Simpson's willing mouth. Slowly, carefully, passionately, the two men licked and sucked each other's organs in that way for several minutes.

Simpson was so preoccupied that he heard no sounds coming from the bedroom door, which had been left partially open. But he did hear Motumbo's muffled murmur of surprise, and he was definitely aware as Motumbo let his throbbing cock slip from his mouth to utter an exclamation. Turning away from the black man's massive dick, Simpson looked around to see what was the matter. Then he heard the giggling from the doorway. All three of the guest teen boys stood there. They had been watching. Their long penises were stiff with excitement.

Motumbo heaved a deep sigh and muttered what must have been a curse in his language. Swinging back around, he flopped back down onto the bed lying alongside Simpson, both men's rods stiff and slapping on their thighs. The boys took this move as some sort of invitation. Chattering suddenly in their language, they piled onto the bed, squirming brown bodies taking up all the available empty space. Motumbo, caught between exasperation and amusement, translated for Simpson the boys' story that the storm had kept them awake, that they were frightened, and they wanted comfort. Simpson looked at their tense rampant cocks and wondered if that were the whole story.

Chunky Bheka had settled in between the two men, sitting crosslegged between their groins, facing the men, a grinning eighteen year old Buddha with a rampant brown cock. Simpson was clearly the attraction, his skin color and hair, the distribution of hair on his torso, even his eyes and lips, all being objects of wonder. Bongani sat between Simpson's legs just below his crotch for a close view of his balls and cock. Khulekani stretched out by Simpson's side, away from Motumbo, and snuggled in close, giggling as he ran his hands on the white man's skin and through his hair, his own stiff brown tube poking the white man's side.

Bheka reached over and seized Motumbo's huge, meaty organ and swung it toward Simpson, stroking it slowly, grinning, while he watched intently as Bongani softly fingered the white man's testicles, covered with fine blonde hair, and weighed his heavy scrotum. Khulekani ran his thin brown hand up and down Simpson's abdomen, pulling gently on the few hairs on his chest and belly, running his fingers through the thatch of dirty blonde pubic hair. Bongani bent over and, grasping Simpson's dick, took the head of it in his mouth, experimentally. Sucking, swallowing a little clear precum, he looked up and grinned, a line of clear fluid trailing from his full lower lip to the head of the white man's dick. Bheka leaned over and took the white man's dick in his mouth in his turn, while his stroking of Motumbo's thick black rod increased. Simpson, for his part, reached down to grasp Bheka's stiff black rod with thumb and the first two fingers and began manipulating it, sliding his fingers up and down the hard brown shaft. With his other hand he kneaded the firm ass cheeks of Khulekani, describing small circles around the boy's anus with his index finger. Khulekani sighed and pressed into the white man's side even closer, now licking and tasting his light colored salty skin, pressing his full lips onto the white man's chest and abdomen, biting gently with his pearly teeth.

Motumbo reached over across Simpson's thigh, able just barely to reach Bongani's stiff black cock as he sat between Simpson's thighs, alternately pumping the white man's cock when Bheka sucked it, and sucking it himself. Then in a moment the boys shifted, Bheka throwing himself forward to lie atop Simpson, grinding his rigid ebony dick into the white man's abdomen, nibbling the white man's nipples with his full rounded lips. Bongani took over the duty of pumping Motumbo as he stretched out between the two men, now kissing and licking Motumbo's deep brown chest and now Simpson's heaving cream colored torso. Khulekani stayed where he was but was now pushed his pelvis back and forth, back and forth, as Simpson had grasped the boy's stiff tool with his fingers and was pumping it vigorously.

Bheka had pushed himself off of Simpson and slid down over the white man's dick, slid down far enough to take it into his mouth, when Motumbo cried out, arching his back and pushing his hips up. Bongani, who had been pumping the African man's heavy meat all this time, slapped the organ over to the side as it began spewing cum, so that it sprayed all over Simpson's belly and chest.

155

Bheka sucked the white man's rod furiously, his plump cheeks sunken in as he created a tremendous vacuum. Then Khulekani shuddered and pushed, crying out, as the white man's fingers brought a surprisingly voluminous orgasm to his thick brown cock. Simpson moaned deeply and pushed his pelvis up into Bheka's mouth; the chubby eighteen year old boy's eyes grew wide but he held on for dear life as an explosion of semen shot up and into his mouth. The boy swallowed as hard as he could, but choked and coughed, expelling a little white pellet of cum from his nose.

It was the start of a long night of pleasure, of writhing brown boys in the arms of the strong older black and white males. Bheka's chubby, rounded brown bottom was invaded by fingers, Bongani's stiff rigid cock was taken into the white man's mouth until he shuddered in a spewing orgasm, Mutombo rolled over onto Simpson, sandwiching a boy and a half between them, Khulekani slid up to put his stiff brown cock into Simpson's mouth and pump it until he shuddered once more...and on through the night. In the small dark hours the five males feel asleep, exhausted, in a tangle of brown and cream, snuggled together like worms for warmth, drifting off into peaceful sleep as the storm outside raged and roared.

- CHAPTER 14 -

Andrew Simpson floated into wakefulness in a nest of warm bodies. Simpson was wedged in tight next to the muscular body of Motumbo, who lay on his belly, lightly snoring. Young Bongani lay on Simpson's other side, while Bheka and Khulekani were entwined on the other side of Motumbo. The storm evidently continued, raising a steady drumming on the roof of the lodge, but the violence of the wind seemed to have settled down.

Simpson smiled remembering the half night of pleasure given and taken with the teen boys, unexpected castaways from the storm. The thought of the tangle of brown limbs around him, the smooth chocolate chests and bellies, made him smile. But then, half turning toward Motumbo and putting an arm around his broad, muscular back, Simpson was seized by another and more powerful erotic urge. Playing with eighteen year old boys had its place. But in that moment, even after a night of coupling, he felt the urge to make love to his strong African lover, to possess the dark chocolate body that lay next to him. As Simpson softly slid his hand over Motumbo's strong shoulders, the contrast between his light and the African's dark skin was beautiful to him, and powerfully sexual. His penis, despite the demands made on it over the last hours, sprang into life, slapping softly against Motumbo's thigh.

The African must have sensed it. His head turned toward Simpson, an eye opened then closed, a smile spread across his face and a low, contented purr rumbled in his chest. A wave of love and longing swept over Simpson, a wave of relief that Motumbo was here in his bed, not in Chele's. Reaching back over the still sleeping Bongani, Simpson grabbed a tube of lubricant from the bedside table and squirted out a gob on his fingers. His breath beginning to come more quickly, Simpson applied the goo to the bottom of the valley between Motumbo's rounded butt, pushing a finger slightly into the puckered anus. Motumbo smiled and sighed, his eyes still closed.

Simpson wiped his fingers on his own cock which was now fully erect, swirling around the head, mixing lubricant with the precum that leaked from it. Then he swung himself over on top of Motumbo, whose legs parted slightly. Simpson placed the slick, blushing helmet head of his dick against the black man's anus and pushed. There was resistance, then a plop as it entered, then a long slide forward. Simpson settled himself flat on the African's broad back, his iron rod completely inside Motumbo's ass, and wrapped his arms around the chest and shoulders of his lover. His quick movement in mounting the black man woke the boys, who sat up in bed, rubbing their eyes sleepily, orienting themselves to the strange surroundings, and discovering to their surprise that the two men between them were fucking.

Two hundred yards away, Thatho and Mthobisi, the eighteen year old African twin boys who were that day's "prize" for the two Swedish men, woke up first. Each sat halfway up in the large bed. In between them the two men slept still, lying on their bellies, pleasantly tired from their night of fucking the boys' butts. Thatho and Mthobisi looked at the sleeping white men between them, then at each other and grinned. Simultaneously, each also looked at the other's groin, each discovering a growing erection. Wordlessly, they seemed to agree on how the morning would start: with a reversal of roles. Thatho grabbed a tube of lubricant and squirted a liberal amount onto his fingers, then tossed it over to Mthobisi, who did the same. Both boys slathered up their young teen cocks, already fully erect, seeming outsized for their skinny bodies, tan cockheads pushing out from the midnight dark foreskin now. Then each boy reached over to rub lubricant onto the men's anuses. The men awoke with a start, instantly realized what was happening, and settled back down with a smile and a sense of resignation. Too tired to manage what was about to happen, they were pleased to let the boys take over.

Each of the boys, fully erect, now swung over on top of the man nearest him and placed the swollen tan cockheads of their dicks against the men's pink anuses. The Swedes grunted as the dicks entered, then gasped as the boys slid all the way in. The boys held themselves up off the men's backs, tan palms flattened against the sheets, so as to see what they were about to do. The boys' brown shoulders and knees rubbed against each other on one side as they began moving in and out, in and out, of the white men who lay beneath them.

Meanwhile, Simpson held Motumbo tightly, pulling his body down into the dark chocolate, meaty body below him. A surprisingly fierce wave of possession began to build in him. Days of frustration at Chele's possession of Motumbo in her bed were his target; Simpson was going to make the African his own. His own muscular body covered the African completely, his hips now pounding back and forth, his pelvis bouncing up and down on the muscular rounded hill of the African's buttocks, a steady and powerful rhythm that became a slamming as he fucked the black's butt as hard as he could. The boys who surrounded them now all sat up in bed, their own ebony dicks stiff at the spectacle of the white man fucking the black man hard. The boys shifted position to see, some looking back behind Simpson to get a better view of his pink and purple rod plunging in and out of Motumbo's hard brown cheeks. But beyond softly stroking their own stiff black rods, they did not touch, sensing that something special was happening between the two men. Simpson continued to fuck with concentrated attention, pistoning powerfully in and out of the African's body who lay beneath him.

For Mthobisi and Thatho, it was a fuck of joy. Having been pounded in different positions and combinations all night, their turn had come, and the grinning, moaning white men beneath them seemed willing to give them that chance. The boys could not look enough, could not take enough in with their eyes, of the sight they were creating. Their thin but muscular bodies were tense and tight, stiff as boards as they held themselves up off of the expanse of pink and white shoulders, backs, and buttocks beneath them. The boys saw their hard teenage dicks, oversized for their young bodies, sliding in and out of the white bottoms beneath them, saw the thick midnight black shafts appear and disappear as they bounced up and down, in and out. The teen boys giggled in between ragged breaths in their joy of the possession and control of the white men they fucked.

And then Andrew Simpson cried out, a wave of ecstasy overtaking him, pounding pushing, bucking forward, squeezing Motumbo as if he would break his chest, shooting jets of cum and love into his ass, roaring and gasping for breath. The three brown boys on the bed with them jumped back in astonishment at the power of the orgasm they were experiencing. And at the same time, Thatho and Mthobisi, laughing and crying "O!" "O!" as the realization came upon them, gurgled and shouted with glee as they pushed forward, squeezing their buttocks together hard to push out their boy cum into the men beneath them, laughing and shouting with joy as their finished their fuck of the two Swedes. In both lodges, two boys and a man collapsed on top of the men they had fucked, sighing, breathing hard, draining the last of their sperm downward. Around Simpson, the boys smiled grandly at one another at the triumph they had just observed, and craned around again to see how Simpson's purple rod was lodged tight in Motumbo's leaking anus.

Motumbo chuckled deep in his chest and, disentangling his arms from Simpson's, shouted "shoo!" in their language to the boys, who gleefully scattered. Simpson pulled off of him and the two lay together on the bed, kissing affectionately, but there was to be no further sex with a gang of rowdy eighteen year old boys frolicking around the room. The two men rose and showered, observed and commented upon all the time by the boys who scampered around, penises either flopping or springing up into momentary states of erection.

The men dressed quickly in dry clothes. Their clothes from the day before had not yet quite dried, nor had the boys', so the young ones would have to remain naked a few hours more. The men stoked the fire and hung the boys' garments more carefully to dry. There was a knock at the door, which Motumbo answered. It was Thabo, well covered with rain gear. A truck idled behind him in the roadway. He shoved two large covered plastic tubs in through the door, smiled and winked, and closed the door again to keep out the rain. The tubs were full of food; it was clear that Thabo was delivering provisions to each of the occupied lodges so that the inhabitants could ride out the storm in comfort. The men and boys fell on the provisions with glee, all gathered around the breakfast table. The boys seemed completely unconcerned for their own nakedness, and Simpson gave himself over to enjoyment of the moment, squeezing arms, rubbing buttocks and bellies, giving hugs from behind, sliding his hands affectionately over the boys' healthy brown skin whenever he could.

160

Toward afternoon the storm began to subside. Simpson found that he could reach Thabo by cell phone as the bad weather broke. Authorities had been alerted as to the damage to the road, and there was some expectation that at least temporary repairs could be made the next day, a surprisingly fast response by the government. However, the economic contribution that DeGroot's made, and the spiritual standing of the mission bus, probably gave some officials a sense of urgency. In the meantime, it was determined that the road in the direction of the airport was relatively sound. Discussion with the Swedes resulted in a plan for Thabo to take them to the airport, as their schedules required their departure, however reluctant they might have been. The two men bade affectionate goodbyes to Little Mandla and to Thatho and Mthobisi, then loaded Thabo's vehicle in the continuing light rain. Waving wistfully, they drove off into the afternoon to return home.

Simpson worked on the plans for a "slave plantation" as much as he could by telephone and in consultation with Motumbo. He continued to marvel to himself at the enthusiasm shown by the Africans and African Americans for the project, and he fully realized that it would hardly be everyone's cup of tea, but he had also come to terms with the idea that his history and reservations might not be shared by everyone.

The boys' clothes dried, but there seemed little point in dressing. Night was drawing on once again, there was plenty of food, the rain was coming to an end, and the lodge was snug and dry. Simpson wrapped up his work and joined Motumbo on a couch, surrounded by naked boys who squirmed and snuggled around them, and listened to the radio which crackled and sputtered in the interference from the subsiding storm. Eventually, it was time for bed. Motumbo and Simpson insisted that the boys spend the night on the couches, where they had started out the previous evening. The two men retired to their own room and enjoyed a mellow night of cuddling, soft stroking, and slow, slow sex. But out on the sofa, the boys took turns enacting the scenes they had observed between the two men, the two slimmer boys fucking the chubby Bheka and Bheka being sucked in turn throughout the night until they fell asleep by the dwindling firelight.

The next morning the boys dressed, anticipating a visit by the nuns. Sure enough, the rain having ceased, the sisters came by to inspect their charges. Men and boys were fully dressed and received the nuns graciously. In another couple of hours word was received that temporary repairs had rendered the road passable, so they began to take their leave. The men hugged the boys, and were hugged in turn affectionately. Motumbo told the sisters that they would visit the orphanage, and that the students could return to visit any time, a proposition that was greeted with enthusiasm by the sisters as well as the young people. In the humid air, the bus trundled off in the direction of the road, sending splatters of mud up behind it, thin brown arms sticking out of windows and waving madly.

A process of cleanup after the storm began, debris having accumulated here and there, some soil having been washed away. There were also the lodges to clean up, Simpson and Motumbo's, and Chele's, from the unexpected visitors, the Swedes' from their sex-soaked stay. Piles of laundry were hauled up to the main lodge, bags of trash were taken to the incinerator. Simpson had taken a sack of trash to be burned behind the main lodge, when a movement near Chele's lodge caught his eye. Turning quickly, he caught sight of Motumbo slipping into the back door. Curious, but also thinking he might lend a hand to cleanup efforts there, Simpson walked quietly over to the lodge. Passing a window, he glanced in and saw Motumbo and Chele embracing, the big African man kissing her passionately.

It shouldn't have come as a shock to him. He knew the two had been a couple for some time, and Motumbo had only recently returned to his bed from Chele's. But a wave of sorrow, resentment, even anger washed over him. Simpson made sure to create some noise as he approached the door, which he rapped loudly. There was a quick scuffle inside and Motumbo opened the door, a big forced smile on his face. Simpson offered a forced smile back at him.

"Can I help? Is there anything more to do here?" he asked with a false tone of bravado.

"Oh, Andrew, just cleaning, just picking up. I, uh, I just picking up this sack," he said, wheeling around and reaching for the closest sack he could find, full of laundry. Behind him Chele stepped into view, smiling broadly at Simpson and waving a small wave with her hand. Simpson smiled back. How did he feel about her? He did not even know. Resentment, yes, but in some deep part of himself he felt he blamed Motumbo more than he blamed the woman for the continuing attraction between them. And yet, how could he object to it; it was an attraction that was there before he and Motumbo had ever met. One twisted emotion after another warred within Simpson as Motumbo, with an embarrassed look on his face, scuttled out of the lodge and up the path to the main lodge.

There was a moment of empty silence between Chele and Simpson. He simply didn't know what to do. Talking to her was out of the question, as they shared no verbal language. He looked at her, unable to see or to show any humor in the situation because of the turmoil in his heart, and he simply shrugged. Sensing what his feelings might be, Chele walked up to him and spoke softly to him in her language, laying her hand softly on his arm.

It happened again as it had a few days before. Chele was beautiful, but Simpson was not attracted to her per se. Had they met in Philadelphia, at a bar, he would have been cordial but uninterested. But she had a claim on his man, she had taken Motumbo inside of her again and again, and sheer jealousy somehow combined with lust and opportunity. Simpson took the woman in his arms, and she went willingly. Then she tugged him a few steps to a nearby sofa, and falling on it she pulled him down on top of her. Simpson simply unzipped his pants and entered her, not violently but with a passion of complete possession, and fucked her rapidly, coming hard and quickly as she slid her hands up his shirt which he still wore. It was over in but a moment. Simpson hung over her, holding himself up off of her, breathing hard, draining his cum down into her, while she continued to stroke his chest and belly, murmuring softly to him. He couldn't meet her eyes. Pulling out as he felt his rod begin to soften, he adjusted his clothing quickly. Then, more from a sense of duty than anything else, he placed his palm on her cheek, smiled, and slipped quickly from the lodge.

Preoccupied, Simpson trudged up the path to the main lodge. He prayed that Motumbo would not smell the scent of his own woman on him. There he found that Thabo had returned from taking the Swedes to the airport, having made a side trip to pick up supplies as well. Simpson helped Thabo and Motumbo carry supplies in from the vehicle and store them, forcing light banter with the two men, trying to resolve his confusion. Grain here, meat there, water on these shelves, it was a work that helped to smooth out his tangled feelings.

As the stores were carried into the pantry room of the main lodge, Thabo tossed a package to Motumbo. Simpson clearly saw what they were: condoms. He arched his brows in surprise and stared at the package in Motumbo's hands. Condoms were hardly ever used at DeGroot's, for anyone who came there to stay for any length of time underwent extensive and repeated medical testing to ensure that they had no communicable diseases, and so had Motumbo and Chele. Motumbo, with some embarrassment, chuckled and hefted the package in his hands.

"No babies, eh Andrew? I not ready yet," then winked at Simpson and tucked the condoms away in a pocket. Simpson could not help but continue to stare. Realization hit him like a brick. The condoms were not prophylactic, they were contraceptive. Motumbo did not yet want a child, and yet...and yet, twice Simpson had had unprotected sex with Chele. He didn't want to think about the implications, but he couldn't help it. Had he known he might impregnate Motumbo's woman all along, in some deep and secret room of his mind? Of course, he had no idea whether such a thing had happened at all. It probably had not...only twice, after all. He shook his head, trying to clear the confusion, and continued the business of emptying the vehicle.

Over dinner, Motumbo seemed to show extra attention to Simpson, perhaps sensing some tension related to being discovered in an embrace with Chele. Chele, who cooked and served the dinner, was friendly to both men, betraying no special favoritism. Maybe it was the friendly atmosphere, or a couple of cocktails, or the physical work of the day, but Simpson slowly settled back into balance, slowly reconciled himself again to the impossible triangle he seemed to have become entangled in. After dinner and conversation, Chele gave Motumbo a peck on the cheek and Simpson an affectionate squeeze and sent them off into the night as she finished tidying up.

Walking through the moonlight back to their lodge, Motumbo squeezed Simpson's hand and held it, arms swinging lightly as they walked like a couple of schoolchildren. Inside the lodge, peaceful for once after the boys' visit, the men embraced, holding each other tightly. They showered together, washing off the soil of the day as they slid hands over soap-slicked bodies in the warm water, kissing in the rain from the shower head. When they slipped into the bedroom, Simpson decided that it was Motumbo's turn to be pleasured, having cum not long ago inside of Chele.

Simpson slid from a tight embrace with Motumbo down to his knees, kissing and licking as he went, sliding his tongue over the smooth, hairless, hard surfaces of the African's brown skin that shown like polished old wood in the lamplight. Simpson nibbled nipples and tongued the African's navel as he went, nuzzling the tuft of crisp pubic hair and, finally settling on the floor, gently cupped the heavy, wrinkled, purple black ballsack. Holding the heavy penis to one side, Simpson took the scrotum into his mouth one testicle at a time, gently rolling it in his mouth and sucking ever so lightly as Motumbo moaned and sighed, running his dark fingers through Simpson's light hair. Then Simpson pushed back a little and stroked the now erect shaft, lined with thick veins, and then took the lighter tan cockhead into his mouth, the cockhead that had emerged from the purple black foreskin. Simpson took as much of the African dick into his mouth as he could; taking it all would be impossible. And then he set up a steady rhythm of sucking and licking while with his hand he slowly pumped the thick, throbbing shaft that would not fit into his mouth. Simpson's free hand ran over the thick thighs, like tree trunks, of the African, then slid around to knead the firm, round, high rolling buttocks.

Motumbo's moaning increased as Simpson's sucking grew harder and faster, his tongue caressing the tender underside of the flared cockhead, his lips sliding up and down the rigid black dick. Then Simpson felt a trembling in the man's thighs, heard a whine and an "O, O, Boss!" from the African, and then Motumbo groaned loudly, pushing his groin forward, and Simpson took the first wave of the thick white cum. Sucking and swallowing, he got all of it down as Motumbo, tacked to the white man's mouth, groaned, bucked, and shivered in his orgasm.

As the two curled into bed together, exhaustion overcame them. For Simpson, all thoughts of Chele had gone, at least for the moment. He held his African lover tightly to him, sliding his hands slowly, very slowly over the warm smooth skin, feeling the texture of the crisp hair, and floated off to sleep on a cloud of contentment.

- CHAPTER 15 -

In the following month, activity picked up considerably on Antoine's offer to sponsor the construction of an old Southern plantation house so that more realistic enactments of slavery fantasies could be done at De Groot's. Andrew Simpson was beyond objecting, although he still harbored reservations. But the staff seemed fully into the planning process and anticipating the added income that the new attraction would bring. Andrew could only shrug in wonder and go along with the plans. Within two weeks, prefabricated building parts were being shipped in and laborers were gathering in a small village of tents to construct the new attraction. Work proceeded into the evening, when the workers would stop and sounds of partying could be heard from their end of the enclosure.

Andrew's thoughts remained conflicted and entangled with Motumbo and Chele through that month. He still wondered what it had meant that Chele had accepted the two quick bouts of intercourse with him without a condom. He wondered what it meant that he, confirmed gay guy that he was, had agreed to that sex—no doubt it was the connection to Motumbo, to being in a vagina that the big African man had been in, that was the attraction for Simpson. And although he told himself to stop it, he still had a twinge of jealous regret every time Motumbo and Chele smiled at each other, every time one ran a hand up and down the other's arm. As it came Simpson's turn to fuck his muscular African lover each night, an edge of frustration and jealousy gave extra power to each pounding of his dick inside Motumbo's butt.

Toward the end of that month it became clear that the plantation structure, being prefabricated as it was, would be completed soon. Simpson was busy online ordering decorations for the interior that might create the illusion of a nineteenth century Southern American slave plantation manor. He was also busy advertising the new attraction, and he wondered what kind of clientele it would attract. Simpson realized that if it attracted Black men who wanted to enact the roles of slaves, then he, as the only White man in residence, would end up taking on the "duty" of slavemaster. He began to realize that the idea excited him, although if very many clients chose that option at once he would have to "delegate" some of his duties to his African assistants or suffer exhaustion.

Somewhat to his surprise, reservations began coming in immediately for the new plantation fantasy, even while there was no slacking of interest in the other adventures offered such as the hunts or the Ball Room. The first reservation was for a white man from America who wanted to bring his eighteen year old teenage son, also gay, with him. They wanted to come in only seven weeks' time. Simpson, seeing requests for later plantation fantasies stack up, accepted the reservation. He announced the start of the new attraction to the staff over lunch one day, to general excitement. Everyone was eager to begin planning how such a fantasy might be played out. Envious of the parties that the laborers had for themselves at the other end of the camp after each day of hard work on the plantation building, Simpson declared that the permanent staff would have a party that very evening to celebrate the new attraction and to talk about how to conduct it.

That evening all the permanent staff gathered at the main lodge for a cookout, with plenty to drink. Big and Little Mandla were there, Thabo, Motumbo and Chele, the young teen boys Thatho and Mthobisi, Strello—and a few others such as Justice and Gift, who came and went for short periods of time. Even Zama appeared, a brief grin breaking across his serious, dark face, to eat a quick sandwich and have one drink before hoisting his shotgun and disappearing back into the night.

The party wore on as such affairs do, with more and more to drink. And given the nature of De Groot's, there was plenty of light stroking, playful kisses, loose embraces among all. Yet it seemed to Andrew that the more everyone drank, the more Motumbo and Chele flirted, despite the fact that Motumbo was, at least for the time being, with Andrew in their cabin. Andrew was dimly aware of being annoyed at their flirtation, but he found himself equally occupied with the increasing attentions of the two young teenage brothers, Thatho and Mthobisi. The eighteen year old boys were unused to even the small amounts of alcohol they were drinking, and were slipping into a quiet, joyful sloppiness, snuggling next to Andrew, leaning and cuddling with him, letting their slim brown arms entwine around him. He had to admit he was enjoying it, and wondered how he could justify that pleasure yet remain irritated at Motumbo for his dalliance with Chele. Simpson watched Motumbo and Chele become more and more intimate the more they drank, until eventually they both rose and, hand in had and with no glance or word to Simpson, the couple staggered out into the night. Well, Simpson said to himself, they have gone back to Chele's cabin to fuck themselves silly. He shook himself, trying to dispel the dull pain of jealous irritation that had settled in him, and turned his attention now fully to the two brown boys who lolled next to and on top of him, giggling softly in their alcoholic buzzes. Another ten minutes passed and Simpson's passion began to arise more and more. Finally he rose and gently took each boy by the hand. Nodding back at Thabo, who winked and nodded back, Simpson led the two boys out of the main lodge and down the path to his own lodge.

Simpson had his hand on the knob of the front door to open it when he heard sounds coming from within. He stopped abruptly, and signaled to the two giggling boys for silence. Simpson opened the door slowly, and could now hear the sounds more distinctly, coming from his own bedroom. He stepped very quietly in that direction and slipped in past the open door. The two boys, suppressing their giggles for the moment, were right behind him, walking softly.

His eyes adjusted to the dim light quickly and Simpson gasped at what he saw. On his own bed, the one he woke up in that morning with Motumbo, he saw the big African man lying on top of Chele, fucking her with long, slow swings of his thick rod. In the dim light of a single candle he could see the dark brown skin of the African gleam softly, a thin sheen of sweat highlighting the movement of muscles beneath. Motumbo's muscular bottom, a shade darker than the rest of his dark skin, rolled rhythmically, the tops of the buttocks rising into rolls and the sides dimpling as he pushed his stiff, purple black penis into the woman beneath him, the muscular bottom relaxing as he pulled partially back out. Chele's brown arms clutched at Motumbo's broad back and muscular shoulders, while the African man's head was down, nuzzling at her neck and ears as he fucked her slowly.

Simpson quickly got over the shock of this spectacle, and he made an impulsive decision. As quietly as he could he tore off his clothes. Behind him, Thatho and Mthobisi watched open-mouthed at the drama that was unfolding among these adults. Simpson took but three steps to scoop up the tube of lubricant from the bedside table, which he used to quickly oil up his rising pink and purple rod. Chele saw the movement and heard the noise first, and gasped, then giggled. Motumbo, deep into drunkenness, brought his head up in confusion and looked around, trying to focus, even as he continued to swing his pelvis back and forth. It was only as Simpson climbed up onto the bed that Motumbo grunted, shaking his head, and seemed to make an effort to rise. It registered with Simpson that Chele at that point held Motumbo tightly to her, and giggled again. It was clear the woman had a sense of what was about to happen, and planned to enjoy it.

Swinging up over Motumbo, Simpson sank his thighs down in between the African man's thighs, which were in their turn between Chele's thighs held wide apart. In a flash Simpson positioned his now iron hard cock at the African's wrinkled dark brown anus and pushed. Unprepared and still a bit confused, Motumbo cried out, but with Chele pulling him down onto her torso and the weight of Simpson above him plus his own incapacity, there was little he could do. The big African man cried out again as the white man's dick slid quickly inside his tight, unprepared rectum, slid all the way in with one mighty push. Simpson landed hard on top of Motumbo, his dick fully inside the black man's ass, his chest now riding the back and shoulders of the muscular stud beneath him, his face positioned to nuzzle the crispy hairs and the velvet skinned neck of his lover. His arms joined in the tangle of the African man and woman beneath him, stroking and fondling, rubbing over warm skin.

Simpson pulled partially out and then back again with a tremendous lunge, and Motumbo gasped again. Then the white man did it again, and Chele whispered something to the African. Now dimly grasping, in his intoxication, what was required, and surrending himself to it, Motumbo began to pump in and out of Chele again, and Simpson adjusted his own fucking of the black man's butt to that rhythm. Motumbo picked up the pace, plunging down into the woman below him, while Simpson matched him stroke for stroke, pulling back as Motumbo pushed forward, slamming down to meet the hard, rising buttocks on their upstroke. Motumbo, pulled close into Chele, softly chewed her shoulder while Simpson looked over Motumbo's other, sweating shoulder directly into her eyes a few inches below, penetrated her eyes as he was penetrating her man's ass, looked into her eyes as he gasped and drooled over Motumbo's heaving shoulder. Up and down, in and out, both men fucked harder and harder until Motumbo, who had a head start, came, crying out, his body twisting into a curl as he pushed down deeply into Chele, shooting his semen into her. He lay there tense and quivering, jetting more of his white spunk into her as Simpson's iron rod pounded his prostate gland from inside, and then it was Simpson's turn to cry out as a wave of sex broke within him and he pushed down hard into the African man's bottom, shooting his semen into Motumbo, gasping and panting as his man juices drained out.

For long moments they lay like that, quivering, panting, breath returning to normal, and then Simpson pulled out of Motumbo's bottom with a plop and sat on his haunches as the end of the bed. Motumbo did not move. Chele pushed him up and off, turning a bit as she did so, and he flopped, snoring heavily to one side. He had simply fallen asleep or passed out in his drunkenness. Simpson noticed in one swift glance that he was not wearing a condom.

Simpson sat there on his haunches for a moment, looking at Chele's sweat slicked body in the dim light, looked at the thin sheen of fluid dribbling from her vagina. Then a noise to the side reminded him of the boys who had come with him, the young teen boys he had planned to have in this very bed tonight. Thatho and Mthobisi stood but a few feet away, naked now, and each slowly pumping and fondling his own fully erect young cock, each organ seeming too big for the skinny brown body. Simpson wondered whether the boys had ever had sex with a female, even if they had reached eighteen. He decided instantly that they would do so that very night. Simpson quickly motioned them over and seizing the nearest one, Thatho, he pulled the boy, now panting with excitement, up onto the bed and positioned him between Chele's legs. The woman giggled and did no more than to gently pull the boy down toward her. Fumbling with one hand, the boy guided his straining penis into the woman's vagina and entered easily, slicked and stretched as it was by Motumbo's attentions.

The boy's eyes grew big and his breath became instantly ragged. He began pumping in and out very quickly, his small, hard, rounded black bottom rolling up and down as he fanned his rigid midnight black cock into the woman. His tight, very dark and wrinkled black ballsack with a few wisps of curly black hair on it could be seen jiggling from Simpson's angle as the boy pumped in and out, in and out. Simpson could not resist, and smacked the bouncing butt with the palm of his hand several times. Inexperienced, Thatho came very quickly, crying out and shuddering, bucking his hips wildly but staying anchored inside Chele's flesh. No soon had his quivering stopped than Simpson pushed the boy over to the side, nearly on top of the comatose Motumbo, and pulled Mthobisi into the same position. A little shyer than his brother but with a penis no less rigid, the boy was quickly in place and commenced the same quick pumping of his dick inside Chele, who by now was giggling with glee and abandon. This time Simpson did not smack the boy's bottom but grasped it and held on, kneading it even as it bounced up and down, squeezing the slab sided buttocks together, cupping the perfect, high roundness of each cheek, his light tan hand making a beautiful contrast against the deeply dark, sweat sheened skin of the boy's bouncing bottom. As with his brother, his inexperience brought Mthobisi to a quick, loud climax, and as soon as his shuddering stopped, Simpson likewise pushed him off to the other side of Chele where he collapsed, breathing heavily.

Simpson sat there squatting on his haunches at the end of the bed, looking at Chele who grinned back, clearly drunk, her legs still spread and the semen of three African males oozing out from it. Simpson felt no physical attraction, but this was about more than that, it was about power and revenge. His organ sprang to life, despite having recently emptied itself into Motumbo's gut, and he slid forward quickly, plunging easily into Chele's gaping and slick vagina, and quickly, with a concentrated sense of purpose, fucked her rapidly until, sooner than he expected, a quick bang of an orgasm took him and he pumped a dollop of his own seed into her. A quick shudder and it was over, the last of his semen oozing down into the gathered pool of African spunk already in her. Exhausted, Simpson toppled over half onto Mthobisi, half onto Chele, and fell asleep in a tangle of dark brown flesh.

The tangle of bodies woke up one at a time the next morning. Mthobisi began squirming and wriggled out from under Simpson, who then woke up, one arm around Chele. He followed Mthobisi to the shower where they washed away the slime and sweat of the previous evening's couplings, grinning at each other in the hot, streaming water. Thatho joined them a few minutes later. Creeping quietly back into the bedroom to find their clothing, they were in time to see Motumbo wake up, shaking his head in a confused way, looking around as if trying to put things together. He was alone in bed with Chele, who was just now stirring, yet what were Andrew and the two boys doing getting dressed nearby? Still shaking the grogginess from his head, he muttered a sheepish good morning to Simpson and the boys as he slipped past them to the bathroom. Chele rose a few minutes later as Simpson and the boys were leaving to get breakfast in the main lodge; evidently she and Motumbo would have some sort of discussion about what had happened the night before…or perhaps they would not.

The day proceeded with plans for the plantation fantasy. Thabo had a long spell of concentrated work on the telephone, receiving and making calls. About mid-afternoon he approached Simpson with some news.

"Boss Andrew," he said, "you know…those young men, the boys, they here not long ago, Bongani, Khulekani, Bheka?"

Andrew smiled in remembering the three cute teens who had been stranded there overnight during a torrential downpour when the bus from the orphanage had to seek shelter at De Groot's. "Yes, I remember them well. Have you any news of them?" he asked.

"Well…you know, Boss Andrew, the orphanage, they try to put they orphans someplace, try to, uh, find work or home for them, you know?" Andrew nodded; he had a suspicion he knew what kind of thing was coming. "Well, they sisters, the nuns you know, they call today…those boys they talk about being here all the time, they say. So they wonder, they ask me, do we have work here for them? Can they come here and stay for work?"

Simpson stared at Thabo. "Do the nuns know what kind of 'work' we do here?" he asked.

Thabo's dark face split into a huge grin. "No, Boss Andrew, I don't think so, they think it a tourist place, maybe for safari you know. Well, that part right, eh?" He chuckled deeply.

Simpson smiled in reply. "What do you think, Thabo? Will we get in trouble if we take them? Are they in fact eighteen?"

"We not get in trouble, Boss Andrew, I think," he replied, "they nuns, they government, they happy just to have somebody take orphans. And yes, they eighteen, but small. And we treat them good, you know, not get them into things before they want to and are old enough. I think," he continued, winking

173

at Simpson, "I think they show they maybe like that kind of work, when they was here, eh Boss?"

Simpson nodded, smiling again, but asked Thabo to ask around to find out how the rest of the staff felt. As it turned out, they were all in favor, and Thatho and Mthobisi especially were in favor and eager to renew their acquaintance with the new boys. Enthusiasm seemed especially high for involving the new boys in the plantation fantasy, where they could serve as a background cast even if they were not focally involved in the adventure. Simpson and Thabo agreed to make final arrangements. Thabo concluded matters over the telephone, and arrangements were made for him to get the boys to bring them to their new home at De Groot's within a matter of days.

The plantation house was nearly finished, and Simpson spent the next few days ordering period-appropriate furnishings and consulting with their partner, Antoine, over finances. Antoine's business would keep him from being there for the grand opening, but it was clear that he intended to return soon to participate in a fantasy. In the meantime, Simpson and Motumbo resumed their life together in their lodge. The night of stolen passion with Chele and the boys was never mentioned, indeed it was not clear to Simpson that Motumbo remembered any of it given his inebriation. Likewise, Simpson and Chele exchanged cordial smiles in passing, and the boys would grin at her in teenage embarrassment, but everyone acted as if the affair had simply never taken place. Was Chele likewise too drunk at the time to remember? She seemed not to partake of alcohol again, at least in such quantities, and once early one morning he found her leaning against the side of a building, massaging her belly—perhaps one episode of too much drink was teaching her a lesson.

In a couple of days Thabo left early one morning to go to the school, and by late afternoon his truck bounced and rumbled back into the compound bearing chubby Bheka and slim Bongani and Khulekani. The teen boys were grinning broadly and evidently glad to be out of the orphanage. The first order of business was to find them lodging. A small lodge was devoted to housing them and the other eighteen year old boys, Thatho and Mthobisi, since the main "prey" lodge was fairly full, and plans were made for the future to add yet another lodge to accommodate the growing population at De Groot's. Around the dinner table at the main lodge that evening, the full nature of De Groot's business was explained to the boys, with special emphasis on the upcoming slavery reenactment. Of course slavery, not being part of their history, had to be explained in detail. They boys alternated between awe and puzzlement at the new vistas that were laid before them, but it was clear that their earlier sexual encounters with Simpson and Motumbo had given them a taste of what was to come which they were eager to accept. Little Mandla agreed to coach the newcomers in what might be expected of them, with Thatho and Mthobisi eagerly offering to help.

The five eighteen year old boys were marshaled by Little Mandla and trooped off to their new lodgings after dinner, while Simpson settled in to another round of paperwork. Motumbo stopped by to say that he was tired and was going back to the two men's lodge to turn in early. They exchanged a kiss and a good night, and Motumbo was on his way. Completing his work some time later, Simpson stood, stretched, turned off the light and stepped out into the night. On his way to his lodge he passed the turnoff to the new boys' lodge and hearing voices coming from there, decided to walk over to see what was the matter.

Knocking lightly on the door, he pushed it open. Little Mandla was strutting back and forth like an eighteen year old general, barking commands. Standing in front of him at attention but with heads bowed, and absolutely naked were the three new boys lined up in a row, with Thatho and Mthobisi likewise naked and standing as bookends on both ends of the line. Little Mandla wheeled in surprise and smiled broadly when he saw that it was Simpson.

"Oh! Boss Andrew, we practice being slave!" he said. "I tell them do this and do that, they must do it. I touch privates, they must let me touch, eh?" Simpson grinned and nodded, and noticed that the semi-erect state of the five young penises attested to Little Mandla's training. Then Little Mandla's eyes widened and he said, "Boss! You help us practice, eh? Be white man," and here he blushed even darker than he was and grinned, realizing that Simpson was already that, "I mean, be slavemaster, eh? You help us tonight, be slavemaster for these new ones, eh?"

Simpson's old aversion to enacting such a part had been crumbling for weeks, and now it gave way completely at the sight of the five naked brown bodies before him, awaiting his command. He nodded and told Little Mandla that he would do it, and suggested that they pretend they were in a slave market, the boys to be examined for any physical imperfections and for their reproductive capacity. Little Mandla explained the premise to the boys, using the boys' native language when necessary. When all was understood, there was a moment of silence. Then Simpson dragged a chair up within a few feet of the line of boys and nodded at Khulekani, in the middle. "Let me see that one," he said.

Little Mandla pulled Khulekani forward. The teen boy giggled but stopped short when Little Mandla quickly slapped his butt and ordered him to be quiet. The boy stopped, now a look of apprehension as well as curiosity creeping over his face. Simpson, sitting on the chair, pulled the boy even closer. He began examining every inch of him, running his hands over the crisp, short hair, rubbing the velvety skinned ears, tilting the head back to look up the clean, broad nostrils, sticking his fingers past the full, luscious lips and prying open the mouth to inspect the perfect teeth and the wet tongue. Running his hands over the boy's shoulders taut with a thin layer of hard muscle, over the lightly padded chest, Simpson dug in here and there with his thumbs, tweaked the nipples, as if probing for any muscular defect. Khulekani began breathing hard, his full, wet lips parted, his hard penis now rising straight up at attention. Simpson's hands slid down the slightly rounded belly, thumbs probed the navel, then pushed into the muscles of the groin, making the tense dark brown penis slap against the boy's brown abdomen. Simpson turned the boy around and ran his hands along the S curve of his spine, noting the development of the hills of muscles along either side of the spine culminating in that beautiful African butt of small pillows rising high and firm. Pushing the boy on his shoulders he made Khulekani lean forward, and parted the boy's butt cheeks. Simpson spat on a finger and inserted it roughly into the boy, who winced but did not cry out, and probed the anal cavity as far as he could go. Pulling his finger out his hands slid down the legs, feeling the strength that was to come to those skinny little dark brown pillars. Then he turned the boy around and worked his way up from the feet, kneading and stroking, digging deeply into the boy's long, muscular thighs before coming to the tight little ballsack which he cupped and then gently massaged. Finally, Simpson grasped the stiff cock, a midnight black against the boy's fudge skin, and began stroking it with thumb and two fingers. Up and down he went while Khulekani gasped and squirmed as much as he dared. The boy ever so slightly began moving his hips in rhythm, back and forth just a bit, milking as much pleasure as he could from the white man's ministrations. His eyes darted in nervous distraction from his own cock, held tightly and pumped by white fingers, to the white man's face before him. And then suddenly he shuddered, quivering as he stood, thrusting his thin pelvis forward. His rigid black cock throbbed in Simpson's fingers, as a long rope of cum came out. The boy gave one more great gasp and then seemed to sink, exhausted from the wave of pleasure that had washed over him.

Simpson then called for Bongani, noting that all the remaining boys were transfixed at the market examination that had just taken place, full lips parted and nearly drooling in each case, while Bongani's and Bheka's vertical cocks and Thatho and Mthobisi's more developed teenage tools stood at full attention. Simpson repeated the whole process with Bongani, who likewise ended in a shuddering orgasm. At that point Simpson, aroused himself to a fever pitch, could wait no longer. Pushing the chair back, he stood.

"I, I must see if these slaves can service me and my servants," he said. He motioned Thatho and Mthobisi to come forward and stand next to him, and then he quickly shed his own clothing, his trousers dropping down around his ankles where he stood. Simpson then motioned for the three new boys to come forward, and as they did Simpson put chubby Bheka in front of him, with Khulekani and Bongani taking Thatho and Mthobisi. Quickly he held his stiffening cock out and motioned for Bheka to take it into his mouth. The boy eagerly did so, and Khulekani and Bongani needed no encouragement to do the same with Thatho and Mthobisi respectively. Simpson put his arms around the naked, warm shoulders of Thatho and Mthobisi and pulled them close, while three black boys in front of them serviced them with their mouths. A quick glance to the side showed that Little Mandla had dropped his own pants and was pounding his big, eighteen year old meat with his hand.

Slurping and sucking, the boys did their work while Simpson and the two teenagers held their heads, rubbed their shoulders, leaned on their backs, and swung their own hips back and forth, back and forth. Little Mandla came first, his rigid iron cock shooting out ropes of semen on the back of Bongani, a drop or two making it onto Bheka. In short order Thatho and Mthobisi likewise cried out, and then Simpson, all three holding the boys by their heads and pulling them close, the boys sucking and swallowing as fast as they could as they took the older males' explosions, excess semen now falling in drops from their mouths and onto the floor. The older males shivered and gasped and then relaxed, releasing their "slaves" from their grasp. A few more moments passed and then there were smiles all around as Little Mandla congratulated the teenagers on enacting their parts well, and everyone thanked everyone else for their services. The new eighteen year old boys seemed especially proud at having done well, although chubby Bheka was surreptitiously rubbing his cock, which nobody had yet done for him. Simpson put his clothes back on and slipped back out into the night; he was confident that Bheka, indeed all the boys, would have more than their share of orgasms that night and for some time to come.

- CHAPTER 16 -

Work consumed Simpson and the rest of the crew as they prepared for the new plantation fantasy. Other customers came and went during the weeks of preparation, each enjoying the different attractions of DeGroot's. The number of new reservations for the plantation fantasy grew at a steady rate, simply astonishing Simpson. Customers were mainly from the United States, and ran about seventy percent white and thirty percent African American. Simpson wondered if he should somehow find more "white help" as he was the only one of his color around, but he resolved to shoulder the burden of fucking brown bodies himself for the time being.

His relationship with Motumbo continued to hang in the balance. Sometimes the African man stayed with Simpson, sometimes with Chele. Simpson wondered whether, toward the end of this time, Motumbo increasingly left Chele's room with a look of concern on his face, and he wondered what it meant. But he did not want to pry into their relationship, despite his jealousy. Simpson simply wanted Motumbo, and could not deny that it bothered him to share the big African with Chele.

Finally, the day arrived when Thabo left to fetch the first plantation fantasy customers, Peter Engquist and his son Leif, from the Twin Cities. The staff spent the day firming up plans and rehearsing for the next day's drama.

Simpson had to chuckle at the eagerness with which the staff "rehearsed," the eighteen year old contingent especially—Little Mandla, Thatho, Mthobisi, Bongani, Bheka, and Khulekani—repeatedly offered themselves up for physical examination and stimulation.

Toward the end of that day, the sound of a distant vehicle could be heard, and soon Thabo was driving into the compound. Once the truck stopped, out stepped a handsome, trim man of about fifty, Peter, who shook hands all around and was heartily welcomed by Simpson and the staff. Behind him stepped his nineteen year old son, Leif. Jaws dropped. Leif was a vision of blonde, blue eyed perfection, looking sort of like a male Farrah Fawcett in her heyday. He had a brilliant smile, and like his father, made a point of learning the names of all the staff. Trousers tented out among black and white alike.

Over dinner that night with Thabo and the guests, Simpson gently inquired into the Engquists' motivations for the fantasy. "Well, our roots are Scandinavian, and none of our ancestors were involved in slavery," said Peter, "but I think we both have always been fascinated by the personal dynamics of those relationships, especially if they involved sex. How would that work, how would it feel? I think we wanted an experience where nobody would really be hurt or demeaned." Leif nodded, and then the younger man added, "And I've always been a chocolate queen, so there's my motive." The group laughed. "Helped me fake an interest in sports when I was a kid," he said. Good food and wine continued into the night, and then the Engquists were shown to the plantation house, where they would actually live for three days. They admired the detail and care with which attempts at authenticity had been carried out. Simpson bade them good night and withdrew to his own cabin.

On the way he passed Motumbo and Chele's lodge—Motumbo was staying with her for a few nights. He heard voices that seemed to be in urgent discussion—not raised in anger, but intense with emotion. He decided not to pry. Saving himself and his friends for tomorrow, he turned in early and slept soundly.

Early the next morning Simpson rose and breakfasted in the main building while Thabo took breakfast to the plantation. Then he dressed in replica nineteenth century American clothing, with much good natured ribbing from the staff. Motumbo stood by and smiled, but seemed a little reserved.

Simpson stepped into the yard of the compound where he found the six eighteen year olds plus Big Mandla and Strello standing around wearing only loincloths. What looked like iron shackles and chains bound their feet and linked them together—Simpson knew they were made of comfortable, lightweight plastic, but they looked real. The group had been joking but snapped to attention when Simpson appeared. He gave them a brief pep talk to remind them of the history and context and then off they went, Simpson in front, the Africans doing their best to shuffle despondently despite their good humor and high spirits.

The group marched a short distance to the plantation house. Going up the steps, Simpson knocked on the door. Peter and Leif, also attired in period clothing provided for their use, stepped to the door.

"Good morning, sirs," said Simpson. "My name is Simpson. I am traveling through on my way to Natchez down the road," and here he tried to keep a straight face—Mississippi was thousands of miles away—"and I have some prime Negroes for sale. Would you care to examine them?" It seemed an improbable story but it served for the fantasy.

Agreeing, the Engquists stepped down into the yard. The Africans stood in a line before them, heads down, trying to look serious. Father and son consulted in whispers, and then stepped apart. Simpson unlocked the fake shackles and pulled away the plastic chains. Peter turned to the two grown men, Big Mandla and Strello, while Peter claimed for his own the whole group of six eighteen year olds.

Walking up to the two men, Peter let his eyes fondle their dark chocolate bodies in front and, stepping around, back. From behind he whisked off their loincloths, letting them fall. Standing behind the two well muscled men, Peter ran his hands over their strong backs, gliding over hills of muscles and along the valleys of their spines. With both hands he grabbed the firm, high, slab sided fudge colored buttocks of each one, deeply grinding his fingers into the muscles of first one and then the other. He let his hands slide down their legs, feeling and probing. And then he walked around to the front.

Mandla and Strello were by then breathing a little harder, their full African dicks semi-erect. Peter cupped the face of Mandla in his hands, running his fingers up through his short crisp hair, then gently prying apart his mouth to examine the teeth. His hands slid down the strong neck, then over the thick lobes of the chest and the raisin nipples, down the quilted muscles of his abdomen, pausing to rest in the bush of curly black pubic hair and then seizing Mandla's now rampant purple black dick. The big man sighed and

181

moaned, but with his training in mind kept his gaze averted and his head down. It was all the big African could do to not pull the white man into a passionate embrace, but this was Peter's game.

"I must see whether you will make a breeder," Peter said, his voice tense. His hand cupped Mandla's heavy balls and then slid around and up to grasp the rampant, nearly quivering black rod. Slowly at first and then more quickly Peter slid his fist up and down the rod, while his other hand braced against Mandla's thick chest, palm splayed flat on the muscled lobes. Faster he beat, and Mandla's hips began moving a little, then more, then with a deep groan the African tensed and a fountain of white sperm shot straight up out of his ponderous dick. It splattered on his brown torso and Peter's vest, as the white man's hand slowed and then stopped. Peter looked directly at the African whose breathing was ragged, then released the organ and turned his attention to Strello.

Meanwhile, Leif wasted little time getting to the fondling, his youthful enthusiasm wanting to cut right to the chase. He quickly stripped off all the loincloths of the youths before him, their eighteen year old dicks all growing very quickly to full erections. "I must test your potency," Leif said, and walked up to Bongani and Bheka, standing at one end of the line. Wasting no time, he grasped their eighteen year old organs one with each hand and began pumping frantically. No foreplay here. The boys forgot their instructions to avert their gazes, and as their breathing turned to gasps their eyes darted from their swollen purple black rods to the white hands grasping them to the flowing blonde hair and handsome face in front of them and then back. It did not take long for them to shout out, forgetting the deference due to their roles, shooting ropes of white cum into the air between them and the white man whose pumping gradually slowed.

Leif moved down the line, the two boys at the end hardly able to wait by the time he put his sticky white fists around their rigid cocks. Meanwhile, Peter had moved on to Strello, "examining" him with the same care he took with Big Mandla, bringing the muscular "slave" to a spouting climax in the same way. All the while, Simpson stood by, his trousers tenting, longing to be part of the scene but deferring to his paying customers. At last, hands and clothing slippery and spotted with cum, but their own bulging trousers testifying to a need for release, Peter said "We will purchase them." Simpson nodded and pretended to accept payment. He waved goodbye as the two white men led their new purchases inside. He wondered what Leif would do with half a dozen willing brown bodies, but he supposed youthful vigor would serve that purpose.

Walking back toward the main lodge, he passed the medical doctor who tested and certified all participants for health. The doctor nodded and smiled, then walked on. Coming up to the main lodge, Simpson found Motumbo sitting outside, lost in thought.

"Motumbo...you have seemed quiet. Is everything alright?" Simpson asked.

Motumbo glanced up, forced a smile, and then looked thoughtfully down. Then he said, "Doctor here, he say Chele pregnant. We use condom, maybe one broke."

As he choked out an entirely insincere congratulations, Simpson's mind worked double time. And it told him these things: First, Motumbo evidently remembered nothing of the drunken debauch in which neither he, Thatho, Mthobisi...nor Simpson himself had used a condom in filling Chele with sperm. Second, the father could be any of them after such an orgy. But third—and here something wild sprang up in Simpson—the odds simply were that he was the father, since he had ejaculated unprotected inside the African woman more than any of them and over a space of days. Time would tell, when either a dark or a light tan baby was born, but from this moment on, Simpson knew: Motumbo, and perhaps Chele, were "his." Not in the old fashioned way of slavery, being enacted in the bedrooms of the plantation. But all his frustration at Motumbo's divided allegiance suddenly vanished. Simpson "had" both of them. He possessed a secret that Motumbo would tumble to or not, but a secret nevertheless. He could share Motumbo now, knowing in an important sense he could claim Chele as much as could Motumbo. Simpson sat down next to his strong African lover and put an arm around his shoulders.

"It's OK, Motumbo. Chele can stay here and we can have the baby here. You can...you can stay with me while she is pregnant." Motumbo looked up and into the eyes of Simpson, then nodded, his eyes moistening a little.

"Thank you, Andrew," he said. Then with a small effort he forced it out: "Andrew...I love you."

- ABOUT THE AUTHOR -

Lance Kyle is a professor in a large university in the southern USA. Lance Kyle is also the author of *Love in Black and White: A Collection of Stories*.

KYLE

LOVE IN BLACK AND WHITE

A BONER BOOK

LOVE IN BLACK AND WHITE

A COLLECTION OF STORIES BY
LANCE KYLE